FROM A MISSILE SILO IN TURKEY where a brilliantly led terrorist band had the power to trigger the most deadly weapon ever conceived by science and built by renegade Pentagon generals . . .

TO THE BOUDOIRS AND BACK ALLEYS OF PARIS where a beautiful woman's body and a mysterious master murderer's itinerary of assassination were both objects of Marc Dean's pressing concern . . .

And though politics and passion were perilous stumbling blocks for Marc Dean, he led his men in a race against time to avoid committing the ultimate crime—and to avert the ultimate catastrophe for humanity. . . .

# THE
# MEGADEATH OPTION

## More SIGNET Adventure Stories

*Price slightly higher in Canada

---

# MARC DEAN
# MERCENARY
## THE MEGADEATH OPTION

### #8

# PETER BUCK

A SIGNET BOOK
NEW AMERICAN LIBRARY
TIMES MIRROR

For Andrew and Eva—another
view of Istanbul!

## PUBLISHER'S NOTE

This novel is a work of fiction. Names, characters, places, and
incidents are either the product of the author's imagination or
are used fictitiously, and any resemblance to actual persons,
living or dead, events, or locales is entirely coincidental.

NAL BOOKS ARE AVAILABLE AT QUANTITY DISCOUNTS
WHEN USED TO PROMOTE PRODUCTS OR SERVICES. FOR
INFORMATION PLEASE WRITE TO PREMIUM MARKETING
DIVISION, THE NEW AMERICAN LIBRARY, INC., 1633
BROADWAY, NEW YORK, NEW YORK 10019.

The first chapter of this book appeared in *The Black Gold Briefing*,
the seventh volume of this series.

SIGNET TRADEMARK REG. U.S. PAT. OFF. AND FOREIGN COUNTRIES
REGISTERED TRADEMARK—MARCA REGISTRADA
HECHO EN CHICAGO, U.S.A.

SIGNET, SIGNET CLASSICS, MENTOR, PLUME, MERIDIAN AND NAL
BOOKS are published by The New American Library, Inc.,
1633 Broadway, New York, New York 10019

First Printing, February, 1983

1  2  3  4  5  6  7  8  9

PRINTED IN THE UNITED STATES OF AMERICA

CLASSIFICATION:  CONFIDENTIAL
            SIGMA SIX

NAME:  DEAN, Marcus Matthew.
DATE OF BIRTH:  06/06/44, Johnstown NY,
        USA.

CATEGORY AND NATIONALITY:  White Anglo-
        Saxon Protestant. American.

PARENTS:  Elmer Roland, MD, former
        aviator. Decd. Mary Elizabeth
        (née Ballantyne), Social worker.
        Decd.

FAMILY:  Older brother (George Alick) (m)
        and sister (Hester Ellen) (m).

EDUCATION:  Graduate of Wilmington,
        Delaware, high school; Bachelor's
        Degree (Yale) languages; Master's
        Degree (USC) political science.

PERSONAL HISTORY:  Divorced. Former wife
        Samantha (née Hurok) daughter of
        USAF Colonel.
        Grounds for divorce: Incompati-
        bility; Mental Cruelty.
        Children of marriage: 1 son,
        Patrick, b.1975.

        No prison record. No smuggling or
        drug offenses. Womanizer. Moderate
        drinker.

OFFICIAL HISTORY:  ROTC (Yale) 1963-66;
        Lt. (infantry) Vietnam 1966-68;
        secretariat member, Senatorial

Committee on International Relations 1969; Peace Corps executive in Biafra, Uganda, Central African Republic 1970-71; AID pacification specialist, Vietnam 1972-73; program evaluator for Eastern Electronics (Orleans, Mass.) 1974; subsequently arms salesman for FN, Omnipol, Vickers, etc. Territory: Africa, Middle East. Became mercenary advisor, leader 1979.

MERCENARY ACTION: (While working as arms salesman) trained volunteers to fight against Soviet and Cuban rebels, ANGOLA (1975); with French mercenaries fighting for Emperor Bokassa, CENTRAL AFRICAN REPUBLIC (1976-77); hired by President Mobutu to defeat Katanga secessionists, ZAIRE (1978).

(As fulltime combat leader) aided Israeli govt. in raid on Palestinian camp, SYRIA; advised Christians in LEBANON; trained and led commando-style raids WEST AFRICA, HAITI and (with secret CIA approval) BRAZIL.

KNOWN ADDRESSES: Apt. 6c, 132 Rue Cavalotti, Paris 18, France. 117 bis, Avenue Yannick Bruynoghe, Brussels 2, Belgium.

MISCELLANEOUS: General surveillance at request of member states. Report unusual activity (SEE ALSO: INTER/INT/6092/USA).

# Prologue

There are not fifty ways of fighting a battle; there is only one, and that is to be the victor.

—André Malraux, *Expectations*

# Danger: Professionals at Work

The Grand Duchy of Luxembourg is noted neither for the number of terrorists within its borders nor for the frequency with which its residents are kidnapped, tortured, or blackmailed. Neatly sandwiched between the frontiers of Germany, France, and Belgium, the country—no more than five-sixths the size of the state of Rhode Island—is an enclave of farmlands which takes in too the headquarters of the European Iron and Steel Federation, the European Investment Bank, and the eldest commercial radio station outside of the United States. The Supreme Court of the European Common Market also sits in Luxembourg.

There were nevertheless seven terrorists in the Grand Duchy at sundown on Monday, June 27, 1983, all of them concerned with blackmail and five at least prepared to torture if necessary.

Two of the terrorists, both men, had driven into the country from Germany, via Saarbrücken and the border town of Remich, in a diesel-powered Volkswagen Rabbit rented from an agency in Frankfurt. The striped barrier poles at the frontier were already raised and the car was waved through without even the formality of a passport examination. If the guards had troubled to look, they would have learned that the passports were Turkish and that their owners came from the town of Erzurum, in the eastern part of the country, but that they were temporarily resident in Berlin. Unless they had made a very thorough search, however, they would not have discovered the two burlap-wrapped Uzi submachine guns concealed beneath the spare wheel, or the pair of 9mm magazines, each loaded with sixty-four rounds, taped beneath the front seats.

Another couple, a shapely brunette and a swarthy young man with a heavy mustache, entered Luxembourg in the southwest, from France. They were dressed in shorts

3

and brightly colored sweatshirts and they were riding in a camping car on a Mercedes chassis. The camper was French-registered, although neither of the supposed vacationers, despite the ID cards they carried, were nationals of that country. As is customary with caravans, campers, and motor homes, the frontier guards made a cursory search of the vehicle's interior. They found nothing suspicious. The small bottles of ether and chloroform—which in any case are on free sale in France—were ranged among the deodorants and after-shave and hair lacquer in the motor caravan's tiny shower cabinet. They were heading, the young man said, for a campsite in Ober-Eisenbach, a hilly, wooded tourist region in the northeastern part of the country known locally as Little Switzerland.

In fact they stopped on the outskirts of Luxembourg city and waited for darkness to fall.

The last three men arrived at the airfield between Sandweiler and Hamm, three and a half miles outside the capital, on the Sabena flight from Brussels. Two of them were Palestinians, although their papers were Lebanese. They had been trained in sabotage at a KGB school outside Minsk, in Soviet Russia, and later by seasoned guerrillas in Qadaffi's Libya. They traveled tourist class, took the shuttle coach to the town terminal, and rented a small panel truck from the local Hertz office.

The third man had flown alone in the first-class cabin. He was a very fat man, almost hairless, and he wore an extremely expensive pale fawn shantung suit, with a silk shirt, a Pierre Cardin necktie, and beige alligator shoes. He took a taxi to the center of the city and checked in at the Hotel Cravat, which is across the street from the slender spires of the baroque Cathedral de Notre Dame, overlooking a ravine.

Luxembourg is built on a plateau one thousand feet above sea level. It is split through the middle—as though some primeval giant had cloven the land with a series of blows from a gargantuan ax—by the Clausen ravine, at the foot of which the river Alzette loops through the capital, separating the old town from the new. Below the cathedral and the Hotel Cravat, the forty-five-degree slopes of the ravine are covered with smooth lawns and the paths of an ornamental garden follow the course of the river five hundred feet lower down. But farther north the walls of the gorge become almost perpendicular and

4

the cliff faces are honeycombed with medieval passages that interconnect casemates hollowed from the rock. Many of these tenth- and twelfth-century defense positions, barred now with steel gates to protect the unwary, are illuminated at night. Below them, steeply slanting roads zigzag down to ancient buildings bordering the Alzette, and the ravine is crossed by bridges at several different levels. Viewed from the belvedere surmounting the ramparts, this descending panorama of stone facades and lamplit roofs, of turrets and spires above the dark surface of the river, lends the city during the hours of darkness the fairytale splendor of a Gothic romance.

The fat man at the Hotel Cravat seemed aware of this. Perhaps he had read one of the brochures issued by the Tourist Information Bureau of the Grand Duchy, advising visitors of the most interesting promenades in the old town. For as soon as he had unpacked his overnight case, he took the elevator down to the Cravat's bar, drank two glasses of Moselle wine in one of the green-rexine-lined booths, and then sauntered out into the early evening. The summer sun was not due to set until nine minutes past eight o'clock, in fifty-seven minutes' time.

He walked past the cathedral and then, instead of continuing across the viaduct that led the road to the far side of the ravine, he turned left up a side street and took a footpath running above the steep roof of the military barracks. For a long time he leaned on the parapet of a tourist viewpoint, staring down into the gorge. He seemed especially interested in the sector where the cliffs were steepest, the shadows darkest, from which the sun had long since disappeared. Here, below huge stone revetments buttressing a slope of roadway, the river curled past a series of long, low buildings enclosed by a high brick wall. The complex was flanked on one side by a warehouse, on the other by a water mill. Between the two, an eighteenth-century bridge traversed the Alzette.

The buildings enclosed by the brick wall (according to the town plan supplied by the tourist office) housed Luxembourg's prison for women.

A quarter of an hour after he had taken up his position, the fat man pushed back a silk cuff and glanced at his gold watch. In twenty-two minutes it would be eight o'clock. He removed a pair of powerful binoculars from a leather case slung over one shoulder and focused them on

5

the depths of the ravine. In a few minutes the pale roof of an automobile appeared on one of the lower slopes of road. It was a white BMW sedan, and although in the poor light below it was impossible to read them, the fat man could see that the license plates were American.

The BMW stopped outside a gray turreted building beneath one of the great rounded bastions linked to the fortifications. Over the gateway, framed in a wrought-iron arch, were the words "École de Danse"—dancing academy. The passenger door of the BMW opened, and a girl about twelve years old climbed out, waved, and went through the gateway. The door closed. The sedan continued down the grade, turned a final curve, and crossed the low-arched bridge to the far side of the river. Outside the prison entrance it stopped. Distantly, the fat man heard the blare of its horn. The gates opened and the BMW rolled inside. Almost at once it was lost to sight behind one of the cell blocks.

The watcher nevertheless seemed satisfied. A smile creased his moon face and he replaced the field glasses in their container. Once more he looked at his watch. It was nine minutes to eight—1951. In one hour the operation would start.

He walked back past the barracks (from the pathway he could look down through the upper dormitory windows to a row of beds where soldiers sat changing their uniforms for civilian clothes in preparation for an evening on the town). But he did not return to the Cravat. Instead, he traversed a network of narrow streets and emerged in a picturesque cobbled square, one side of which was taken up by adjoining five-story brick buildings crowned by peaked slate roofs and pepperpot spires. These—neither of them much wider than a New York brownstone—were the royal palace and the national assembly. In front of the palace, which rose directly from the sidewalk, were two sentry boxes with a single soldier in front of each.

The fat man grinned patronizingly. A block away, he crossed a broad street busy with home-bound traffic and walked up a short graveled driveway to a nineteenth-century house set back from the road. Only the words "Pavillon Royal," in discreetly small red neon lettering over the portico, revealed the fact that this was a restaurant—one of the best in Europe. The fat man installed himself at his reserved table and studied the menu. It was exactly eight o'clock.

At a quarter to nine, the Frankfurt-registered Volkswagen Rabbit passed the restaurant and crossed the great single-arch bridge that spanned the Clausen between the cathedral and the radio station. There were four people—three men and a dark-haired girl—in the small sedan now. The heat of the day had been dissipated by a breeze blowing up from the German side of the Moselle, and the sky above the ornamental gardens was shading from blue to violet. The Volkswagen turned left by the European Iron and Steel Federation and spiraled down to the old riverside area on the far side of the ravine. Two hundred yards before the prison, the motor appeared to be misfiring. The driver halted by the blank wall of a granary, propped open the hood, and leaned in to tinker with the ignition.

Three minutes after a clock in one of the towers above the gorge had chimed the hour, the prison gates opened and the white BMW emerged. It was driven by a woman of around thirty-five, bespectacled, freckled, with straw-colored hair in a ponytail. The license plates had been issued in Nevada.

The car turned right and crossed the river by the ancient low-arched bridge. The woman shifted down and turned to climb the grade. The driver of the Volkswagen seemed to have fixed whatever had been wrong with the motor. He slid back behind the wheel and followed the white sedan up the hill.

The young girl—clearly the BMW driver's daughter—was waiting outside the dancing school. By the time she had scrambled in beside her mother, the Volkswagen was close behind. Together, the two cars zigzagged to the top of the ravine, crossed the palace square, turned into the street that passed the Pavillon Royal, and drove up the slight grade that led to a public park. It was a wide, tree-shaded area, the lawns crisscrossed with paths and bordered by tropical shrubberies, where huge fairs were held in August and at the time of Mardi Gras. Behind it, also generously planted with trees, was a neighborhood of quiet residential streets, with large houses standing well back in manicured gardens. The BMW cruised slowly around a wide crescent and braked just before a driveway with open gates. The Volkswagen pulled out to overtake—and precisely at that moment a panel truck shot backward out of an entrance on the opposite side of the road. It was very neatly done. The VW swerved, as if automatically to avoid the truck, and its right-front fender crunched against the BMW just forward of the windshield. The bigger car staggered and squealed to a halt, the bodywork stove in against the offside front wheel.

Three of the passengers in the Volkswagen jumped out at once and ran around to help the child and her mother out onto the sidewalk. "Are you all right? Are you all right?" one of the men asked the child anxiously. "Are you sure you are not hurt?" the brunette asked the mother.

"I guess not. Maybe just a bit shaken. That wasn't a very smart thing to do," the American woman said angrily. "I ought to be sore as hell—"

"That damned fool in the truck! Shooting out with no warning . . ." One of the men strode away to berate the driver of the offending vehicle, who had pulled to the side of the roadway and was about to get out and see what had happened.

At that moment the girl from the Volkswagen cried, "Kamal! He must be hurt! Look!" The driver was still slumped over the wheel.

"Must have hit his head on the windshield; knocked himself out," another man said. "We'll have to report to the police. Got to, if anyone is hurt. Better find a phone and call an ambulance, too."

"You can phone from my house. I live right here," the American woman offered. "Jesus, you guys should drive more carefully."

"Thank you. We will arrange about the cars later," the second man said. And then, turning to shout again at the two in the panel truck: "And don't try to sneak off until we come out again. We have your number!"

Extricating the supposedly unconscious driver of the VW, two of the foreigners carried him across the sidewalk and followed mother and daughter up the driveway and into the house. The girl from the Rabbit brought up the rear. As though it was an afterthought, she glanced once at the men in the panel truck and then ran back to the stalled VW to retrieve her purse. Slung from a shoulder strap, it was of polished brown leather and appeared over-full. Beneath the flap were two small bottles, one blue and one brown, and a wad of cotton. It was quite dark now.

The shadows of leaves dappled the lamplit sidewalk. The downstairs windows of the house were alight. Hurrying up the steps, the girl followed the others indoors.

The hands of the electric clock on the BMW's facia stood at 9:23.

At 9:30 the lights in the house blinked off once, twice, and then stayed on again. The driver of the truck started his engine and backed up the driveway to the front door. Three men and a woman came out carrying between them two heavy bundles, which they loaded into the rear of the truck. Then all four of them scrambled in afterward and slammed the rear doors. The truck turned out of the driveway and headed back downtown. Lights still burned in the lower story of the house, but nobody came out to inspect the damage to the crippled cars.

Passing the Pavillon Royal, the driver of the panel truck thumbed his horn button to sound five long, distinct blasts.

At his reserved table inside the restaurant, the fat man heard the signal. For the third time, he looked at his watch: 9:45. They were dead on time. How agreeable to work with professionals, he thought. He had consumed three aperitifs, a quantity of hors d'oeuvres, and a plateful of mountain ham. Now he was attacking the house specialty: a dozen freshwater crayfish with rock-hard shells, half drowned in a dish of lobster sauce. There was only one month in the year in which this local delicacy was prepared—and this was the month. He dipped his fingers fastidiously into a bowl of warm water, picked up the silver shears and the small silver-headed hammer beside his plate, and began dismembering his seventh crustacean.

"My dear old girl," a deep, exaggeratedly English voice said behind him, "you can complain like billy-o about your short-haul flights, but you can't say they do *us* any harm. I mean to say, twice as many opportunities for the lovebirds to curl up in the jolly old nest, what!"

The fat man stiffened. He glanced swiftly over his shoulder. A very tall, powerfully built black man and a slender blond air hostess in blue Lufthansa uniform were being shown to a nearby table. "Nothing like a spot of the local brew to limber up the old tum for the feast to follow," the black man said. "What'll you have, lovey?"

Subsequently the fat man at the next table behaved in a curious way. Leaving a small sheaf of banknotes beside his plate, he rose to his feet and hurried from the restaurant without calling for the bill or even finishing his meal.

Outside, the wind had freshened. It would be hours before the moon in its last quarter was visible and the sky was bright with stars. Lamps along the footpaths illuminated trees and lawns at the foot of the ravine as the fat man returned quickly to his hotel.

The panel truck was already past the railroad station and the airport, on the road to Grevenmacher, a resort town on the banks of the Moselle, where it formed Luxembourg's border with Germany. Five miles short of the river, the driver pulled in to a rest stop behind a French-registered camper. The blanket-wrapped bundles that had been carried from the house were rolled into the double-bed compartment above the trailer's cab. The girl and the original driver climbed into the cab, leaving one of the Palestinians cradling an SMG in back of the vehicle.

The two Turks and the remaining Palestinian got back into the panel truck and headed for Grevenmacher, the bridge over the Moselle, and Germany. The camper drove northwest, toward Ettelbruck and the heavily wooded country beyond.

"Admirably planned and executed," the CIA regional director said two days later in Washington, D.C., "but a banal kidnapping case just the same. The wife and daughter of a minor U.S. official are abducted in Luxembourg. So what? So why bring us into it?"

"The husband—Andrew Healey—is on forty-five thousand."

"That's what I mean. Guys at that level don't pay ransoms."

"Not in money perhaps. Hijackers and kidnappers sometimes demand their payoff in alternative currencies." The lean, lined man behind the desk was National Security assistant to the President of the United States. Beside him, a wide window looked out over roofs and red walls toward the great dome of the Capitol gleaming pale against a rainy sky. "That's why the case is so sensitive."

"Secrets, you mean? Treason? What does this guy do?"

"He's one of a team of rocketry technicians based in Luxembourg. They travel Europe, servicing our IRBM silos, checking out the gadgetry, making sure the missiles would lift off if the button was pressed."

"I see." The regional director was a small gray man with a military bearing and a clipped mustache. His name was Alexander Mackenzie. "You say Healey was out of town at the time of the snatch?"

"And working. His group was on their way to a silo on the slopes of Mount Ararat, in eastern Turkey. Maybe eight miles, maybe ten, from the Soviet frontier."

"Turkey! I know it's a NATO country, but I thought . . . ?"

"It's one of the old missile sites constructed at the time of the Cuba crisis. They can be reactivated at any time. This one has been." The National Security assistant sighed. "It should not have been. It's against all our agreements with NATO. And the missile that's in place"—he shook his head—"the warhead on that illegally sited bastard is so secret, and so deadly, that even the President doesn't know of it."

"I see what you mean by sensitive," Mackenzie said dryly. "So like you said earlier, it's my sector: we'll pull in this Healey, and—"

"The roving maintenance teams," the NSC man cut in, "travel in special trucks loaded with highly technical software. Kind of a super army command car. The crew of Healey's wagon was found by the roadside yesterday in northern Greece; they'd crossed the sea from Taranto the previous night. All of them had been shot to death."

"Jesus!" Mackenzie sat up in his chair. "You mean this same kidnap commando from Luxembourg hijacked that command truck?"

"I mean," the presidential assistant said somberly, "they hijacked the missile."

**I**

Men are so stupid that the violence they repeat ends up by seeming to be their right.

—Helvetius, *Maxims and Concepts*

# 1

# Putting the Heat on Healey

Andrew Healey was thirty-eight years old, a spare man of medium height whose sandy hair was already thinning on top. His forehead, nose, and chin were each prominent, which gave his face the look of a sculpture executed by three different artists. Behind thick-lensed shell-rim spectacles, his pale eyes were studious.

On Wednesday, June 29, those eyes opened to blink at a khaki burlap panel that was shuddering and vibrating some four feet above them. Healey frowned. He was surrounded by noise—a loud rattling rumble with the subdued roar of machinery beneath it. Beneath him too. He was lying on a hard surface that was jouncing him about like a penny on a drumhead. It was abominably hot.

He sat up. At least he tried to sit up, but he was unable to move his hands and feet and he fell back into a prone position as the surface supporting him gave an extra violent lurch. He moved his head: above and behind, dials, levers, and coils of wire gleamed; in front, beyond the silhouettes of two men in uniform, a shimmer of glass and bright, bright, aching blue space.

The mechanical noise altered. A surge of increasing volume, abruptly cut, a fractional pause, a renewal of the roar higher up the scale. He was in a vehicle; the driver had just shifted down. Yes, the hard surface under his body pushed upward at an angle, lifting him with it. They were climbing a steep grade with a poor surface. But how and where . . . ?

Healey tried again, more forcefully, to sit up. At once it was as though a lead counterweight inside his skull had swung up and struck him behind the eyes. He flopped back with the agonizing pain and discovered that his hands and feet were bound. He was trussed up, suffering the king of all headaches, lying in some kind of truck that was grinding up a rough road. A truck that was . . . ?

God in heaven! The truck, the command truck! Memory came flooding back, and with it the sickening sense of failure. And the horror.

Jesus! Anson, Brown, Weinberger, and the others . . . the stalled pickup in the hills behind Dhrama . . . the driver signaling for help, and the men with machine pistols who had appeared from among the trees, firing without warning, mowing his men down the moment the command truck stopped . . .

He remembered nothing after that murderous, blazing volley. Had he been hit? He thought not; only his head hurt damnably; he imagined he could feel, behind his left ear, a lump against the floor of the vehicle. He nodded—the spot was tender—and the movement sent another nauseous wave of agony searing through his skull. He uttered a stifled groan.

"Hah! He is waking up," a guttural voice said somewhere behind him. "I was afraid that you had hit him too hard, Kamal."

"I know what I am doing," a second voice said sulkily.

Healey groaned again. *Never, ever stop at night for what looks like an accident or a breakdown,* his colonel said before he was sent to Luxembourg. *If the road is blocked, back up as quick as you can and take another route.* After all the training, the security brainwashing, and the monthly recap lectures, he had fallen for it the first time it happened, walked straight into it with his eyes wide open like the greenest hardware apprentice. And now his team had been liquidated, the truck with its secrets and its built-in software stolen, and he himself made prisoner . . . for what purpose?

Slowly this time, he shifted his head. The truck had been stolen, all right, but he was still in it. His eyes roved around the familiar interior. Beyond the heads and shoulders of the men in the front seats, the glare from a cloudless sky struck him like a blow.

"Nesuhi!" the guttural voice called again, louder this time. "Our guest is awake. Maybe we should stop and wise him up some? We may need his help soon."

The head of the man beside the driver turned. "Okay. There is a clump of trees in a dip half a mile ahead. We will stop there. I could do with a leak anyway." Automatically, Healey's mind registered the details: they were speaking the English of men who had learned the language

16

from movies; the careful pronunciation with the slight American intonation told him something. Kamal, the sulky one, could be an Arab or a Palestinian. The name Nesuhi was Turkish; so was the accent of the man with the guttural voice. Healey and his team had been on the way to Turkey.

Perhaps, he thought groggily, they still were. He could think of no valid reason why any terrorists would want to steal the truck. He and his crew carried no arms. The electronic gadgetry fitted inside the vehicle was almost exclusively checkout material: data banks that would be useless if you didn't know how to program your questions and lacked the equipment they were designed to verify; control systems that were meaningless with no missile to service. Before he had time to reflect any further, rough hands pushed him upright and the truck swerved off the road and braked heavily. His nose wrinkled in disgust as he smelled the sour stench of vomit that had dried on the front of his jacket. He still had no recollection of how or when he had been zapped.

Two of the kidnappers carried him from the command truck and dumped him on the ground. He screwed up his eyes in anguish at the glare of sunlight. Then they were shaded by a grove of cedars lining a shallow depression that scored a great slope of mountain. On either side the dirt road snaked away around ravines eroded from the bare rock. Below them, the land dropped steeply to an undulating plain whose contours shimmered indistinctly through the haze. Even in the shadow of the trees the heat was stifling.

There were five of them, Healey saw when it was no longer too painful to keep his eyes open: the two Turks, in their mid-thirties, swarthy and muscular; Kamal, the sullen Palestinian; the driver, whose hooked nose, black mustache, and angry stare gave him, too, an Arab look; and a squat, powerfully built Japanese with a color that was almost orange. His name, Healey learned later, was Matsuzaki.

The driver was urinating on the far side of the road. When he returned, zipping up his fly, his place was taken by Nesuhi. A small point—Healey's trained mind was working again—but perhaps an important one: even with a prisoner bound hand and foot, they were unwilling for more than one man to be away at a time. To Healey this suggested that they were both organized and disciplined. Ruthless too, he remembered, thinking of his slaughtered companions. Not the kind of ramshackle group that could be taken by surprise or divided psychologically by a clever talker.

"My turn next?" he said huskily, trying to make it sound light.

"Later," the driver said.

"But I really need to." Healey squirmed as much as his bound limbs would allow. "I haven't been since—"

"Shuddup. I said later."

Healey saved his breath. The pressure on his bladder *was* becoming uncomfortable.

Matsuzaki had walked back to the truck. He returned carrying a small Philips portable tape recorder in an imitation leather case. "I figure maybe it's time we entertained our guest," the driver said.

"Sure. It's tough, tied up like that," said Nesuhi. "And after the program, I guess it'll be safe to set Mr. Healey free." He unflapped the pocket of his military-style bush jacket and fingered out a regular tape cassette.

"Sinatra? Streisand? Elton John?" Healey was still trying to raise the tone to a jokey level. *Once you're on personal terms, you're halfway home,* the colonel had said. "A new version of 'High on a Windy Hill' maybe?"

None of his captors smiled. "Listen," the man with the guttural voice ordered. He took the cassette, unfastened the recorder cover, lifted the plastic lid, and slipped the cassette inside.

"More intelesting than Miss Stleisand." Matsuzaki spoke for the first time. "Play him, Paul."

The man with the guttural voice let the recorder lid fall. He stabbed a rectangular button marked "Play."

A woman's scream cut through the rasp of cicadas beneath the cedars. It was a panic-stricken sound, starting on a note of incredulity and then rising, rising, to halt on a choking sob. *"You can't do that! You can't! You wouldn't dare!"* the voice cried despairingly.

Healey stiffened. His whole body felt suddenly weak and drained, as though all the blood in his system had cascaded down to his feet. The voice was certainly more "interesting" than Barbra Streisand's: unmistakably, spine-chillingly, it was the terrified voice of his own wife, Margery.

Paul had stopped the tape. He pressed the button

marked "Fast/Fwd" and watched carefully as the spool behind the small observation window sped past the calibrated scale. He stopped the tape again. Once more he thumbed the Play control.

A younger voice, higher-pitched, more frightened still. *"Oh, don't do that to me! Don't! Please . . . please, please, please!"* And then an agonized shriek ending in the word *"Mamaaa!"*

Healey was shaking. His twelve-year-old daughter, Carole.

For the third time, the tape was moved, stopped, played. A short extract. Carole's voice crying: *"Leave my mommy alone!"* A slap, a sob. And then Margery screaming again.

"You fucking bastards," Healey said. "You murderous, callous, motherfucking sons of bitches."

The driver laughed. "Motherfucking is good," he said. "But whose mother?"

For the first time in his life, Healey realized the exactitude of the cliché "his blood ran cold." Dark hairs grew on the back of the driver's hands. The fingernails were rimmed in black. He saw hands like those pawing at Margery, the brassiere strap snapped and the breasts springing free. He felt the lithe, warm body of Carole; saw it contorted with pain, mouth open, eyes staring. The hands held . . . what? A hot iron? A flame? An electrode? He wrenched his mind away from the images. "It's not true," he cried desperately. "The tape's been faked. You're trying to fool me."

"We expected you to think that," Paul said. "Premier reaction in shock: disbelief. Happily"—he smiled—"we have the means to persuade you that we're not kidding. Fetch the radio, Matsu."

The Japanese returned once more to the truck and came back with a suitcase that was evidently heavy. Opened up, it revealed the dials and tuners of a powerful shortwave radio. A speaker was incorporated in the lid.

Two of the men set up a tripod that supported a tall telescopic aerial. The cicadas, which had fallen silent when the screams were produced by the recorder, restarted their chorus.

Matsuzaki turned knobs and made marginal corrections to the slide controls. Ten minutes later, he repeated some call sign into a microphone sprouting from the radio chassis. After a moment, there was a reply. It was overlaid by static, distorted by several different kinds of interference, but it was clearly a man's voice, speaking in what sounded like Arabic. "Ahmed, Kamal," Matsuzaki called. "Hassan speaks with you, okay?"

The driver and the man with the sulky voice approached the mike. For perhaps half a minute they spoke with the anonymous Hassan, while Matsuzaki tuned out as much interference as he could. Then, after a pause, a female voice, not Margery's, not Carole's: *"Are you receiving us well? Is everything okay?"*

Paul took over the microphone. "Loud and clear," he said. "All systems go, as they say. As we hope they'll go on saying." For the first time, Kamal's face lost its sullen expression. He giggled. "The only thing," Paul continued, "our guest suspects that the tape may have been doctored."

*"What?"*

"He thinks the cassette is faked. The . . . husband."

*"You want us to make another?"* the female voice asked. *"It's all set up; the nearest people are too far away to hear anything."*

"Maybe you should. Something a little more . . . extreme . . . this time. It has to be convincing."

*"Just as you like. You want to stay tuned in while we do it?"*

*"No!"* Andrew Healey shouted. "If you still have . . . If you've got my wife and child, whoever you are, let me talk to them. Let me hear their voices."

Another pause. And then, abruptly, Margery's voice, overlaid by the child's, the two of them speaking at once, anxious, frightened, pleading.

*"Andy! Have they got you too? I can't hear you. I—"*

*"Daddy! Come and help us! I don't want them to hurt—"*

Both voices were cut off at the same time, as a hand was clamped over Healey's mouth to prevent him replying.

Seconds later, Paul spoke again. "Alicia? Everything all right at your end? Not too much trouble? Everything under control?"

*"Everything,"* the woman's voice answered. *"Hassan and Marcel have made the point, I think. They're quite well-behaved now."*

"Great. Call you again once we're inside. Keep cool."

Paul nodded and the Japanese switched off the radio and shut the suitcase.

Healey was white-faced. "All right," he said hoarsely. "You have my wife and child. You . . . you tortured them to make that tape. You have me. You murdered my men and stole the truck. What in the name of God do you want? If you're so damned efficient, you should know that I have no money apart from my pay."

Ahmed, the Arab driver, laughed. "We have more money than you'll ever see," he said. "We don't want your miserable dollars."

"But . . . ? Presumably this is some kind of a ransom deal?"

"That's right," Paul said affably.

*Once you're on personal terms . . .* "I don't get it," Healey said. "You kidnap me, but it's not against a cash ransom. At the same time, you kidnap my wife and daughter. But you hold us in different places. There's nobody left to negotiate with. What the hell does this *mean?*"

"You're supposed to be some kind of a scientist. Interpret the facts. What do you think it means?"

"I imagine," Healey said after a moment, "that since you took the truck as well as me—and you must have had your own transport to stage the ambush—then both the truck *and* myself are important to your . . . plan. It would seem, therefore, that the tape you played me is"—he swallowed—"some kind of a sample. Perhaps what you would call a foretaste of what would happen if . . . if I . . ." His voice died away.

"I told you the guy would have brains," Paul said to the others. "You can untie him now; he won't dare walk out on us or make any hostile move now that he knows we have his wife and kid. And what could happen to them if he steps out of line."

"Very well." Healey squirmed from left to right to allow the two Palestinians to cut the ropes binding him. "Look, I've got to urinate before I can say another word. It's . . . I'm bursting."

"Go ahead."

As he crossed the road, wincing at the blood coursing back through his cramped limbs, Healey filed away another small fact that testified to the terrorists' organization and attention to detail. Clearly they had deliberately forbidden him to relieve himself, knowing that the discomfort would increase the distress he experienced, hearing the cries of Margery and their daughter. If, as the colonel had said, he was halfway home, it was a hell of a long journey he had to travel. . . .

"All right," he said when he returned. "You're holding my family, using the threat to torture them as a lever, in the hope of forcing me to do something, to help you in some way, right?"

Paul nodded. "No harm will come to them, they will not be hurt any more, if you cooperate. We are trading their safety against your help."

Healey sighed. "What is it that you want me to do?"

Paul glanced at Ahmed. Ahmed told him what they wanted him to do.

Healey blanched. "Jesus God!" he cried. "You . . . I . . . Holy Mother of Christ, I couldn't do that! I couldn't." He shook his head and repeated, "I couldn't."

"Not even if your refusal brought about the mutilation, perhaps the slow death, of . . . Margery and Carole?"

The scientist flinched at the deliberate use of the first names. Another example of their psychological technique. He compressed his lips. "It's . . . out of the question. Impossible. I don't have the necessary knowledge," he shouted suddenly. "My security rating isn't high enough. I'm just a maintenance engineer."

"Rather a specialized one," Paul said softly. "We happen to know your security rating . . . and that you do have the knowledge. It would be entirely within your competence to do what we want."

Again Healey shook his head. "No way," he said.

"Very well." Paul turned back to Matsuzaki. "Set up the radio again and call Alicia. Tell her to arrange something a little more painful. And maybe we should have it live this time."

The Japanese reopened the suitcase.

Healey watched them reassemble the aerial. In the heat, the blood was thundering behind his eyes. The rattle of cicadas ceased.

"Alicia?" the Japanese said. "Matsu. Paul would like another word with you."

"Wait!" Healey cried as Paul moved forward. "Let me think about it." The five hijackers were motionless, staring at him in the silent, heavy atmosphere beneath the cedars. Very far off, somewhere beyond the sun-bleached curve of mountainside that dropped away from the road, he could hear the faint tinkle of sheep bells. "I need time," he said wildly. "Give me a couple of hours."

Ahmed looked at his watch. "You have one minute," he said.

# 2

# In the Country of the Blind

"Hijacked the *missile?*" Alexander Mackenzie echoed. "Henry, you can't be serious! Those silos were designed for IRBM's, weren't they? Minuteman 1, if I'm not mistaken. Six-thousand-miles-plus, with a warhead up to one megaton. Do you know how much those things weigh? Do you realize the kind of transportation they need? Are you aware of the security—?"

"I didn't say the missile had been taken anyplace," the National Security assistant interrupted. "I said it had been hijacked—captured, if you like."

Mackenzie stared at him. "I don't understand."

"It's still in its silo on the slopes of Mount Ararat. But the bunker crew and the personnel staffing the site are no longer members of the U.S. forces."

"Good Christ!" Mackenzie said.

Henry Carpenter nodded. "Exactly. We have quite a situation here. What appears to have been an armed raid—a successful armed raid—on an American site in a NATO country. A lethal missile in the hands of extremists. It's the kind of thing the administration has feared for years."

"You mean nuclear blackmail?"

"Not exactly. It's blackmail, all right, but it's not precisely nuclear." Carpenter took a pipe from the pocket of his tweed jacket and clamped his teeth around the stem. He unrolled an oilskin tobacco pouch. As he looked down, the creased flesh on either side of his thin face sagged into jowls that gave him the air of a tired bloodhound. Mackenzie waited for him to continue.

Carpenter said, "You'll be one of a very small minority, Alex, but I'm going to put you fully into the picture, shoot you the whole sorry story from A to Z."

"It's an idea," the CIA regional director said dryly.

"Okay, I'll take it from the top." Carpenter rammed tobacco into the bowl of his pipe with one thumb. He looked up and across the desk, his gray eyes somber. "It started with the Pentagon, of course. Tell me what military screw-up doesn't."

"You said something earlier about this Turkish site being reactivated 'illegally'?"

"Sure I did. It's part of this damned undercover war that's been going on for years between the hawks and the doves on the Joint Chiefs committee. Hardanger's the man responsible."

Mackenzie sighed and compressed his lips. Major General Eric Hardanger was one of the last of the tough-line, MacArthur-style army chiefs whose anticommunist zeal extended to the preference of a hot war over a cold. Hardanger, an advocate of the preemptive strike ever since the days of the Berlin airlift, had indirectly caused Mackenzie's field agents more headaches than the past four secretaries of state added together.

"I won't clutter up your mind with the administrative details," Carpenter continued. "You know as well as I do how planners and staff authority can be bypassed with the command structure we have. I'll just say that Hardanger and a handful of his hawk cronies have succeeded, first in reactivating this site, second in equipping the IRBM inside the silo with a warhead that is . . ." He paused, at a loss for words, struck a match, and held it to the bowl of his pipe.

"You said something about the blackmail . . . that it wasn't exactly nuclear?" Mackenzie offered.

"Damn right I did." Carpenter sucked at the pipe and blew out smoke. "Warhead on that Minuteman is packed with Tabun nerve gas."

"Jesus!" The CIA man sat bolt upright in his chair. "But that's the most deadly and lethal of all—"

"I am informed," the National Security assistant said evenly, "that with an air burst over the center of the city, the gas in that warhead would annihilate the entire population of Moscow within ninety seconds."

"And the missile is targeted on Moscow?"

"Yes."

Mackenzie had turned pale. "Do the Russians know the site has been reactivated?"

"Of course they do. It's only a few miles from the border."

"And they haven't raised a stink?"

Carpenter shook his head. "I guess they figure it for part of the normal NATO buildup. They're doing the same thing. One more or less—especially in an existing site—isn't even worth a protest note. What they won't know is that the site has been reactivated without the knowledge or permission of the NATO Council's Defense Planning Committee."

"And they won't know about the Tabun warhead?"

"We think not. We hope to Christ not."

Mackenzie pushed back his chair, stood up, and walked to the window. "Henry," he said with his back to the room, "how do *you* know?"

"That's easy. Hardanger himself told me. The hijackers communicated directly with him. He and his pals had to confide in someone, so they came to me."

"Shit, Henry!" Mackenzie swung around and stared at the desk. Behind him, pigeons fluttered against the evening sky. "You realize what that means? If they contacted Hardanger, that means the terrorists do know the reactivation's illegal; they probably do know about the Tabun warhead." He spread his arms in a helpless gesture. "I'd like to know how those hawks got hold of that stuff. I thought we signed that convention against manufacturing chemical-warfare agents years ago."

"Sure we did," Carpenter said wearily. "The Strategic Arms Limitation talks have been going on for years too, but I don't see any Vickers or Krupps or Lockheeds going out of business; I don't hear of any munitions factories putting their workers on relief. Don't tell me, in any case, that the stuff's not stockpiled someplace." He relit his pipe, which had gone out, and added, "Face it, Alex . . . these bastards have us by the balls."

"You say they actually hijacked . . . that they're in possession of the whole site, the missile, the bunker, everything within the perimeter?"

"Right." Carpenter fanned smoke away from his face with one hand. "They have the strongest lever anyone ever had on a U.S. administration. And because the Ark's illegally sited and illegally primed—"

"The Ark?"

"The missile. They code-named it Ark. You know, Mount Ararat and all that."

"You mean Hardanger's equipped with a sense of

irony? I don't see too much of a role for the dove in this scenario."

"He's too dumb to have figured that one out." Carpenter brushed the point aside. "Because everything about it is illegal, the terrorists know we dare not rake anyone else in on the deal. Because they know—they must know—the President is ignorant even of the existence of the Ark, they can rely on Hardanger and his gang keeping the whole thing under wraps. Like I say, they have us over a barrel. There's only two courses of action open to us."

"There never are more than two," Mackenzie said. "Give the hijackers what they ask for . . . or beat the shit out of them."

"Yeah. But there are complications with this one."

"Such as?"

"The two sides of this particular equation; the terms of the ultimatum."

Mackenzie waited. Behind him, the pigeons cooed outside the window. Above the steel filing cabinets on the far wall of the office, a pendulum clock ticked loudly. Carpenter laid his pipe in an onyx ashtray. His bloodhound face grew more solemn still. "Mubarak, the Egyptian President, is presently in Paris attending some international ecology conference," he said. "In just over two weeks' time, he flies to Israel to resume, hopefully to conclude, the final round of peace talks with Begin. The hijackers' terms are simple: either we arrange to have Mubarak assassinated before he leaves France . . . or they fire the missile."

"Jesus!" Mackenzie went back to the desk and slumped into his chair. "Henry, you wouldn't happen to have liquor stored someplace in your office, would you?"

Carpenter pulled open a drawer and took out two glasses and a quart of Jack Daniel's. "You see what I mean?" he said, pouring.

"But . . . ?" The CIA regional director passed a hand over his brow. "I mean, granted this monstrous suggestion is seriously intended, why bring us into it? Why not arrange the killing themselves? Why not hire professionals?"

"They are hiring professionals, in a sense," Carpenter said gently. "Specifically, you and your operatives. They want the assassination planned and carried out by the Agency."

"Good God!"

"As to why they don't do it themselves: you tell me."

"Who are these madmen? Do we know who we're dealing with?"

Carpenter shook his head. "Not so far."

"But . . ." Once more Mackenzie hesitated. "Okay, they rubbed out the crew and stole the command car; somehow they made it inside the Ararat perimeter and neutralized the guard; somehow they got wise to Hardanger's shenanigans and contacted the guy with this crazy blackmail routine. But the whole idea is preposterous. It doesn't make sense." He rose from the chair and began to pace the room.

"I'll allow that determined men could raid and take over an isolated site. Guarding the perimeter of these posts isn't a particularly high security task; not much stricter than the staffing arrangements for any U.S. military depot, dump, or airfield in the NATO sphere. And why not? Because, so far as firing a missile goes, there are so many fail-safe mechanisms built into the control system and the silo that it carries, in a way, its own security. Even if people do penetrate a silo, they can't possibly fire the weapon."

"They can if they hold a nuclear expert like Andrew Healey," Carpenter said, "with the means to blackmail him into helping them."

"Oh, Christ, yes. The kidnapped wife and child." Mackenzie sat down again. "How many people know of this threat, Henry?"

"Hardanger and his three fellow hawks, damn them. You. Me. And of course the hijackers."

"And about the missile?"

"The same people. And the junior officers, the transport crews, guards, and so on who packed and shipped and installed the Ark. But it would have been just another item of hardware to them; they wouldn't have attached any significance to one more Minuteman heading overseas."

"I see. Each man down the chain of command carries out his specific duty; nobody sees the whole picture or adds up the parts to make a whole."

"Except our terrorists," Carpenter reminded him. "Remember that old saw: in the country of the blind, the one-eyed man is king."

"Okay, okay. But the whole deal is still preposterous. There may be enough Tabun to wipe out the population of Moscow in—what was it? ninety seconds?—but even if

28

they succeeded in firing it, the missile wouldn't get within a thousand miles of Moscow. Lifting off within a few miles of their frontier? It would be on their early-warning screens within seconds—and destroyed before it reached operational height."

"Along with New York, Los Angeles, and Detroit maybe," the National Security assistant said. He cleared his throat. "But there is one aspect I haven't yet mentioned. The missile is being retargeted: it's not aimed at Moscow anymore, but at Tehran."

Mackenzie drained his glass and held it out for a refill. "Where there is no early-warning screen," he said faintly, "where the missile *would* explode on target with devastating human and political results. The least of which"—he stood up and drank again—"beyond the murder of several million innocent people, would be the certain and total poisoning of U.S.–Middle East relations for years to come. The worst of which could be the not improbable launching of World War III."

"Exactly."

"So what do we do? Call in the army and the air force and blast these sons of bitches off the face of the earth? Mount an Entebbe-style raid and hope to get away with it before the missile takes off?"

Carpenter stood up and faced the CIA man across his desk. "Uh-uh. We can't do either of those things."

"Why not, for Chrissake? Shit, Henry, if we—"

"Because," Carpenter cut in crisply, "operations like that can be kept secret from the enemy but not from your own side. It couldn't be done without the consent of the Joint Chiefs and the NSC. And once the Pentagon knew of the threat, there would be a leak. Bound to be, with the number of people involved."

"You mean if the hawks confess . . . ?"

"It'll go both to the Pentagon and to the White House. And there's a double danger in that: first, if the nerve-gas secret leaks, nobody will believe that the President and the administration knew nothing about it. World opinion will be outraged, NATO chiefs will be furious because it's against our agreement on the arming of warheads, demonstrations all over Europe will weaken our position and play into the Comrades' hands. Second, the terrorists have warned that if there's the smallest press leak on the actual threat, or any move to alert Iran, they'll launch the missile anyway."

"But we can't just do nothing!" Mackenzie said helplessly.

"Sure we can. That's all *we* dare do: nothing."

Mackenzie stared at him.

Carpenter splashed more liquor into their glasses. "Look," he said, "faced with this kind of extortion, there are but three options: do what they ask and knock off Mubarak—"

"You'd even consider that?"

"We have to. Consider it, I mean. Number two, find some way to immobilize the missile without the terrorists on the site knowing it's being done. Three, work out a way of rendering the terrorists incapable of launching the Ark when the ultimatum expires. But there's a risk in all of those too. Any kind of raid could turn sour on us, the way the choppers did with the Tehran-embassy hostage situation. And as you say, if the Ark did go into orbit, we'd be through forever in the Middle East. On the other hand . . ." Carpenter shrugged. "On the other hand, that may be their aim anyway, to louse up our position in the area. If your guys did in fact organize an assassination, if it came to that, there's nothing to stop these fuckers blowing the story wide open afterward. Another foul CIA conspiracy against the peoples of the free world. You know the kind of thing."

"Sure," Mackenzie said feelingly. "I know exactly the kind of thing." For the second time he drained his glass. "So?"

"So the President's got to be kept in the dark. You know who'd be in the White House, quick as a rat up a drain, if there was any question of him being in the know, any talk of a Nixon situation or an impeachment. We have to avoid that at all costs."

"No quarrel about that, Henry." The CIA man smiled.

"For that reason—and because of the extreme sensitivity to any hint of U.S. involvement in this kind of deal—I'm suggesting that we, the United States of America, do nothing. To put it brutally, what we need is a fall guy: someone, or some organization, capable of pulling the chestnuts out of the fire for us. But someone we can disown at once if anything goes wrong." Carpenter picked up his pipe again. "Excuse the mixed metaphor," he said.

30

Mackenzie was frowning. "Specifically, you mean . . . ?"

"Specifically, I mean, first, that we double-check, satisfy ourselves that the threat's genuine, that it could be carried out. And then, if it is, we call in outside help."

# 3

# Alarm Ignored

The guards at the Greek-Turkish frontier post knew the command car well; it had been passing each way every three months for several years. For the last five visits, Andrew Healey had been the officer in charge. And his efforts to divert them to an unfamiliar route northward through Edirne were unsuccessful. The terrorists knew precisely the routine he followed; they must have had his team under observation more than once.

"Called in substitutes for the wings and center, *kapitan?*" The guard raising the barrier pole was a football fan. He smiled genially as he waved the vehicle through.

"Sometimes we're . . . obliged . . . to take on different personnel," Healey said, conscious of the Stechkin machine pistols aimed at him from the rear of the truck, the aerosol of hydrocyanic-acid gas held by Paul, sitting next to him in the passenger seat. One brief squirt from that could produce a convincing enough heart attack to stall off a frontier guard. He hoped—if ever anyone checked out the command car's movements—that the very slight emphasis he had permitted himself would be remembered.

Healey himself, along with the five hijackers, was now wearing the spare lightweight summer fatigues that had been stowed in a locker in back of the vehicle. Paul, who was visually the most convincing American, wore a bush jacket with a lieutenant's shoulder bars and the "flaming onion" Ordnance Department insignia; Nesuhi was kitted out with the chevrons of a technical sergeant; the Japanese and the two Palestinians, supposedly PFC's, stayed in the shadows among the command car's software.

It was almost dusk when they reached Istanbul. On the European side of the Bosporus, the unbelievable domes of Saint Sophia and the sixteenth-century Suleiman Mosque snared the last rays of the sun beneath their Turkish minarets. Crossing the new bridge that spanned the channel separating the Black Sea from the Sea of Marmara, they found themselves blocked in the homegoing traffic jam that choked the streets of Scutari. By the time they broke free, it was quite dark and the water was brilliant with reflected lights from Galata and the pleasure boats moored along the Golden Horn. But soon they were clear of the suburb and Paul urged Healey to put his foot down along the highway leading to Izmit and Adapazari.

They bypassed Ankara forty minutes before midnight, heading east between fields of corn and tobacco. Ahmed was speaking on the radio. Healey couldn't catch the words over the whine of gears and the rattle and thump of the bodywork over poor surfaces.

Sometime later, on a deserted stretch of road beyond the town of Tokat, Healey was ordered to pull off the highway and park in a clearing by a lake bordered with dense woods. Ahmed was still talking into the mike, reading figures off a scale held beside a map. Within five minutes the helicopter planed in over the clearing.

It was a small European-made ship—a Westland or a French Seacat, Healey thought—designed as an LOH with a crew of only two. Paul leaned across and switched on the headlights of the truck. In the twin shafts of brightness tunneled from the dark, Healey saw the branches of trees threshing in the downdraft from the machine's rotors. A rope ladder tumbled from the open perspex hatch in the nose. Momentarily the chopper hovered a dozen feet over the glade as a tall, thickset man in uniform climbed down and jumped to the ground. He raised a hand. The ladder was hoisted out of sight and the helicopter rose and wheeled away into the night.

Before the clatter of its rotors had faded, the man was by the command car's cab. The uniform, Healey saw with no particular surprise, was that of a full colonel in the U.S. Army. Its wearer (he learned later) was a Canadian named Furneux.

"Everything okay?" the newcomer asked. He had a harsh voice, not very deep, with a rasping, almost sneering quality to which Healey took an instant dislike.

"According to plan," Paul replied. For an instant, Healey wondered if the terseness of the answer implied that the Turk too disliked Furneux. But he concluded subsequently, with regret, that the crisp, military-style speech was simply one aspect of the terrorists' organizational discipline.

"Let's see the map," Furneux said. Ahmed leaned forward with a clipboard holding a sectionalized survey behind cellophane. He switched on the truck's roof light. In the illumination, Healey saw a heavy, thick-featured, rather coarse face centered on a large nose webbed with the tiny red veins of the habitual drinker. The eyes, prominent below thick brows, were pale and small.

"Okay," Furneux announced when he had studied the map. "So how far we got to go? Four-eighty, five hundred miles? Fine. We rest up a coupla hours someplace along the way, and we arrive there at dusk tomorrow as per schedule. You can't average much more than thirty on these hick roads anyhow." He turned and stared at Healey. "And this is our meal ticket, huh? This is the bum's gonna show us all the way in, that right?"

"Playing ball the way the rules are written," Ahmed agreed.

"I should say so, the trouble we been to!" Furneux opened the door of the cab and climbed in. "You piss off in back, Paul. I want to sit up front here with Pretty Boy, see nothing goes wrong." He chuckled. "Senior officers should ride in front anyway. And as for you, Pretty Boy, you only got to remember one thing: you drive real careful and do what you're told . . . or your wife and kid get their tits cut off. Okay?"

Healey made no reply. An hour later, when they were approaching Erzincan, he said, "I guess you people must realize you don't have a hope in hell of pulling this off?"

"Don't give me that shit," Furneux growled. "It's all laid on. With you playin' ball—and you will—we can't miss."

"I got your friends across the Turkish frontier okay," Healey said. "We made it through Istanbul and bypassed Ankara. Okay. I may even be able to talk my way past the guards and into the perimeter. But the moment you start pulling any funny stuff, the second a shot's fired, a number-one-priority general-alert signal goes out from the silo. The NSC warns NATO. And you'd have Starfighters from Erzurum overhead in ten minutes; Third Army shock troops from the Erzincan base parachuted on your backs in half an hour."

"Fuck the Turks' Third Army," said Furneux. "Let me

tell you something, Bright Boy. You want to get anyplace in this sad world, you got to be positive, you got to be sure of yourself. Now, me, I'm so sure of myself that I already contacted the general responsible for the installation of this goddamn missile and told him we *already* beat the shit out of his lousy garrison and took control of the silo; I warned him that a single countermove on his part would like touch off the blue paper at once. We'd launch that baby right away. So you can bet your bottom dollar that the schmucks in NATO will already have been told off to ignore any alarm from Ararat."

"You're crazy," Healey said. He shifted down to steer past a herd of goats nibbling the brushwood at the side of the cratered road. "He'll check back the moment he gets your message. What makes you think he can't use NSA's Military Command Center and speak at once with the officer commanding the site via a KH-11 satellite and one of the Sixth Fleet electronic-surveillance ships? Christ, he can even *see* the site on one of the satellite-serviced video screens in the Center if he wants." The truck bumped around a sharp curve and took the downgrade slanting toward the distant lights of the town. "Within two minutes of your message arriving, the site will be on alert red; as soon as they see it's a lie, you'll have half the armed forces in Europe waiting for you."

Furneux laughed. It was an ugly sound. "You underestimate us, Bright Boy. The message—it's on a tape cassette—has already been *sent*. Because it's a long way from here to Washington, D.C. But it won't be *delivered* until just before we attack. That's why timing is vital: so he'll actually see us in charge and warn reinforcements to lay off when the alert is given, he won't get the message before we move in, figure it for a phony, but bugle in the U.S. cavalry just as a precaution."

Healey said nothing. There was nothing left to say.

He had in fact no knowledge of the Ark's super-deadly warhead; he only knew that the missile had been replaced in an all-systems-go condition and that it was his job to check that those systems worked. Equally, he knew nothing of the appalling threat that would be delivered with the cassette they had been talking about when it was placed in the hands of General Hardanger; he had been told simply that if he wished to save his wife and child he must retarget the missile and if necessary explain how to fire it.

He had not the slightest clue as to the terrorists' identity or what cause they claimed to serve; he was ignorant of their plans once he had gotten them past the security guards at the entrance to the Ararat site. Their own security was such that—apart from constant checks relating central European and eastern standard time, with references to "the attack" and "the cassette"—they had revealed nothing whatever about the operation in front of him. He imagined, however, from a certain sureness, a total confidence in their attitude, that whatever the plan was, it had been very meticulously worked out and that they were all familiar with the layout of the site. The thought worried Healey more than anything: aerial photographs or telephoto pictures in the case of this particular site would be practically valueless; there was only one way they could have gotten sufficiently detailed information to mount a valid plan of attack. From someone on the inside.

In other words, the hijackers had an American or a NATO ally.

Approached from the west, Mount Ararat presents a silhouette not unlike Mont Ventoux, in Provence—a simple peak reached by a gentle slope on one side and a steeper one on the other. There is the difference that Ararat attains a maximum height of sixteen thousand feet, whereas the French summit is some ten thousand feet lower. But visually this is minimized by the fact that the Turkish mountain rises from a stony plain that is already several thousand feet above sea level. DEWS* reflectors are strung along the pre-Alpine chain to the east of Ventoux, but the missile silos connected with them do not house Minutemen and the warheads are not packed with Tabun nerve gas.

The site surrounding the Ark in its lair had been carefully chosen. The silo was blasted from the bedrock in a giant fissure or gully half a mile across, where untold ages of wind, rain, and frost erosion had stripped layers of sedimentary strata from a fault gashing Ararat's volcanic bulk.

Guards patrolled cliff paths one hundred feet up on ei-

*Direct Early Warning System. The chain of front-line radar posts designed to alert NATO commanders in case of nuclear attack.

ther side of the cleft, and there was a small bunker equipped with two machine guns where a dried-up riverbed made a natural exit. But the only manmade barrier was at the end of the narrow, twisting ravine that led unexpectedly to the site—a double chain fence, floodlit after dark, that stretched from wall to wall on either side of the guardhouse and the gates. In the rainy season, torrents rushing down from the bare rock faces formed a natural barrier where they roared over a series of cascades in the riverbed.

Healey's command car had passed north of Lake Van, swinging around a blinding white hotel that stood, part of Turkey's new tourist boom, at the intersection of the road leading to the Iranian border post on the southern slopes of Ararat. Thirty miles farther on, Furneux ordered him to stop. Behind them, the sun hung low over a featureless plain scattered with boulders and patches of shale. In the distance, between them and the mountain, a cluster of goatskin tents marked the site of a nomad encampment.

"Okay, you guys," Furneux rasped, "ready the equipment."

The five terrorists in back of the truck unstrapped packs and bundles that they had carried aboard with them. Besides the Stechkin pistols, Healey saw, each of them now had a short-barreled Kalashnikov AKM automatic rifle with a thirty-round magazine and an ammunition belt. There was in addition a Russian RPG-7V grenade launcher with four of the five-pound high-explosive antitank rockets it was designed to fire. Furneux picked up one of the pear-shaped missiles and fitted it experimentally over the end of the tube.

"What makes you think you won't be walking into an ambush?" Healey tried a last attempt at dissuasion. "Those bodies—my men that you massacred—they'll have been found. Do you imagine they won't be identified and a general alarm for this truck put out?"

"I *know* they won't be identified, Pretty Boy," Furneux said. "They'll have been kitted out with civilian clothes and fake ID papers before they're found. Only the general who gets our cassette will be able to make the connection, and by that time we'll be in there and he won't dare do nothing about it."

"The fellows at the site"—Healey tried another tack—"they've done you no harm; they'll be expecting this vehicle at dusk, as you know. Surely you don't have to shoot them? With those weapons, you could—"

"Shuddup," Paul said from the back of the car.

"Why kill them too? They'd surrender once they saw—"

"Be quiet!" Furneux shouted. "Do what you're fucking told and button your lip. You already heard extracts from that tape of your wife and kid. Another word outta you and we'll make you listen to the bits in between."

Healey swallowed and said no more.

The sun sank. The shadow of the command car lengthened along the dirt road leading to the mountain. Very faintly, once more, Healey could hear the melodic strains of sheep bells from the skinny flock around the encampment.

Furneux looked at his watch. "Get goin'," he ordered. The American started the motor and they jolted forward.

Within ten miles the boulders had increased in numbers and in size. Soon they were threading their way through an enormous jumble of igneous rocks, some of them as high as a house. A track leading off to the right was signposted with a freshly painted board bearing U.S. Army formation codes in neat black figures and lettering. A mile away, the entrance to the ravine showed dark against a rock wall still gold in the sunset. "The boss delivers the cassette in twelve minutes' time," Furneux said. "Wait outside the gulch until I give the word."

Healey nodded. The Canadian was obviously superior to the five men who had hijacked the car; now there was a "boss" above him. Clearly it was a big-time operation as well as one that was disciplined and well-organized.

The minutes passed slowly once they had braked outside the gap in the cliff face. Glittering crystals of muscovite, quartz, and feldspar dimmed among the volcanic outcrops as the light faded. The sky paled; an eagle or a buzzard hung motionless, black against the blue, in the thermal rising from the ravine. There was no sound but the stealthy ticking of metal as the command car's motor cooled.

At last, after a final time check, Furneux said, "General Hardanger will be downing his first cup of coffee in his big house on the banks of the Potomac River. A Filipino houseboy brings in the mail. With it there's a small package containing a cassette. It was just delivered by hand, and the note with it will send the general shouting for his recorder. Get goin', Pretty Boy: we gotta be through those gates and visibly on top before he wises up NSA and their satellite. He ain't goin' to enjoy his second cup of coffee!"

Healey started the motor and drove into the ravine. It twisted left, right, and then straightened out as the walls receded and the entrance to the site came in view.

The road was metaled here. A large board supported on two white posts announced in Turkish: "Defense Department Property. Danger: Keep Out!" Fifty yards farther on, red lettering warned in Turkish, English, Arabic, and French: "U.S. Army. No Unauthorized Entry Beyond This Point."

Above the right-hand side of the ravine, the great bulk of Mount Ararat towered into the darkening sky. "That must have been some flood!" Furneux said.

"How was that?" Paul asked.

"Noah and his fuckin' menagerie, you ignorant wog. You wouldn't know."

"Paul and myself both come from Erzurum," Nesuhi said stiffly. "We are Christians, entirely conversant with the fables in the so-called Old Testament."

"Well, bully for you. Maybe you can explain how come this desert was covered all at once with ten thousand feet of water? And what the fuck those animals had been feeding on before he shoved them into the ark."

"I'm sorry?"

"Aw, forget it." Furneux stared through the windshield. In the dusk, a flat-roofed guardhouse was visible behind the chain fence. Beyond it there was a sector of wooden huts, a helicopter pad, a vaned wheel at the top of a mast over a well. The entrance to the silo was farther down the valley, hollowed from the bedrock.

Arc lights spluttered to life above the fence as the truck approached. In the sudden brightness they could see white helmets and gaiters standing by the gates. Just within the wire was a third notice: "All Passes to Be Shown."

The gates swung open. Healey stopped the command car inside. One of the M.P.'s stepped up on the driver's side. " 'Evening, Captain, sir," he said, saluting. "Another visit from the family doctor to check that the patient's still alive?"

"That's right," Healey said. For an instant he toyed with the idea of blurting out the truth, of tipping the man off and salving his conscience with the concept of duty done. But what *good* would it do? He would certainly be killed;

the guards would still be murdered . . . and they had told him what would happen to Margery and Carole—the instructions already given to the terrorists holding them—if he made one single false move during the raid on the site. He bit his lip and then said, as he had been instructed to say, "A different team this time; the usual gang are on furlough. We have the top kick showing the new guys the ropes."

"That so, Captain?" the M.P. said without interest. "Better check out the ID material, then—just in case they're Russian spies!" He laughed perfunctorily and held out his hand.

Astonishingly, the hijackers did have papers good enough to pass the most thorough scrutiny. Healey held them out with his own. Their weapons hidden, Paul and the others stared incuriously from the rear of the truck. A second M.P. strolled out and came to the far side of the vehicle. For the first time he noticed the insignia on the uniform Furneux was wearing. Snapping a salute, he said, "Colonel, sir. Excuse me. I didn't—"

"That's all right, Sergeant," Furneux said easily. "I wasn't expected, I know. Unofficial visit."

"I'm afraid I have to ask you for your identification and pass, sir, just the same. Orders . . ."

"Of course you do. Quite right." Furneux opened the door and jumped to the ground. He was holding a leather briefcase. "They got buried in among the papers in here. I want a word with your duty officer, anyway." He started toward the guardhouse, and then halted and swung around. "You carry on, Healey," he said. "I'll walk to the silo as soon as I'm through here."

Healey swallowed again. "Yes, sir," he said dully. He banged the stick shift into first and drove on. It was important to secure the entrance to the silo—Furneux had told the others—before any attack was made on the guardhouse. If the latter was alerted first, an alarm would be sounded and steel shutters would automatically seal off the entrance to the bunker, making it difficult if not impossible for the hijackers to complete their task.

It didn't take very long. The weapons, well hidden while they passed the gates, were primed and ready. Paul was now sitting next to Healey with the RPG-7 tube over his shoulder. Ahmed had already placed the grenade in position; Nesuhi, Kamal, and Matsuzaki cradled their AKM's.

There were two guards on duty by the concrete entry to the tunnel in the rock. Two officers—a captain and a lieutenant—ran up the steps to greet the maintenance crew when they saw the familiar command car approach. Healey was deafened by the blast of flame erupting over the open sides of the truck behind him. He saw the officers hurled back down the steps as a hail of 7.62mm slugs from the Kalashnikovs ripped into them. One of the guards spun around and crumpled to the ground, leaving a mess of blood and bone splinters and gluey fragments of brain on the concrete behind where he had been standing. The other man drew his pistol as he fell, but Ahmed drilled him through the forehead with a single shot from his Stechkin and the guard's bullet tore harmlessly through the truck's soft top. Before that, Paul had fired the RPG-7.

The projectile, streaking from the barrel at 330 feet per second, accelerated to three times that speed as the four stabilizer fins opened and the rocket motor cut in with a roar. The HEAT warhead exploded against the entrance wall with a livid flash and a stunning detonation, pulverizing the officers' bodies and dislodging fragments of rock from the cliff face above. Unhurriedly, Ahmed positioned a second grenade in the tube.

Paul actuated the firing mechanism at once. The missile was well placed: it burst halfway down the left-hand side of the entrance, buckling the steel guides channeled into the stonework and jamming the automatically operated armor-plate shutter when it was only halfway to the ground. Echoes of the shattering explosion were still ringing in Healey's ears when more uniformed figures appeared through the dust and smoke whirling around the entrance. They were carrying lightweight submachine guns, but the terrorists, with all the advantages of timing, position, surprise, and knowledge of what was going on, gunned them down before they could loose off more than a token volley. Slugs ripped through the command car's soft top and spanged off the armored fenders, but nobody was touched.

Healey sat behind the wheel, numbed with horror. There was nothing he could do; he was a technician—none of his training had prepared him for this kind of situation. His helplessness was so evident that the terrorists left him alone in the vehicle while they ran through the thinning smoke to the interior of the bunker. He heard more shots, and then—from way behind him by the guardhouse—a single flat explosion, more of a thump than a detonation. He didn't know it, but Furneux, having stalled with his inadequate papers until he heard the opening of the attack, had now taken care of the men he had maneuvered into the building with a plastic concussion grenade. What he did know was that, at the first sign of trouble, the two duty officers deep in the bunker would have been automatically sealed into their subterranean redoubt. These were the men with orders never to leave their posts under any circumstances whatever, the men who held the two keys which alone could open the armored locker containing the direct-line phone to military headquarters, the steel hatch behind which the Ark's red firing button was secured. The keys had to be operated independently, each man using a personal combination of his own, and there was a complex sequence of manipulations that had to be carried out by each of them before the red button became operative, even after an order to fire had been received.

The duty officers would have been sealed in by now . . . and no RPG-7 grenades were going to blast open that inner entry. Healey presumed the terrorists would know this (they certainly appeared to know everything else about the site); he wondered dully how they intended to cope with the fact. He was to find out very soon.

Ahmed, Paul, and the others emerged from the smoking gap in the cliff face. Blood splashed the chest and one sleeve of the Palestinian's combat jacket, although he himself appeared to be uninjured. Elbowing Healey out of the way, he climbed behind the wheel, swung the command car around in a circle, and drove back to the gates. He braked to a standstill outside the guardhouse.

As the dust settled, Furneux was visible in the doorway, stooped over an unconscious guard he was dragging into the open air. Two men had already been stripped of their uniforms and laid out on the packed earth at the side of the building. "All right, you guys," he ordered. "There's two more inside. Bring 'em out and get the gear off them." He glanced at the Rolex on his wrist. "It's time we started in on the serious stuff."

Healey stared at the five guards laid out in a row in the dust. They looked pathetic and defenseless in their socks and undershorts, mouths agape and eyes turned up so that only a thin crescent of white showed between slitted lids. Furneux stood gazing down at them, deliberating. Somewhere behind the guardhouse, a cricket shrilled in the darkness; above it, stars shone brightly beyond the black bulk of the cliff.

The Canadian seemed to come to a decision. "Okay, Paul; this one," he said, touching the youngest guard with his foot. Two of the terrorists came forward and dragged the young man out of the line. Furneux turned and beckoned to Ahmed. "Take care of the others," he said curtly.

With Matsuzaki, Nesuhi, and Kamal, he picked up the youngest soldier and carried him back into the guardhouse. Ahmed reached into the command car and recovered his machine pistol. He slid off the safety and walked over to the four unconscious men. As casually as a man tearing the cellophane wrapper from a cigarette pack, he brought the Stechkin up to hip level and pressed the trigger. Flame stabbed the night as the weapon's staccato detonations beat back from the rock walls of the canyon. The guards' prone bodies jerked and twitched as the slugs smacked into their flesh; beneath them, blood spread and then sank into the dry ground below small spirals of dust. Ahmed hosed the deadly stream of lead from left to right and back again until the Stechkin's magazine was exhausted; then he tossed the gun back into the command car and walked to the guardhouse. Behind the vehicle, Healey fell to his knees and threw up.

When he appeared, with staring eyes and twisted mouth, at the doorway ten minutes later, the surviving guard had been spread-eagled on the trestle table with his wrists and ankles wired to the four corners. "You'll never get away with this, you murderous bastards!" Healey shouted hysterically. "Don't you think there are automatic alarms? Don't you think the two guys in the bunker will have alerted Washington on the hot line?"

Furneux was bent over the trestle table. He looked up. "Don't act so dumb, Pretty Boy," he said.

"They'll send reinforcements, they'll send in a whole division, they'll call on the air force and blast you—"

"Shuddup. I told you: what you just seen, the general will have seen in fuckin' Washington; because of that cassette, he'll be watching this site through the infrared cameras on that satellite. Ain't gonna be no reinforcements within a hundred miles of here. He won't dare."

"You'll never get into the bunker," Healey said desperately. "The duty officers are sealed in there. There's no way you can—"

"Pack it in, stupid. Why do you think we kept this guy alive?" Furneux hooked callused fingers under the waistband of the boy's shorts and ripped them open. "They got arc lights here, don't they? There's a generator with juice in the wiring, ain't there?" He reached across to a desk and picked up a lamp, tearing the cable loose to expose naked ends of copper wire. He stooped to slam the plug at the other end of the cable into a wall socket.

"Finest discovery of the age, electricity," Furneux rasped. "By the time we've finished with this kid, there won't be a secret about this goddamn camp that we don't know about—including the way to override the controls that lock those bunker doors." He grinned wolfishly. "And including just how much *you* know about the works of the baby inside that fuckin' silo," he added.

Nothing is perfect in this sorry world except the calamity. In the things they destroy and the things they spare, they accomplish always and equally a work that is both refined and definitive.

—Jean Giraudoux, *Littérature*

# 4

# A Delicate Mission

Marc Dean was completing a sand castle on a beach that lay to the south and west of Cape Cod when the quiet-spoken young man in the dark blue Brooks Brothers suit trod across the line of wrack that signaled the high-water mark and approached him. The young man was pink-faced, but his gray eyes were unsmiling. He looked oddly out of place in his city clothes among the suntanned, sandy bodies and the children playing in the shallows beneath the summer sky.

Dean's ex-wife, Samantha, lay reading a book with her head pillowed on a rolled-up towel that was balanced on a picnic hamper; Patrick, their eight-year-old son, squatted on his heels, supervising his father's handiwork with a critical eye. None of them noticed the young man in the dark suit until he stopped by the pile of discarded clothes at one side of the hamper. "Shouldn't there be steps up to the drawbridge, Dad?" the boy asked. "The sand's hard enough to—"

"No, no," Dean interrupted. "They could only withdraw the self-propelled guns and the artillery tractors if there was a slope that . . ." He glanced up, seeing the stranger. "Was there something you wanted?" he asked. "Are you looking for somebody?"

"Mr. Dean?" the young man said. "Marcus Matthew Dean, late of Eastern Electronics, presently domiciled in Europe? Paris, to be precise? I'd be grateful, sir, if I could have a word with you."

"If you're well enough informed to find me here," Dean said, "you'll know where I'm staying . . . and you'll know that I'm on vacation. If you must see me, call at my hotel around six. Okay?"

"I'm afraid the matter's urgent, sir." The young man looked at his watch. "It's almost noon, and . . ." He allowed the sentence to tail away into silence.

Dean sighed. "If you must," he said again. "But make it short."

The young man coughed. He shuffled his feet. There was sand clinging to the soles of his highly polished black oxfords; a damp salt mark already stained the heels. "My instructions were to speak to you in private," he said awkwardly, with a glance at Samantha and the boy.

"Jesus," Dean said. "Excuse me, honey. I don't know what the hell this is all about, but, okay, we'll take a walk down to the water's edge and back. If you haven't made your pitch by then, you'll have to call again another day," he added to the man in the blue suit.

Samantha had put down her book as soon as the newcomer spoke. She sat up now and watched the two men stroll down the slope of sand between the oiled sunbathers and the family parties and kids playing softball among the upturned boats. Her divorced husband was in pretty good shape, she thought—almost reluctantly—taking in the muscles that rippled beneath the bronzed skin of Dean's back, the wide shoulders, and the lean, hard frame. At thirty-nine, six feet tall, and an even one-eighty, he could still put to shame most of the handball show-offs and lifesavers on the beach. The tautness of calves and biceps, the narrow hips under those white briefs . . .

Samantha put the thought of Dean's hips out of her mind. Suddenly the sun seemed too hot. She drew on a terry-cloth robe and started to repack the hamper.

If there had been a beauty-competition judge evaluating the feminine components of the beach population, Samantha herself would have rated a slot high up on the list. She was a honey-blond, the shoulder-length hair held back with a wide tortoiseshell comb, the voluptuously curved body sheathed in a black one-piece swimsuit that accentuated the tanned and healthy glow of her skin. Her eyes were wide and her mouth generous, but there was a troubled frown disturbing her features as she put up a hand to shade those eyes from the sun and survey the two figures pacing the wet sand where the wavelets creamed in to the shore.

Samantha was the daughter of an air-force colonel; her father and Dean's had been buddies in World War II. She had sued for divorce when he had quit the electronics corporation of which her father was a director and become a full-time combat leader whose skills were for hire—a mercenary, to put it brutally. The mental cruelty cited in her petition lay, according to her counsel, in the danger to which Patrick would be exposed, having for a father a man for whom death was a business commodity. It was in vain that Dean had protested that air-force colonels too dealt in death, that the electronics company manufactured gadgetry for nuclear rockets, that his wife had made no complaint when he was fighting in Vietnam: the judge had sided with Samantha.

The trouble (she reflected, strapping down the wicker lid of the hamper) was that on a personal level her feelings had never changed. And she knew that he was still in love with her. Physically, she still found him irresistible. Well, almost irresistible; whenever he returned stateside to see Patrick for the periods prescribed by the court, he made a spirited attempt to effect a reconciliation. And each time this happened, supercharged with sexual desire, they risked ending up in bed. But so far the covers had never actually been rumpled: on each and every occasion, something to do with his damnable job (Samantha shook her head, gathering up beach towels) had rocked and finally capsized the boat. War games with the child, who in fact had an artistic bent, quarrels over the boy's education, disagreements on fundamentals, the unexpected arrival of Dean's contacts—anything that reminded her of his profession could be a rock on which the reconciliation foundered.

Until the arrival of the young man with the pink face and the unsmiling eyes, this visit had gone better than any. Samantha lived in a village near Orleans, Massachusetts, but Dean had insisted that neutral ground would allow them less chance of being affected by echoes of the past. He had taken them to this small coastal resort near Narragansett and—she had to admit it—the first of the two weeks had been wonderful. It was an unwritten rule between them that no mention was ever made of his military activity. But this didn't guarantee there would be no disputes. The past seven days, nevertheless, had gone like a breeze. Dean hadn't been involved in a mission for some time: he was relaxed, attentive, good with the boy, and considerate to her. The court decision giving him access to his son did not of course require Samantha to be present when they met, but usually, since he made no objection and in fact welcomed it, she went along—mainly to counterbalance any "bad effects" on Patrick that she figured his father might have. On the current visit, for the first time since the divorce (how long ago was it? three years? four?) she was there because she wanted to be. As near happy as she could remember, she had even begun seriously to consider a reconciliation herself. If only she could persuade him to quit. If only he could see her point of view. If only she could convince him. If only . . .

It was conditional, but a future with Dean had once more seemed at least a possibility.

Until the man in the Brooks Brothers suit arrived.

Dean had been born on June 6, 1944, date of the Normandy landings, the biggest military operation in history, so perhaps it was hardly surprising that he leaned toward the martial arts. The birthdate, on the other hand, made him a Gemini, the sign above all others that imposed on those born under it a dual personality. Gemini . . . the fighting twins: one good, one bad; one generous, one selfish; one tender, one tough. It had been Samantha's hope when they married that she could nourish and enlarge the more romántic, sensitive side of Dean's nature; her complaint when they divorced was that the ruthless man of action was in the ascendancy. She had even extended the dichotomy to his first and middle names: Marc was the rugged one, for the boys, the veterans, the people he met in his job; Matt was the man she loved, the guy who could share with her the mystery of the stars on a November night, who could conjure from a harpsichord the beauties of Bach and Scarlatti.

It was Matt who had walked to the water's edge with the stranger. As soon as she saw his face, she knew with a chill of disappointment and despair that it was Marc who had returned.

She stood up. "Honey," he began, "I'm awfully sorry, but . . ."

"Well?"

He wouldn't meet her eyes. There was sand in the hollow between her breasts, and a dark fragment of wrack that adhered to one firm slope of flesh. He had to resist the temptation to reach out and remove it. "I have to go see a fellow," he said. "It's important. But it's not far, just along the coast a little way. I . . . I guess I should be back at the hotel by midnight."

Samantha's expression was stormy. The man in the blue

suit had wandered a few paces away; Patrick was with two friends, playing sea hawk on an upturned dory. "You won't find me here," she said.

"Ah, come on, honey. Don't be like that. You know—"

"I know one thing," she said fiercely. "If you go away with that man, neither Patrick nor I will be here when you come back."

The house was on Weaver's Hill in Greenwich, Connecticut—a single-story red-brick chalet with deep-overhang eaves that were painted white. It stood among similar though not identical properties in a tree-shaded suburban street. There was a small pool beside the carport; single lengths of chain slung between white posts guarded the clipped lawn that ran down to the road. The punched aluminum name tag attached to the mailbox read simply: "A. A. Mackenzie."

The second initial stood for Archibald, but if there was any Scottish blood in the regional director's ancestry, it didn't show in his voice or in the military precision of his speech patterns. He sat talking to Henry Carpenter in a small room overlooking the backyard. There were glass-fronted bookshelves along one wall, and two comfortably worn leather armchairs in front of the desk. A large television screen in one corner displayed a printout of the latest news bulletins from AP, UP, and Reuter.

"This fellow Dean," the National Security assistant was saying, "you are sure—absolutely sure—that he's . . . well, that he's the best possible choice?"

"As sure as I can be," Mackenzie replied. "Clearly I cannot guarantee it one hundred percent. But as far as security rating, screening, and all the normal vetting goes, he comes out tops. The man was decorated more than once in Vietnam; he went back as an AID 'pacification' specialist in '72 after a spell with the Peace Corps. He was infiltrated into Cambodia and sent secret information back to Westmoreland when we were bombing the Ho Chi Minh Trail. He worked with a senatorial committee on international relations before he . . . before he was seduced into his present occupation. He's a brilliant tactician; he's bested hijackers before."

"And you figure he'll accept this assignment?"

Mackenzie fingered his clipped mustache. "We shall find out very soon," he said. "The check you ran on this threat—the genuineness of the terrorists' boast, the feasibility of retargeting the missile, whether this man Healey is competent to do it—it was positive all the way, I suppose?"

Carpenter sighed. "All the way," he said. "Tom Argyle, the Rand Corporation whiz kid who's been advising Hardanger, confirmed every point. He knows the site, he knows the missile, and he knows Healey. Specifically, he knows precisely the extent of Healey's own knowledge—and he's had access to the guy's dossier: everything from his IQ rating, through his refresher-course results, to an up-to-date analysis of his 'maximum-danger' capability. They could fire the damned thing at Tehran, all right."

"And they are already there, in total command of the site, the way they said?"

"Sure they are. Hardanger ran satellite checks the moment he got that cassette. He actually witnessed the last part of the takeover." Carpenter shook his head. "Murderous bastards."

"Any developments since?"

"Nothing beyond the time schedule conveyed to Hardanger on the direct line from the silo. He called off the Turkish unit that would have answered the automatic alarm, said it was a technical failure and that everything was okay. He stalled the U.S. Army detail that was to have relieved the guard yesterday. An unidentified chopper landed half a dozen more terrorists on the pad this morning. They're wearing GI uniforms, making just like the genuine guard, four-hour tricks and all."

Mackenzie's fingers drummed on the desk. "And the number of people in the know?" he asked. "Still the same group?"

The National Security adviser nodded, reaching in a pocket for his pipe. "Same old gang. Hardanger. McClintock. A colonel named Weiss who's a missile specialist. The Rand man, Argyle. You and me."

"That's six already . . . and we're about to make it seven, with Dean. The risks of a secret leaking increase geometrically, rather than mathematically, with the number of people who know it. I shall have to make it a condition that any men Dean hires are kept in the dark."

"Kept in the dark? But you can't expect—"

"I mean, Henry, kept in the dark about the ultimatum and the means the terrorists are using in the hope of making us accept it. Of course, if it comes to an Entebbe-style raid, then naturally they'll have to know that a *site* has been occupied. But they must on no account be a party to the fact that there's a missile there, or know anything about its warhead or the blackmail arising from that."

Carpenter was stuffing tobacco from the oiled pouch into his pipe. He said, "But your man Dean may have to call in *official* help—Interpol, police departments in Greece and Turkey and Luxembourg, program evaluators from the NSC computer. If he's to track down and identify these people as a first step, I mean."

"None of them need know the real reason for his questions. But that's why we dare not ask for assistance from NATO: they might insist on reasons. Talking of the ultimatum: there *is* a deadline?"

"Certainly. Before Mubarak leaves Paris. Effectively that gives us fourteen days. He flies to Israel on July 17." Carpenter struck a match and held it to the bowl of his pipe. "You were speaking . . . when we first met . . ." he said between puffs, "of irony. I agree that Hardanger . . . is unlikely to possess that quality. But . . . the same cannot be said . . . for whoever is directing the hijackers."

"Meaning?"

"In view of the fact that the missile's code-named Ark, it cannot be an accident that this particular date was chosen for the expiration of an ultimatum that could destroy the world."

Mackenzie was looking puzzled.

Carpenter shook out his match and dropped it into an ashtray. "Genesis Eight," he explained. "The fourth verse. 'And the Ark rested in the seventh month, on the seventeenth day of the month, upon the mountains of Ararat.' "

The regional director nodded slowly. "Yes," he said. "I see."

"And then later, Alex: 'And all flesh died that moved upon the earth, both of fowl, and of cattle, and of beast, and of every creeping thing that creepeth upon the earth, and every man: all in whose nostrils was the breath of life, died. And every living substance was destroyed which was upon the face of the ground.' "

Mackenzie shuddered. "As good a description of the final holocaust as we shall get," he said. "You mean that the choice of date is a subtle way of tipping us off that they do know what's in the warhead of that damned missile?"

"Yes, I do. Think of the planning that went into the site takeover, the kidnap, the selection of alternatives. Think of the chopper bringing the extra men. This is no rag-bag anarchist commando we're dealing with here, no band of dissident Palestinians or Armenians with chips on their shoulders. This is a big-time operation backed with a hell of a lot of money. And the brains behind it may be twisted, but there's no doubt whatever of their quality."

Before Mackenzie could reply, a bell shrilled in the hallway outside the room. He pushed back his chair and got to his feet. "That will be young Carter with Dean," he said.

"Carter? He doesn't know why he's been detailed to bring Dean in?"

"Of course not," Mackenzie said testily. "He's a very junior operative: that's all he does, locate people and bring them here or to Langley. He hasn't even been on overseas assignment yet. That's why I chose him. He doesn't have any two and two to put together." He led the way to the front door.

Marc Dean looked angry. In a cab from the beach to Narragansett, during a helicopter flight from there to Greenwich, and now on this latest trip, made in a black Cadillac with blinded windows, he had been able to get nothing out of the young man named Carter except that the National Security assistant to the President of the United States wished to see him; that it was urgent; that it was secret; and that it had to do with some kind of mission.

Carpenter's face was familiar to Dean from newspaper photos. He had never met Mackenzie, had no idea that Carter worked for the CIA. "Perhaps, sir," he said stiffly to the NSC adviser, "I might be permitted some idea now of why I have been brought here? I was on vacation; this business has already provoked family trouble."

Carpenter took Dean's hand and shook it. "I can answer in a single phrase—not original, I'm afraid," he said genially. "Your country needs you. It was good of you to come, Dean."

"It seems I didn't have much choice," Dean said.

"Well . . . things may seem more reasonable when

you've heard what we have to say. Shall we retire to your sanctum, Alex?"

"Certainly," Mackenzie replied. "That's all, Carter. You can return the car to the pool now."

"Sir." The young man with the pink face turned on his heel and strode back to the Cadillac.

Mackenzie took them through the sparsely furnished modern hallway, past orange and brown and olive-green single-panel doors, to a kitchen in back of the house. An agreeable odor of baking, which greeted them as he opened the door, was overlaid with the bitter smell of charred cooking. "Oh, my God," he exclaimed. "I sent my wife over to have coffee with friends while we talked. I forgot that I promised to keep an eye on the oven!" He yanked open the stove, releasing a cloud of black smoke, and snatched out a tray of burned cookies. "That's another evening in the doghouse," he said, laying the tray down by an open window. "Let's get out of here."

He opened a door between the dishwasher and the deep freeze and took them down a flight of steps into a cellar. Behind the racked bottles and empty baggage and vacation gear was another door that had to be opened with three separate keys. The room inside was no more than six feet square, a cream-walled cube with a copper-screened fluorescent light in the ceiling. Three tubular-steel chairs and a computer console on a metal table stood on the wall-to-wall General Services Administration carpeting.

The room—which Mackenzie had seldom used since he had been transferred from New York to the southeast European theater—was enclosed like a cherry stone in its fruit by an eighteen-inch stressed-concrete shell through which no sound and no electrical signal could escape. The insulation was pierced only by the conduit feeding current to the light and by a thick cable linked to the computer. Mackenzie closed and locked the door. "Don't want to seem melodramatic," he said apologetically. "It's very unlikely that my home has been bugged or that some villain has a directional mike trained on my study. But you can't be too careful. Especially on this deal."

"If I knew who it was talking . . . ?" Dean began.

"Sorry. The name is Mackenzie. We haven't met, but I know you; you've worked with Quinnel more than once, haven't you? Hugh Quinnel? Tall, lanky guy looks like an overgrown schoolkid?"

"Quinnel? Sure I have. This is a CIA routine, then?"

"Quinnel works for me." Mackenzie avoided a direct answer. He settled himself at the keyboard of the console, punching in his access identifiers and connecting the computer outpost to the CIA's central data bank at Langley. The lines of greenish characters assembling and then rippling away on the screen in answer to the top-secret queries he was feeding to one confidential sector of the bank meant nothing to Dean or Carpenter. But soon he swung away from the console and shook his head. "Nothing new," he reported. "Just a confirmation of the deadline and a warning that any leak would be as good as pressing the button. Sit down, gentlemen. Sit down."

Dean's brows were raised. If this spare gray man was Quinnel's boss, if Carpenter was involved and there was talk of "pressing the button," it looked—bearing in mind the sealed room and the other precautions—as though he was onto something very big indeed. But why him? If it was that important, why were they taking such trouble to bring in secretly a mercenary, a man disdained by the military, disowned by the politicians, ignored by the administration? A man who officially didn't even exist. Perhaps for that very reason, Dean thought to himself wryly. He was all at once interested, waiting eagerly for an explanation.

"Before I say any more," Mackenzie began, "I have to have your solemn word as a loyal American citizen that nothing said between these walls will ever be repeated anywhere by you. And your signature to a document which is in its essence an oath to that effect."

Dean smiled lazily. "No problem, sir," he said. Covertly regarding the man's crisp pale hair and wide blue eyes, the determined mouth and chin set in those rugged features, Henry Carpenter felt, for the first time since General Hardanger had contacted him with his fearful dilemma, a lessening of the weight on his shoulders. At least, he thought, whatever the means by which he lived, this was a person to be trusted.

When the formalities were over, Mackenzie summarized the situation, from the illegal installation of the Ark with its terrifying warhead, through the kidnap of Healey's wife and child and the invasion of the site, to the ultimatum and the unthinkable alternatives it offered. After he had finished, there was a short silence, and then Dean said,

"My God! As you say, sir, they seem to have you over a barrel."

"We want you to help us, Dean," Carpenter said.

"You can name any figure you like"—Mackenzie.

Dean scratched his jaw. "Couple of questions I'd like to put to you first," he said.

"Go ahead."

"First . . . well, I guess you have satisfied yourselves that the threat is valid; that these people can do, have the power to do, what they threaten?"

Mackenzie sighed. "Unfortunately, yes. Hardanger's tame Rand expert has confirmed it. So far as the site is concerned, we've seen there."

"Second, with all the huge resources of NATO, the U.S. Army and Air Force, the Pentagon planners at your service, why call on me?"

Carpenter told him why. "It's vital, absolutely vital, that the President's kept out of this," he added. "And that means the Pentagon has to be kept out of it too—except for the three men we have told you about. I'm sure you can see that."

"You couldn't sacrifice this guy Healey? Nuke the silo and wipe out the threats in one go? You wouldn't have to face either of your alternatives then."

"That was the first thing we thought of," Mackenzie said. "Naturally." He shrugged. "The silo's proof against anything less than a five-megaton burst directly on target. With the Russian border so close . . ." The sentence was left unfinished.

Dean was looking dubious. "I'm a combat leader, a military adviser if you like," he said. "Not an undercover planner or a dirty-tricks expert. I'm sorry. I'm afraid this isn't my scene."

"With your experience, surely you could turn your talents toward—"

"I don't think so."

"The challenge doesn't interest you?"

"All challenges interest me," Dean said frankly. "So long as they're in my field. I don't think this is."

Mackenzie tried another tack. "Quinnel tells me, from his own knowledge of you, that you have invariably refused any assignment when you knew that it might work against the interests of the United States."

"I'd like to think that was true, sir," Dean said.

"Well, I'm asking you to show us the other side of that coin. To *accept* an assignment, knowing that it is very much *in* the interests of your country. I appeal to your loyalty as an American, Dean."

"You're putting me in a very difficult position."

"Not as difficult as the one we're in," said Carpenter.

Dean smiled resignedly. "Well . . ." he said on a rising inflection.

"You will?" Mackenzie pounced. "Splendid fellow!"

"Seems you're not the only ones over a barrel!" Dean said.

He began to take notes as Mackenzie amplified the details of their predicament. "They'll be committed to memory and destroyed before I leave here," he promised.

Later, the CIA regional director said, "There are only two solutions possible if this extortion is not to succeed. One, to find some way of immobilizing the Ark without the hijackers on the site knowing it is being done; and two, to work out a method of rendering the terrorists themselves incapable of launching the missile on the chosen day. The second alternative would be largely a matter for your own judgment; on the first, you could count on any technical assistance or advice—the entire resources of NSA if necessary—that you wanted."

"But they'd have to be kept in the dark about why I wanted it?"

"Right. The same restriction applies to the team you choose to help you—and any organizations supplying arms, information, computer data, or police assistance."

"Okay. I'm free to select whatever team I like?"

Mackenzie glanced at Carpenter, who nodded. "With one proviso," Mackenzie said. "I'd want to vet anyone you chose. I'd want the right of veto. And I'll emphasize again: your team must *not* know about the Tabun warhead or the ultimatum; the most they can be told is that a missile silo has been taken over by terrorists."

Dean said, "Suppose neither of your two alternatives proves workable?"

"In that case," Henry Carpenter said soberly, "we have *no* alternative. On a lesser-of-two evils basis, the ransom demand will have to be met and Mubarak must die."

"You want me to work out a contingency plan for that too?" Dean sounded shocked.

"I'm afraid so," Mackenzie said. "We'll supply the guy who pulls the trigger, though."

"But I'm the patsy if anything goes wrong?"

"I guess I can't deny that," the CIA chief admitted after a short pause. "The whole point of using . . . outside . . . help is to keep the President and the administration in the clear."

The combat leader repressed a smile. He was shrewdly aware that one—just one—reason *he* had been corralled for this job was the fear that the terrorists, even if their demand was met, might renege on the bargain and reveal that the U.S. had organized the murder of the Egyptian President. If, as seemed possible, the long-term aim of the operation was to cause the maximum embarrassment to American prestige, such a betrayal would be highly likely. In which case, better a mercenary scapegoat than the Agency!

For another half-hour the three men considered ways and means, examining the possibilities, running over the dissident groups conceivably responsible for the outrage. It was crazy, Dean thought to himself: here they were, discussing a world threat of unimaginable gravity as casually and nonchalantly as men deciding whether or not to have a second highball before they went in to lunch. Yet if the issue had been of relatively minor importance—whether a sports delegation could properly be sent to racist South Africa, for instance—they could have been on their feet and shouting!

Finally, when the menace had been analyzed to the point of exhaustion, Dean asked, "Shall I be working through Quinnel when we get to the operative stage? I presume you'll want day-by-day contact, even if you're officially out of the picture?"

Mackenzie shook his head. "We have to keep the number of people in the know to an absolute minimum," he said. "Also, you've worked with Quinnel before. In the intelligence world, that could make a link between you, the hijackers, and the Agency, if you were seen together. But we do of course require continuous contact. As the silo's in an area that's part of my sector, I'll handle it myself: I'm leaving for Europe tomorrow. We'll keep in touch through heads of station in Turkey, Greece, Luxembourg, France, wherever you will be. I'll give you numbers to call."

"I'd better leave for Europe tomorrow myself," Dean said. "Time's mighty short on this one."

"You're already booked on Pan-Asiatic."

"Pan-*Asiatic*?"

"Via Los Angeles, Tokyo, Delhi, and Ankara. I don't really believe anyone would have my house under surveillance, but it's best to be sure. So long as nobody connects you with me, or the Agency, or even Europe at this time, you'll have a slight advantage over the outside help these bastards must have."

"Right now," Dean said, "I'd appreciate a ride north and east to the beach where you found me: I promised my son and my ex that I'd be back before midnight."

But the suite he had reserved was in darkness when he arrived at the hotel. His bags had been packed and left on the rack by the door. Through the open window he could hear the surf breaking along the empty shore. Of Samantha and Patrick there was no sign.

"Mrs. Dean and the young gentleman, sir?" the night porter said. "But they checked out"—examining the register—"yes, early this evening, sir. Madam said you'd understand." And then: "No, sir. They left no forwarding address."

# 5

# Advantage Striker

The flowered carpeting in the upper corridors of the Hotel Georges V in Paris is very thick. The fat man, who was, like many large individuals, uncommonly light on his feet, made no sound as he approached the door of suite 712B. He was immaculately dressed in lizard shoes, a superbly cut off-white sharkskin suit, and a dark shirt buttoned at the neck. Although the city was sweltering in a heat wave and the shade temperature in the Avenue des Champs-Elysées was thirty-five degrees Centigrade, the suit was uncreased and the fat man's hairless face was as dry and smooth as the marble top to the console supporting the flower arrangement at the end of the corridor.

Inside 712B, the two girls he had ordered deftly removed his clothes and helped him onto the massage table he had installed between the desk and the sofa in the *salon*. They were about to begin the subtler, more intimate part of the operation when there was a musical burble from the phone on the desk. The fat man sighed. "Hand it to me, Ghislaine," he said to the redhead.

"Your transatlantic call, Monsieur Hamid," the voice of the switchboard girl said in his ear.

The brunette "masseuse," staring at the huge hairless body as she waited with the cologne-soaked cotton in her hand, was unable to make much of Hamid's end of the conversation.

"Yes," he said. "Yes, but I told you not to call me here . . . It's what? . . . Oh, I see. Well, well. That might be very smart of them or it might be extraordinarily foolish. We shall see. . . . Dean, did you say? Marc Dean? With a completely free hand? . . . Yes, I know him. We have, as a matter of fact, met. I shall have to warn our friends on the site. . . . I agree: it's most important that Alicia, Marcel, and Hassan are instructed to be especially careful with our guests. I shall attend to that myself."

Hamid, who had been sitting up on the massage table, now swung his fat legs to the ground. "As for the accommodating Mr. Dean," he said, "I shall contact certain other friends and leave the matter in their capable hands. Don't forget to keep me briefed on his movements." He hooked the receiver back on its lightweight base and handed the phone to the redhead.

When the two girls had attended to his needs, he paid them and sent them away. Wrapping himself in a scarlet silk robe, he sat down at the desk and made three phone calls himself. One—it took a quarter of an hour to get through—was to a country number in Luxembourg. Another was to an apartment in Belleville, one of the city's poorer quarters, where the population was largely Arab. The third call was taken by a woman in uniform. She lived in an attic studio near the Sacré Coeur, high above the roofs of Montmartre. The studio was unusual in that there was a loft above it—and between the peaked slate dormers above the loft there rose an extraordinarily sophisticated complex of radio antennae.

As soon as Hamid had finished speaking, the woman pushed open a trapdoor above her bed, pulled down a counterweighted ladder, and climbed to the loft. Beneath the dusty, sloping beams in one corner, a high-powered ultra-high-frequency transmitter-receiver was installed. She plugged leads into a square photographer's junction box that was connected to the electricity supply in the flat below, and activated the set.

A very slight hum became audible over the distant boom of traffic seven floors below. Dust motes danced in a ray of sunlight slanting through the grimed skylight. The woman was sweating: it was hot and airless in the confined space beneath the dormers. She switched on a flexible reading lamp and twisted it to illuminate the dials and levers on the radio console. Red and blue pilot lights glowed as she manipulated the tuners.

Sometime later, settling a headset over her ears, she turned aside to grasp the rubber-covered handles at the foot of a steel shaft controlling the rotation of a directional aerial on the roof above. She maneuvered the aerial until the signal she was receiving was at maximum volume, and then turned back to make an adjustment to the transmitter. A blue pilot faded and died, to be replaced by a green one.

The woman leaned forward and spoke into a microphone that sprouted from the console.

"A message from Number One," she said. "They are calling in outside help: a mercenary named Dean. It seems he is not without a certain competence."

She listened for a short while to a voice quacking in the cans, and then said, "He could be alone or with a small team. The guard is to be especially alert for any unusual movement outside the perimeter. Orders have been given for the elimination of this obstacle before your sector is reached. But it is as well to be prepared. The trailer has already been warned."

Another pause. And then: "Of course. Immediate destruction on sighting. Call back at the usual time. I have to leave now: I am on duty."

She removed the headset, switched off the transmitter, and returned to the apartment below. Fifteen minutes later, she was smiling professionally at potential customers in a luxuriously furnished office beneath the colonnades that bordered the Rue de Rivoli.

# 6

# Dean Detained

Marc Dean arrived in Istanbul on Day Three of a two-week countdown to the ultimatum expiring. The first attack came on the morning of Day Four.

Dean had been directed to an Arab enclave on higher ground not far from the famous Topkapi Museum. In one of the bazaars beneath the cypresses surrounding that huge complex lived Mahmoud Yusuf, the assassin wished on Dean by the CIA. Yusuf was a Palestinian—an ex-member of the Palestine Liberation Organization who had quit because he believed Arafat should be tougher, much tougher with Israel. He was also (Dean reflected sourly) a natural for the fall guy if everything else fell through and the plan to kill President Mubarak was put into action.

The Arab was surprisingly lighthearted for a professional triggerman. It was only the subjects of his black humor—the Israeli attacks on Beirut, bomb outrages in Paris, anti-Semitism in Europe—that pulled Dean up short from time to time. Yusuf agreed to visit Dean's hotel that evening, to study maps of the airport sector from which—according to Mackenzie's contacts in the French DST counterintelligence service—Mubarak would leave on July 17. "The plan may never have to be activated," Dean told him, "but it has to be watertight, I mean like one hundred percent, and ready to put into operation at very short notice. We'll go case the airport itself next week."

Yusuf's sallow, mustached face split open in a grin. "Maybe I can find time for a little night life," he said. "This city boasts nothing but cabarets . . . and these are staffed entirely by girls from England, France, and Holland who thought they had been hired as dancers. Can you imagine?"

"Only too easily," Dean said. "Is there a shorter route back to the center than the way I came? Could you show me from here?"

"Only too easily," Yusuf echoed. "Come: I show you."

From the door of the small flat-roofed house where he was a lodger, he gave the combat leader directions. The route led through a network of narrow streets—a sort of Turkish casbah—past the Haseki Hamami baths and the Mosque of Sokullu Mehmed Pasha, built by the sixteenth-century architect Sinan, to a business quarter nearer St. Sophia.

Dean was on foot. As he drew farther away from the alley where Yusuf lived, the lanes became wider but more crowded, so that sometimes he had to shoulder his way through the press to make any headway. And even here the thoroughfares were still too narrow to permit the passage of an automobile.

He was in sight of an arch through which, some way below, he could see boats crowding the bright waters of the Bosporus, when the first sign of trouble appeared.

For some time he had been aware—or thought he had been aware—of crisper European-style footfalls behind him among the anonymous shuffling of the slippered Muslims. It sounded as though he was being followed by a man—two men?—wearing heavy leather-soled shoes. When he turned to look behind him, he was unable to single out any individuals from the throng, but he was almost sure now: he varied his pace; the footsteps quickened or slowed down in time with his own.

Alert for the sudden attack in a quarter he suspected was rarely penetrated by westerners, he kept to the middle of the street. But now there was trouble ahead too. Three men, tough-looking characters in tarbooshes and striped shifts, were barring his way to the arch.

Dean glanced swiftly around. Hole-in-the-wall stores lined each side of the lane, tiny *caves* and kiosks in which carpet sellers, tinners, jewelers, and vendors of sweetmeats plied their trade. To his right, a narrow entry led for fifteen yards toward a high blank wall with a gate in it. Beyond palm fronds on the far side of the wall the domes and minarets of the great Suleimaniye Mosque bulked against the summer sky. And behind Dean—yes, he had not been mistaken!—two more thugs approached. Both wore heavy boots beneath their robes; one held a knife half-hidden in his sleeve.

The busy life of the street, scenting violence, was visibly melting away into shops and doorways. The high singsong of the Muslim population, arguing, gossiping, bargaining, faded to a murmur of anticipation. Dean ducked into the entry and swung around to face his attackers. If you're outnumbered in personal combat (he had always advised the men he was training), hit first and hit hard, as soon as you know the bastards are after you, or even before. If you strike first, you may take them by surprise and reduce the odds against you, apart from which it gives you a psychological advantage and it gives them a false idea of your strength. If you *have* made a mistake, you can always apologize afterward. On the other hand, if you leave the initiative to them, there may not be any afterward.

Well, he himself was outnumbered now. It was five to one, and he was unarmed. Here was a chance to put his own theories to the test!

Dean leaped at the nearest man, who was running into the cul-de-sac ahead of his companions. The three who had been guarding the arch were still some yards away. He slashed the thug across the throat with the edge of his right hand, slammed a short left into the robe at belly level, and then, before he could as much as raise his arms, seized the man's head and brought it crashing down to meet his jerked-up knee. The Muslim hit the ground like a felled tree, blood from his broken nose spraying the cobbles.

The combat leader stamped on the back of the man's head as he crouched to meet the attacker with the knife. This one was a professional, a killer—the wicked blade held hip-high, the honed point jutting upward to rip the guts. But Dean knew about that one. His toe flashed out to connect with the hood's knuckles. The fingers opened involuntarily. The knife clattered to the ground . . . and Dean sprang in to close quarters. Savagely he hauled the man's shift up and forward, pinning his arms and half-stifling him. He jammed the attacker against the wall, kicked again with all his force, and thudded three fierce rights to the dirty undershirt he had exposed. The killer rolled away screaming, a hand pressed between his legs.

Only with the first two thugs down could the remaining trio move in. That was why Dean had chosen to face them in the entry: you lose the advantage of five-to-one odds if the space available allows only two to advance at a time (coda to his unarmed-combat course, he reflected as he prepared to meet the second wave). But the reinforcements were bigger and tougher than the original attackers. One held a stick weighted with lead; the other two carried knives.

The stick man and one of the others moved forward shoulder to shoulder, leaving the third man in reserve. Their plan must be to drop him with the blackjack and then slash with the knives. Dean had no illusions about their intentions. This was no rolling in an alley for the cash in his billfold. The aim of the operation was death. His death.

Desperately now, he stared around him. He couldn't use the kick technique again against the knife: the man with the stick would cripple his leg before he connected. He turned abruptly and ran back to where the cast-iron bracket of a streetlamp projected from the wall above his head. He leaped upward. His outstretched fingers touched the rough metal, failed to grip, slipped. He jumped again, frenziedly, as the assassins raced in. This time his hands grasped the bracket and held firm.

Swinging like a pendulum, he brought up his knees, straightened his legs, and then slammed his heels as hard as he could against the chest of the leading thug. There wasn't enough force behind it to do any damage, but the man was caught off balance and lurched back to collide with his companions. For a moment they staggered between the walls of the alley.

It was the opportunity Dean had been waiting for. He swung back, hard . . . harder still forward . . . back again . . . and then, lifting his bent legs once more, he launched himself up and over. His body lanced through the air above the heads of the attackers. There was a confused blur of activity as he hurtled over. Something struck his thigh. A razor-sharp blade sliced through one sleeve and pierced his forearm. Then he had landed on the cobbles with a jar that shook him from head to toe. But he was in the street again, facing his assailants from the rear.

In the instant before they grasped the situation and whirled to meet him, he acted. Fear and anger and surprise lent him a formidable strength. Seizing the nearest thug by the shoulders, he spun him forcefully sideways.

There was a tinsmith's shop on the corner of the entry, with a brazier for melting the solder outside. The man cannoned into this, knocked it over as he fell, and received its cargo of glowing coals in his lap. His cheap cotton robes blazed up instantly, choking his screams into silence as he threshed on the ground in a flaming heap.

Dean's eyes were glittering now in a face that was twisted into an expression of malevolent glee. This was the kind of challenge he craved: he had shortened the odds; now he had a chance to win. "Three down and two to go," he panted. "All right, you motherfuckers, come and get me!"

They were already coming. He twisted a tall pyramid of cooking utensils off its display stand and shoved it toward them. The remaining knife man charged into it, staggering aside as the pots and pans clanged to the roadway. Dean raised his arms to ward off a crippling blow from the club. There was a numbing impact that paralyzed his left shoulder, and then he was at close quarters again, grappling with the assassin, pulling the man across his body at the same time as the thug with the knife recovered his balance and stabbed viciously upward.

The club-wielder stiffened suddenly, gave a curious choking gurgle, and then slid limply from Dean's grasp.

Dean sensed the hot gush of blood through the lightweight leg of his pants. Before the last attacker could bend and pull his knife from the belly of his unintended victim, he picked him up bodily, raised him above his head, and hurled the man down on the overturned brazier. In a second, he too was ablaze, rolling frantically on the cobbles among the clattering pans in a futile attempt to extinguish the flames devouring his garments and searing his flesh.

The tinsmith was yelling blue murder, but the other inhabitants of the quarter had gathered in groups on the far side of the lane, where they stood respectfully watching the action unroll. Dean straightened his ripped bush shirt, bound a handkerchief around the gash on his forearm, and walked briskly through the arch and down toward the Golden Horn. He had gone less than fifty yards before a merchant emerged from behind a clothing stall and offered to replace his bloodstained trousers ("At a price which leaves me out of pocket, *effendi*: it is through admiration for your valor that I make this sacrifice").

Dean grinned and paid the extortionate price demanded. Half an hour later he was threading his way between the closely packed tables of an open-air café built on a stage projecting over the Bosporus.

It was hot in the bright sunlight, and the glare from the

water was hard on the eyes. Dean was relieved to see that the man he had come to meet was sitting in the shade beneath a striped parasol—a very large black man with a dazzling smile and muscles that rippled beneath the flowered T-shirt he was wearing.

"What happened, squire?" he asked in an exaggeratedly English accent. "I was beginning to think you'd been seduced by a belly dancer or tempted into a house of ill fame that was full of Eastern promise."

"Somebody tried to tempt me into the morgue," Dean said somberly. He stared out over the blue and white and yellow boats crowding the waterfront. "There's nothing new in that, Ed—but I'd sure like to know how come they were expecting me, how it was they were able to lay for me when I only hit town last night and didn't know where the hell I was going to be until this morning."

# 7

# A Negative Brief

Edmond Mazzari had been born in the Congo when it was Belgian. Enlisted in the army as a sergeant, he had been sent to Oxford University, England, as part of a government-sponsored scheme to train an officer cadre capable of running the country once independence had been won. Mazzari had left Europe with a bachelor's degree, a command of British English that would have staggered the late P. G. Wodehouse, and a strong dislike for the wheeling and dealing that was corrupting the politicians of Brazzaville and Kinshasa. Preferring himself to choose those in whose service his military skills could be used, he had become a mercenary. Working with Marc Dean on many of his most perilous missions, he had also become one of the combat leader's closest friends.

His confidence in Dean and his judgment was such that he had flown immediately from Hamburg to Istanbul, without a single query, on receipt of a laconic telegram simply stating the date, the time, and the address of the waterside café where they met.

"All right, old lad," he said when Dean had provided a brief rundown on his brush with the killers, "give now with the background: why should your gentle self be jumped by the fezzed gentry? Why has yours truly from the breast of his loved one in distant Krautland thus rudely been plucked? As your esteemed countrymen say, what is the jolly old pitch?"

So far as he was able within the terms of his mandate from Mackenzie, Dean put Mazzari in the picture. It was hard for him not to take his old buddy entirely into his confidence, but he said nothing of the missile or its nerve gas warhead. "A crowd of heavies from who-knows-where raid an abandoned silo in eastern Turkey and take it over . . . and then the Central Intelligence Agency hires *us* to get it back? There's something rum there, something very

70

rum indeed," Mazzari said. He looked keenly at Dean. "That's not the whole story, squire, is it?"

"I'm sorry, Ed." Dean was discomfited. "My terms of reference . . . I had to sign a paper . . . I hope you understand."

"Not to worry," Mazzari assured him. "We'll take it as read that it's a regular deal: your word's good enough for me." He plucked his lower lip, staring into the crimson depths of a Campari-soda on the table in front of him. "All the same . . . a NATO silo, a gang of your actual hijackers, the Agency relying on the hired help? That smells of some kind of ransom to me. My guess would be that the site's not so bloody abandoned, that these johnnies are threatening to do something nasty if the Agency doesn't come across. Organize the release of some political prisoners perhaps? Free some other terrorists? Something like that?"

"No comment," Dean said wretchedly.

Mazzari grinned, the white teeth flashing in the shade beneath the parasol. "Point taken," he said. "Just the two of us—or does the Treasury Department run to a trio?"

"Don't talk about any sector of the administration," Dean warned. "Not even in whispers. We come strictly out of secret allotments that don't have to be approved by Congress. No . . . I plan to organize a compact group, just guys we've worked with before."

"Hammer?"

Dean nodded. Sean Hammer was a tough little Irish-American ex-con who had been his other trusted lieutenant on the majority of his more dangerous assignments. "And Kurt and Emil and Wassermann and Daler," he said. "Plus the hit man I saw this morning—who's been wished onto us by the Agency—and maybe one other."

Kurt Schneider was a solid and reliable seaman, a North German who helped his brother run a waterfront bar and a boatyard when he wasn't ferrying Dean's crew on some secret errand. The explosives expert, Emil Novotny, was a naturalized Pole whose command of the saltier expressions in his adopted tongue was legendary. Although he had the most responsible position (he had inherited his father's Seventh Avenue tailoring business), Wassermann was the first of the mercs to arrive in Istanbul—a short, meaty man with a florid complexion and a fringe of dark hair curling around his bald crown. Wassermann was a world-class marksman, a sharpshooter who would be an invaluable asset in the terrain Dean expected to cover.

Alfred Daler, the last to show, was an enigma. According to his papers, he was Norwegian, yet all the many languages he spoke were embellished with a villainous cockney accent. Among the mercs there were many theories as to his origins, but he remained a mystery. What was important to Dean was that Daler was remarkably unremarkable: he was a thin man of medium height, with thinning hair, nondescript features, and anonymous clothes; he could pass as a national of any country in Europe, except perhaps Italy or Greece, until he opened his mouth and the accent came out. But since he spoke seldom, and then only with the minimum of words, even this was of little importance. The man's two strongest attributes —that he had immensely powerful arms with wrists of steel and that he was utterly reliable—were evident only to those who worked with him.

Alexander Mackenzie had run a secret check, via Interpol, the FBI, the NSC data banks, and various European intelligence organizations, on all these men. On Dean's insistence, he had given his consent—reluctant in the case of Daler, on whom no information was available—to their recruitment. In order to attract less unwelcome attention, Mackenzie was staying in a small hotel in the suburb of Usküdar, on the Asiatic side of the Bosporus. Dean, for the same reason, was lodged nearby. On the evening of Day Four, he met the CIA regional director in a small park on a stretch of high ground overlooking the channel. "I have to ask you for a release from one part of my undertaking," he said.

"A release? What release? What part? Why?"

"These men are not brainless idiots," Dean said earnestly. "They are not the kind of gun fodder that generals regard simply as statistics or colored pins on a map. They can *think*."

"So?"

"So I can't expect them to believe that a band of terrorists has occupied an *abandoned* missile silo and that we've been briefed to get it back."

"Why not?"

"Because their immediate reaction will be: 'Okay, let's

take our guns, go in there, beat the shit out of the bastards, and reoccupy the site.' "

For a few minutes Mackenzie paced the deserted garden. The ground was dusty and the leaves of unwatered lemon trees hung limp in the heavy air. It was dusk. The crescent of bright lights locating the Golden Horn were reflected across the dark water. "I'm not sure that I see your problem," he said at last. "You mean that because you can't make a frontal attack on the place—"

"I mean I have to give them a valid reason for not making that obvious move. The only believable reason is that there is a missile in the silo and the hijackers threaten to fire it if we attack. If I tried to pull anything else, the guys would know damned well that I was stalling, holding out on them—lying, if you like. And if I don't have their confidence one hundred percent, I might as well turn in the job right now."

Mackenzie halted, gnawing the lower margin of his clipped mustache.

"They don't have to know where it's targeted," Dean urged. "Or the kind of warhead that's fitted. They don't even have to know about the ultimatum or the danger to Mubarak. But they have to know why we can't just take that place by storm."

Mackenzie sighed. "Well . . ."

"Among other things," Dean said, "we'll have to backtrack on the kidnap of Healey's wife and child, and follow up the course of the hijacked command car. Why would they want to pressure Healey if there wasn't a missile on the site?"

"I guess you're right," Mackenzie admitted. "The 'need-to-know' routine is less applicable in the case of volunteers, who sign on on a personal basis." He stared out across the water. The wake from a passing ferry had shivered the reflection of the lights along the Golden Horn. "Very well. Just the fact that a missile risks being fired, then. Nothing else, is that clear?"

"Yes, sir," Dean said. "Thank you."

And later, addressing the six mercenaries in the back room of a third hotel where Daler and Schneider were staying: "For the moment, that's all I can tell you guys: terrorists have raided this site and taken it over; they threaten to launch the missile in the silo if any attempt is made to displace them; it's up to us to find some way of besting them or neutralizing the missile before they can do this."

"Why should they be takin' over the site, but, if it wasn't to fire the missile?" Sean Hammer's seamed, nutcracker face was crumpling into a puzzled frown. "They must be usin' it as a lever, some kind of blackmail, sure."

"Yeah," Novotny agreed, "ain't no piss-ass point fighting to grab hold of the fucker if they don't aim to use it."

"What you mean, cock"—this was Daler—"is that they threaten to fire the thing for some reason or other, unless some terms or other are met, but that they'll launch it anyway if any attempt is made to retake the site. Is that it?"

Dean said, "None of that's our business; our briefing is to find some way of neutralizing the missile, the site, or the hijackers, before any blast-off can be maneuvered. That's all."

"What missile is it, anyway?" Novotny demanded.

"A Minuteman 1, I've been told."

"An IRBM, by Christ!" Novotny whistled. "To me that spells the comrades—Magnitogorsk or Moscow or even Leningrad. Why the fuck would a gang of terrorists want to wipe out those places? Most of them are *financed* by Moscow, for God's sake!"

"To put pressure on the U.S., old lad," Mazzari said. "They would only have to threaten to fire it, after all."

"Yeah," someone else said. "That should be enough to get them any damned thing they wanted."

"Will somebody kindly tell me, in this case, why the United States government it should not make use of its own highly paid and expert forces?" Wassermann spoke for the first time. "By me it is a very odd circumstance indeed when the world's most powerful country descends (you should excuse the word) to the hiring of a team of mercenaries to do its dirty work."

"Shit, yes. Abe's right," Novotny said. "There's something screwball here, and that's for sure."

"Listen, you guys," Dean began, anxious to change the subject, "there's no point beating out your brains—"

Wassermann was looking at him very straight. "It's just that I like a man he should put *all* his cards on the table," he said levelly. The emphasis was slight but unmistakable.

"I've told you all I know," Dean lied. "You can think about it as much as you like, but it's just a waste of time to keep on rabbiting. Now, shut up while I fill you in on the first stages of the operation.

"It's maybe the craziest mission we ever undertook," he admitted after he had made a few preliminary remarks. "Because right now I don't have any idea—not a hint or even a clue—how the hell we're going to play it. Sure, we skip out to Ararat and prospect the site, just in case there might be some way to organize a frontal assault before they could put the Ark into orbit. But after that . . ." He shrugged. "Your guess is as good as mine."

"Okay, Marc," Sean Hammer said after a short silence. "You're after tellin' us that we'll be playin' it this time by ear. It'd give us some kind of lead if we knew who the hell we were dealin' with, would it not?"

"Sure it would. But we don't . . . So far as I know . . . I've not been told . . ." For once Dean was floundering.

"What are the hijackers asking for?" Daler said reasonably. "If we knew what their demands were, it should give us a clue to their identity, surely? I mean, like if it was for the release of certain prisoners, you'd know at least what political color the terrorists were. Maybe even what group they belonged to."

"You're right. But so far they haven't declared themselves. And I haven't been told anything about their demands." Once again Dean prevaricated. He was beginning to wish he'd never heard of Mount Ararat or the deadly present-day Ark that was resting within it. "All we can do right now is, like I say, case the site. If we draw a zero on that—and I figure we will—then we follow up every other lead we have: the Luxembourg kidnap, the command-car hijack, the frontier crossings, in the hope that something, somewhere will tip us off to the identity of these killers. If it does, maybe we'll learn enough about them to find their weak point. And use it."

"And if it doesn't?" Daler asked.

"Then we report back and ask for alternative orders," Dean said evasively. On Mackenzie's instructions, he was saying nothing of the contingency plan to assassinate the Egyptian leader, and Mahmoud Yusuf was to be kept separate from the other mercs.

Mackenzie himself had left for Ankara and the American embassy, from where he could correspond in code with Henry Carpenter and General Hardanger without the contents of his message leaking. He was obliged, he told

Dean, to inform them of his decision to allow mention of the missile in the combat leader's briefings. And in any case he had to find out if there were any developments vis-à-vis the hijackers. Should they have revealed something of their long-term aims—or for whose benefit these were to be implemented—then clearly the information would be of the utmost value to Dean and the CIA man "running" him.

Before midnight, Dean had his second meeting with Yusuf. In the privacy of his hotel room, they studied the plan of the terminals of Orly Airport, Paris, and roughed out an M.O. that would give the Palestinian a choice of several sightlines if the Egyptian party in fact followed the schedule already communicated to Mackenzie by the DST.

Early the next morning, Dean and his six companions boarded perhaps the most bizarre form of transport that had ever carried them toward a possible theater of operations: with tickets bought by their leader the previous day, they joined a coach tour that was to take sightseers on an eastern Turkish itinerary that would include Lake Van, the ancient Armenian capital of Ani, and Kayseri, in central Anatolia, where the attraction was the extraordinary lunar landscape of Cappadocia.

On the shores of Lake Van, Dean and his men were shown such exotica as wrestling camels and the famous curly-haired swimming cats of the region. "Even more astonishing, gentlemen and ladies," the Metak Holidays guide assured them behind his microphone at the front of the coach, "is the Cappadocian hinterland, where for centuries early-Christian fugitives lived in secret underground cities, leaving behind them multiplied painted chapels hewn from the rock."

"I should be so lucky," Wassermann said, scrutinizing the brochure netted with other papers on the back of the seat in front of him. "It's like nothing else anywhere, it says here. 'An astonishing rocky landscape carved by time and ancient artists.' And not a synagogue in sight!"

There were, however, Soviet watchtowers surveying the complex of churches from the far side of a gorge that formed the frontier at Ani. None of the other tourists on the coach could understand why the tall, fair, tough-looking American and his friends would want to leave the package by the new hotel on the poorly surfaced road that led to the Iranian border post on the lower slopes of Mount Ararat.

They would have been more astonished still if they could have watched the subsequent activities of the group. There was a four-wheel-drive Steyr-Puch Pinzgauer parked in the yard in back of the building: a tall, square, jeeplike vehicle with a soft-top body that was mounted on a platform above the wheels with their ribbed heavy-duty tires. "She'll climb anything, ride over any terrain," the young man from the military attaché's office had told Dean when Mackenzie had organized the pickup. "Amphibious, too— though I doubt if you'll find too much evidence of floods around Ararat at this time of year!" Discreetly, he made no inquiries, asked no questions about the use to which the small truck would be put. Requests for help from the Agency could always lead to headaches: it was best to do what they wanted as rapidly as possible, keep your mouth shut . . . and duck.

Clearly, however, money had changed hands. Although voices could be heard and there were sounds of activity from the hotel's kitchens, nobody appeared to question Dean's group, no faces appeared at the windows, and there was no reaction when they climbed into the amphibian and Schneider twisted the key that was already in the ignition to drive them out of the yard and away.

It was some fifteen miles along the dirt road before the U.S. Army signs manifested themselves alongside the infrequent fingerposts. They traversed a belt of upland forest, and then, in the center of a barren plateau strewn with outcrops of rock among the scrub, they came to a smooth blacktop arrowing toward the foothills. Dean consulted a large-scale map. "I guess we can go as far as the second hairpin before there's any risk of the motor being audible on the site," he said. "After that, we're on foot. But keep her in third and fourth as much as you can, Kurt, okay?"

Schneider nodded and eased the stick into position.

Nobody spoke as the Pinzgauer began to climb. They were all tired; they had traveled more than six hundred miles in the coach; it was now the afternoon of Day Six; and the heat had not diminished. There was nothing to say anyway. They didn't know exactly where they were going or what they would do when they got there.

By the time they reached the second sharp curve, the

conical sixteen-thousand-foot peak of Ararat had disappeared behind a shoulder of the mountain. Schneider parked the truck in what looked like a disused quarry, and they left the roadway to attack the steep slope beyond which they would look down on another loop of blacktop . . . on the far side of which was a slant of mountainside from whose crest they should—according to Dean's map— be able to survey the site.

"The Dear knows," Hammer said piously, "this is the quarest bloody scouting party I ever heard tell! Would you look at the picture the lot of us make, for God's sake!"

Dean's mercenaries were indeed a strange sight—for anyone who knew the way they customarily looked when they were on assignment. Normally the combat leader insisted on lightweight battle dress with no insignia of rank, black berets, and combat boots, believing that neat and orderly dress bred the discipline that was as necessary to men whose skills were for hire as it was to conscripts or national formations. Today his men were unarmed. They wore an assortment of tourist gear that ranged from Wassermann's unsuitable shorts and Hawaiian shirt to Novotny's unspeakable jogging suit in red and blue stripes. Dean was dressed in pale ducks and a bush shirt; Hammer—who had one artificial leg—was the only man to wear conventional pants with an alpaca jacket. All of the mercs, however, were shod with rubber-soled basketball shoes, and each carried binoculars and a 35mm camera.

It was exceptionally hot, although they were spared at this height the humidity that was so enervating in the lower regions of Anatolia they had passed through. Most of the slopes they were climbing were bare rock made slippery by centuries of frost and rain and wind erosion, or scree-covered inclines rendered treacherous by fragments that had fallen from the weathered cliff faces above. By the time they approached the second crest, their clothes were plastered to their bodies by the sweat that ran beneath their collars, coursed down legs and arms, and rolled between their shoulder blades. Wassermann, who was overweight, and Hammer, with his stiff leg, suffered the most; only Mazzari, striding lightly and silently ahead of the others, seemed unaffected by the heat.

"It is lucky," Wassermann observed, "that I am not carrying a Winchester repeater, say, or a Mannlicher elephant rifle. In such a case, a man would be fortunate his finger it should not slip on the trigger and he shoots off his own fucking foot."

"Shit, yes," Novotny agreed. "With a pack and a shooter and a cartridge belt in this, you'd never make that motherfuckin' crest."

"And it ain't," Hammer panted, "as though there's anything to do when we bloody get there!"

"The Grand Old Duke of York," said Daler.

"Come again?"

" 'He had ten thousand men; he marched them up to the top of the hill . . . and he marched them bleeding well down again,' " Daler misquoted.

Schneider said, "By Jesus, he is being a little too hot here for my comfort, I am telling you."

"Too right, cock," Daler said. "No way could a guy—"

"Shut up—and quit beefing, all of you," Dean snapped. "This is what we get paid for, isn't it? Now, get on up to that crest"—Mazzari had already reached it and was lying prone—"and keep your eyes open, noting everything the way we planned. I don't want to hear another word until I give the signal to withdraw."

Very cautiously Dean and the five others crept up to the ridge. Lowering themselves face downward, they peered between jagged outliers of granite at the scene spread out beyond the foot of the far slope. It was here, some two hundred feet below, that the new road curved between rock walls into a defile that gashed the valley floor. Where the gorge widened out, they could see the line of concrete posts supporting the arc lights above the chain fence. A small Sealion helicopter stood on the pad beyond the guardhouse ("French Army surplus," Dean noted mechanically, focusing his field glasses).

As the farther reaches of the site sharpened into definition, the entrance to the silo—chipped by the explosion of grenades, with the buckled steel shutter still jammed in the opening—came into vision. Not far away, the command car shimmered in the heat.

Two jeeps with the white five-pointed U.S. Army star painted on their hoods stood near the pad. Men dressed in the white helmets, gaiters, and webbing belts of military police stood by the gates and patrolled the fence. There was a patch of freshly turned earth behind the guardhouse, but otherwise the long, narrow site showed no signs of the raid that had taken place only a few days before. Apart from the men guarding the perimeter, the dusty canyon was deserted. On either side, sheer faces of volcanic rock trembled in the pitiless glare of the sun.

Dean wiped the sweat from his eyes with the back of his hand and focused the binoculars afresh. Two hundred yards beyond the savaged entrance to the underground redoubt, a step in the valley floor marked the shelf over which in winter the stream cascaded. He could just make out the farther edge of the pool, now almost dried up, below. Beyond it, the gulch narrowed again, the floor became steeper. He estimated the drop to the floor as between twenty and thirty feet.

He swept the glasses from end to end of the site, and then from side to side all the way around the perimeter. The heat beat back at him from the scorched rock walls. The blood drummed in his head, and there was a pain behind his eyes. Apart from the supposed U.S. guards, nothing below moved. No leaf stirred, no blade of grass wavered, no bird's wing disfigured the immaculate blue of the sky.

Dean bit his lip. There could be no doubt about it: the site had been well chosen. Too damned well chosen, he reflected bitterly. Even for trained mountain troops there was no possible line of approach beyond the blacktop that snaked through the gorge toward the gates. For a small band such as his own, a frontal attack on the gates and the guardhouse was the only conceivable course of action.

But even if that could be won, and won quickly . . . Dean shook his head. He knew there were a number of complicated maneuvers, involving both the duty officers, that must be carried out before a missile could be fired. And he knew too—estimating the distances involved below—that no team he could raise, that *anybody* could raise, would be capable of fighting its way past the gates and the guard, down the driveway, and into the sealed redoubt, before the alarm was given, those maneuvers carried out, and the button pressed to launch the Ark.

His first line of attack was therefore useless. The six-hundred-mile coach trip from Istanbul, the two days wasted on the journey, the exhausting hike up the lower slopes of Ararat, had all been in vain. Wearily he signaled the mercs to withdraw from the ridge.

# 8

# Cook's Tour

It was soon after Dean and his men returned to the little Steyr-Puch amphibian that they had what seemed at the time to be their first piece of luck. In back of the truck, each man had left the overnight bag with which—to support the role of coach tourist—he had been traveling. Dean's, however, was the only one to carry a small but powerful two-way radio. At 1700 hours he was due to tune in the secret wavelength that relayed him, via the embassy at Ankara, to Mackenzie, wherever he was. The first of the two fixed-time daily calls, at 0800, had brought nothing new. This one was more fruitful.

"They're running out of food," Dean told the mercs when the transmission was terminated. "Ordinarily they would have gotten a fresh consignment when the guard details were changed two days ago. Since nobody's been near the place from the moment it was raided, stocks of provisions are exhausted. They've asked for a flatbed truck to run in a fresh supply tomorrow morning."

"Would that not be an opportunity, faith, for a coupla well-armed men to penetrate the site?" Sean Hammer asked. "Hidden, maybe, under a false floor in the truck, or something of that sort?"

Dean shook his head. "They're too smart for that. They've stipulated the model of truck they'll accept—a Zastava S-12 pickup; that's a Russki four-by-four with no sides and no tailgate. No chance for anyone to hide beneath the flatbed, either: you can see through from one side to the other between the gas tank and the chassis."

"Could the food not be poisoned, then?"

"They thought of that too: they took care to say that they'd be eating in relays. If the first group became sick, they'd simply eat no more . . . and fire the missile, they said."

"Poison the bugger they're blackmailing," Daler said,

"this Yank technician, I mean, and they *couldn't* fire the bleeder."

"Just tell me," said Dean, "how we ensure that one particular portion goes to one particular guy. In any case, by now they'll have beaten out of him the mechanics of launching, I should think." He shook his head again. He smiled reluctantly. "Goddamn nerve! You know what? They actually specified the restaurant that must supply the chow! Place back in Erzurum, on the road to Ankara."

"Is that a lead?"

"A lead?"

"If the guy knows this town well enough to have a favorite restaurant there—and one of them must, obviously—then couldn't that mean he's a Turk, that he comes maybe from there? And wouldn't that at least be something we could follow up?"

"Yeah," Dean said. "Sure. But there are so many angles, so many possible leads . . . and so few of us, so few days to act in. But you're right, of course: it *is* a lead of a sort."

"Old lad," Mazzari said suddenly, "I have an idea."

"Welcome to the club already," Wassermann said. "Not many people qualify, but there's always room for more."

Dean said, "Okay, Ed, let's have it."

"The jolly old comestibles, squire," Mazzari said. "The fatted calf and all that. They may have a Turk from Erzurum playing end-stop. We don't."

Dean stared at him. "So?"

"What I mean—there'd be no question of substituting one or more of us for the waiters, or whoever, slated to deliver the mouth-watering delicacies to the site. If one of the bods hails from the actual town, he might even know the types anyway."

"Go on," Dean said.

"But the odds are that he wouldn't know the chaps who toil and spin in the back room, he wouldn't be familiar with the sacred kitchen staff, would he?"

"No, I guess not. But I don't see what you—"

"And although it might be a trifle odd to see one as a waiter in central Turkey, not an eyebrow would be raised to learn that there was a black man slaving in the kitchen, would it?"

"Just what are you getting at, Ed?" Dean asked.

"I'm suggesting that the chef is so proud of the stuff he

dishes up that he goes along with the waiters when they deliver, just so's he can make sure the jokers on the site know how to cook it, or prepare it, or heat it up, or whatever."

"And the role of chef is played by E. Mazzari, late of the Congo, okay? But what good would it do? You'd be at risk more than somewhat—and even you couldn't take on the whole gang single-handed."

"Absolutely not. No question of that, squire. But it would at least give us an inside view. I could suss out the form on the far side of the wire, find out how many of them there were, take a shufti at the hardware they have, generally case the bloody joint, as you fellows say."

"I don't know . . ." Dean was dubious.

"It might not be much, but it would at least be *something*," Mazzari urged. "Perhaps there's a weak point, only obvious from within. Even if there isn't, we'd know once and for all that any kind of direct attack would be hopeless. As things are now, we only *think* it would be hopeless."

Dean spread his arms and then let them fall to his sides. "This is the damnedest mission I ever was on," he said. "All right, you twisted my arm. What can we lose but your life? But for God's sake," he added seriously, "be doubly, trebly, quadruply careful, Ed. These guys are not playing marbles; they already showed they're totally ruthless; they must be playing for pretty big stakes."

"Yeah—just what *are* the stakes, Cap?" Novotny asked.

"Maybe Mazzari will find out," Dean said.

Low cloud veiled the summit of Ararat the following morning, and the heat, which had not diminished, was now damp and oppressive. The Russian-made pickup was stacked with polystyrene containers that insulated the food from atmospheric conditions. The terrorists had been explicit in their demands: they had specified vacuum-packed bread, butter, canned fruit, cheese, eggs, coffee, and precooked dishes such as pilaf, kebabs, and couscous—precisely two meals, one light, one heavy, for each member of the band from Day Seven through Day Fourteen, when the ultimatum expired. One of Mazzari's questions was thus answered at once: simple division told them that there were now eighteen men on the site—the original half-dozen, plus Andrew Healey, the helicopter pilot, and the ten-strong commando he had flown in.

There were other pointers. "No wine and no liquor," Dean noted. "Together with the choice of food, that spells local talent to me, and followers of the Prophet at that. Turks maybe—especially if they're familiar with Erzurum —Palestinians perhaps, or extremists from Libya. The guys who attacked me in Istanbul were certainly Muslims."

The idea, he reflected (though he said nothing aloud), stacked up with the selection of President Mubarak as a target. Tehran too fitted the bill as an alternative: there were plenty of warring sects, inside and outside Iran, who were violently opposed to the Ayatollah Khomeini.

Three men and no escort, the terrorists' radio message had warned—and if anyone stepped out of line, all three would be killed. Mackenzie had not thought it right to expose waiters from the restaurant in Erzurum to risk: the driver and his mate were Turkish members of the embassy personnel in Ankara who resembled them as much as possible. Mazzari, in a white chef's jacket, perched among his supposed gastronomic creations on the tail of the Zastava.

The truck crawled up the loops of blacktop and made the entry to the gorge. At the far end of the defile, two hundred yards before the chain fence, the gate, and the guardhouse, the dusty route was barred by six men with machine pistols. They were wearing U.S. Army uniforms—a tech sergeant and five G.I.'s—but they could never have been mistaken for Americans. It wasn't the swarthy skin and drooping mustaches and thick, curling hair that gave them away. There were plenty of naturalized Mexicans and men of mixed blood carrying arms for Uncle Sam. It was something indefinable, some special, sullen insolence in their bearing, a fuck-you-Jack attitude and a total callousness of expression that placed them definitively outside the scope of any normally disciplined professional army. That and the fact that they were hatless.

"Out of the truck, ten paces away, and the hands well in the air," the man with the sergeant's chevrons ordered when the driver had braked to a standstill. "Try any funny business and you're dead, all of you."

These men were unbelievable, children in fancy dress, Mazzari reflected as he lowered himself to the ground. It was no more than a coincidence that their toys were lethal, with thirty rounds of 7.62mm high-velocity ammu-nition in the chargers. "Over there with the other two . . . move!" the "sergeant" snapped.

*Why do you address me in borrowed robes?* Mazzari had taken English Literature as a subsidiary at Oxford and the tag from *Macbeth* sprang readily to his lips. He remembered just in time that he was supposed to be a Turkish kitchen hand, and joined the two embassy men in silence.

All of them were carrying Turkish ID papers—Mazzari as an immigrant from East Africa—and all their clothes had local labels. While three of the terrorists kept them covered, the others frisked them expertly and then turned their attention to the truck. Each carton was opened and examined, the hood was removed and the motor checked, the cab searched, and the underneath of the chassis scruti-nized. It was twenty minutes before the inspection was over and the advance guard satisfied that no arms or ex-plosives were being smuggled into the site. "Right: back aboard and keep driving until I tell you to stop," the leader ordered. "Ten miles an hour. No more, no less. And don't forget, there are six guns trained on you."

"How could we forget, boss?" Mazzari said, trying his best to look scared. "Shucks, we ain't no hit men: you got no call to be leery of us; we're just the delivery boys."

"Shut up and get back among that merchandise," the man said.

Two of the hijackers swung up and perched on the steps at each side of the cab; the other four joined Mazzari on the tail. The Zastava moved slowly forward in a cloud of dust.

When it was fifty yards from the chain fence, men in military-police gear swung the gates open. The driver hesi-tated, looking over his shoulder. "Keep going," the man in sergeant's uniform told him. "You showed your passes al-ready!"

The truck continued its snail-pace progress past the two jeeps, beyond the helicopter pad, a group of army huts, and a shed housing the generator (Mazzari wondered if a well-placed explosive charge—or a grenade even—could put the machine out of action and foul up all the control systems in the air-conditioned silo. No, he thought: there was bound to be an emergency system inside the redoubt, if only to keep it operative under conditions of attack).

After they had crossed a bridge spanning the dried-up riverbed, the walls of the gorge closed in. Some way before the cascade, they were told to stop. Mazzari regarded the bomb-splintered entrance to the silo and the damaged steel shutter without comment. There would, he knew, be armored elevators inside to carry the duty crews down to the subterranean chambers, where there was no sound but the subdued hum of the plant ventilating each sector with cool, dry, sterile air smelling faintly of ozone, no vision but the hieroglyphics on ground-glass radar and computer screens, and communication with the outer world only by means of the secret radio transmitters installed among the winking lights and steel lockers of the control room. The sinister aperture through which the slender nose of the Ark would be visible doubtless pierced some inaccessible slope of the mountain on the far side of the ridge.

Four more terrorists appeared from inside the underground complex and helped to form a chain along which the cartons were unloaded from the truck and passed into the interior. Mazzari's offer to hump some of the heavier packages into the silo was sternly refused. He stood by the rear of the Zastava with a notebook, ostensibly checking off each container as it was unshipped, but in reality taking stock of everything that he noticed.

There had been four men dressed as M.P.'s on the gate. With the half-dozen who had searched them and the quartet from the silo, that left three terrorists plus the technician Healey inside the redoubt. But if Mazzari had hoped to catch sight of the American, perhaps exchange some message or pass a word of encouragement, he was doomed to be disappointed. He had just hurriedly noted the fact that there were a mortar, two RPG-7's, and a couple of heavy machine guns at the entrance to the site, and that the terrorists seemed to be armed with Kalashnikov rifles and Russian machine pistols, when a heavyset florid man in the uniform of a U.S. Army colonel emerged from the tunnel carved from the rock.

Mazzari took one look at the small, mean eyes, the network of tiny veins webbing the skin on either side of the nose, and he knew that so far as he was concerned, the game was lost.

He turned hurriedly aside, surreptitiously tearing the page from his notebook and stuffing it in his pants pocket.

But his size and the princely, slightly arrogant tilt of his head could not so easily be concealed. The man in colonel's uniform stopped dead, staring. "Holy fucking Christ!" he swore. "What the bloody hell's going on here?" He turned savagely on the terrorist with the sergeant's stripes. "Ahmed, you half-assed wop cunt, have you gone crazy or something? Don't you know who this is?"

"I am sorry. I . . . I don't understand," the hijacker stammered. "You mean this man? But he's the cook from—"

"This is one of *them*, you moron; one of the guys we've been warned about. This is one of that bastard Dean's sidekicks!"

In the sudden silence that fell, Mazzari straightened up. "Furneux!" he said. "I knew you'd sunk pretty low, but I hadn't realized you kept this kind of company."

"Pack it in, nigger," Furneux grated. "This time you've gone a step too far. This is the end of the road for you, boy."

Two of the terrorists raised their guns. "It's okay, Kamal, Nesuhi," Furneux said. "Don't shoot. I want this black bastard alive. Just." He waved the ten men forward. "Take him," he ordered.

Mazzari leaped to the far side of the truck. He glanced swiftly around him. Apart from the entrance to the silo, which was blocked by Furneux and two other men, the nearest cover was the generator shed, and that was more than a hundred yards away. His only chance was to make the shelf at the top of the waterfall, which was about half that distance—but even then he would have a thirty-foot drop to survive. He had to try, though. He had no illusions about Furneux. The Canadian was a mercenary, vicious, spiteful, and unprincipled. He had once worked with Dean on a West African adventure. After the mission was over, the combat leader—finding the man a braggart, a racist, and the first to take cover when the going had gotten tough—had sworn never to employ him again. They had met once since then, when Dean's team had foiled a Communist plot to take over a small buffer state in Indochina. Furneux had been on the other side then, and the defeat still rankled. He had no love for Dean or his friends.

The knowledge lent Mazzari speed and vigor. What was it that his chief always said? *When outnumbered in per-*

*sonal combat, always strike first . . . it gives the enemy a false idea of your strength.* Well, two of the hijackers were covering the Turkish driver and his mate, and Furneux still blocked the entry. That left it eight to one. And these men were no tenderfeet. It would have to be a hell of a strike if he was to get away with it, Mazzari thought grimly.

As three of his adversaries advanced around the tail of the truck and the remainder circled toward the front, he threw himself forward and seized the nearest man, picking him up bodily and hurling him chest-high at the others. They staggered, momentarily off balance, and the man who had been thrown fell to the ground.

Mazzari was in there like a flash, a dark, towering windmill of fists and feet. He planted a thumping right in the solar plexus of one man, felled the second with his left, and delivered a shrewd blow with the sole of his foot to the head of the terrorist who was attempting to rise from the ground. Before they had time to react, he whirled around to face the five rushing in from the front of the truck. He jumped in and began trading punches with the two nearest as the others fanned out to encircle him. Two murderous lefts and a right uppercut rocked them on their feet, but there were blows raining on the big man now from either side. A blackjack thudded into his upper arm, numbing it to the wrist. Brass knuckles split open his temple and then his cheek.

He turned and tried to place his back to the truck, but the first three men were on their feet again; one scrambled across the tail and leaped on Mazzari's shoulders locking an arm around his neck. Mazzari threw him off as a dog shakes water from its coat, but for an instant his guard was down and his face and torso became the target for a hail of blows. Blood from a broken nose sprayed the front of his white jacket.

Some of the attackers were bleeding too. There were grunts and yelps of pain as Mazzari's one-man tornado lashed out left and right, knuckles and feet and the hard edge of one hand cracking against bone and smacking into flesh. Then someone dropped on all fours behind him, he was shoved violently in the chest, and he fell.

At once they were all in there, kicking and punching. He rose to his feet with a roar of rage, dragging four of the hijackers with him. Astonishingly, he shook them off, and ran staggering toward the cascade. But even a man of Mazzari's titanic strength and stamina could not hold out forever against eight toughened hoods. One of his arms was now useless, he was half-blinded with his own blood, and his immense reserve of energy was exhausted. Before he had covered ten yards, they had caught him and he was submerged again.

Ahmed had run back to the silo entrance and returned with a Kalashnikov. Holding it by the muzzle, he swung the weapon up and then down like a sledgehammer. The terrorists separated and the butt of the gun smashed against Mazzari's head, just behind the ear. At last he lay still, facedown in the bloodied dust.

Furneux moved forward with a satisfied smile. He nodded to Ahmed. "All right," he said. "Go in and finish him."

# 9

# Action Indirect

Arnaghi Hamid stood beneath the hot shower in one of the two bathrooms attached to his suite in the Hotel Three Falcons in Copenhagen. The water cascaded over his shoulders, streamed down the swelling convexities of his huge frame, and swirled around the feet that he could no longer see. Steam rose from the scented foam that eddied above the drain hole, dewing the glass panels of the shower with droplets heavy with sandalwood and musk.

For ten minutes Hamid remained there, reveling in the soft battering of spray against his upturned face. Then he wrapped himself in a white robe of Turkish toweling and padded through into the bedroom. It was a long room with deep windows and orange folkweave drapes. Beyond the twin beds there were easy chairs, a sofa, and a modernistic teak desk with a copper-shaded counterweight lamp hanging low above it. He stood in front of a full-length mirror and stared at his reflection. The great, pale, fleshy body was almost totally hairless; only around the nipples at the tip of the womanly breasts, a few dark strands sprouted. Hamid frowned. His lizard lips puckered into a tut of irritation. He was a perfectionist: either one was hirsute or one was not; he detested compromise, any kind of halfway house. Fastidiously he took a pair of manicure scissors and snipped off the offending hairs.

Half an hour later, immaculate as ever in razor-creased blue mohair, his dry skin perfumed with cologne, he was ready to ride the elevator nine floors down to the breakfast bar at the foot of the hotel's concrete tower. There were two entrances to the room, each at the end of a short passageway with a clothes closet at one side and a bathroom at the other. Clearly the place was designed for couples who were not prepared to wait in line for a session in the tub! Hamid hesitated, tucking a silk handkerchief into the sleeve of his elegant jacket; then he chose the door by the unused bathroom: spilled water in the other passageway could dim the polish of his crocodile pumps. As he left, he became aware of an insistent noise that had been in back of his consciousness for some time. He had forgotten to turn off the shower. He shrugged and opened the door. No doubt one of the chambermaids would attend to it later.

The breakfast bar was dark, with pink-shaded lamps. Beyond the cigar kiosk and the reception desk in the entrance lobby, he could see through glass doors the chauffeur of a Rolls-Royce chamoising the windshield on the rainswept forecourt.

Hamid sat at the counter in front of pineapple juice, coffee, fresh rolls and butter, cellophane-wrapped packages of pumpernickel and black bread, honey, ham, crisp curls of Gouda cheese, and a plate of bacon and eggs. Like most immensely wealthy men, he was miserly over trifles. When he had finished eating, he pocketed a vacuum-packed slice of rye bread and two small sealed cartons of liver pâté and processed garlic sausage that lay untouched on a plate before him. One never knew when they might come in handy; they were paid for, in any case.

He looked at his gold watch. The woman was due in the residents' lounge on the second floor at any moment. He slid from the stool and headed for the elevator.

She was already waiting for him—the slate-gray uniform neatly pressed, dark hair curled above the collar, the makeup expertly, not too noticeably, applied. She was forty years old and looked younger, with a deep, pleasant voice from which most of the French accent had been suppressed. "They caught one of them on the site," she said. "A black man. He came in with the Turks bringing food. Fortunately Furneux had seen him before and recognized him."

Hamid looked around the big room with its leather armchairs and magazine-strewn tables. It was deserted at this hour. "I have seen him before too," he said. "A West African named Mazzari?"

She nodded.

"Just so. Well, I suppose it was to be expected. The man has been . . . attended to?"

The woman nodded again. "According to plan."

"Good. What news from America on your radio in Paris?"

"Nothing specific, Monsieur Hamid. The secret is being

kept. Dean is getting nowhere. They are running around in circles."

The fat man chuckled. "Excellent! And our CIA friends?"

"You know about the renegade Palestinian, Yusuf, whom they have so to speak wished on Dean? . . . Well, now their assassination project has been activated. Just in case."

"Ah!" For the first time Hamid looked genuinely interested. "And what do we know of that?"

"Very little, so far," she said. "It appears to be a contingency plan that has been in existence for some time, so there is no need for planning or discussion. The order has simply been given to proceed . . . and then wait for a yes or no at the final moment. But our contact has so far been unable to obtain names or details."

"Just so long as it's efficient," Hamid said. "I have great faith in the efficiency of the Agency. We have already arrived at Day Eight. They still have a week to perfect their plan before that final affirmative is given . . . as it will be. You are returning to Paris this afternoon?"

"Yes. On the four-fifteen flight. Shall you be coming?"

"I have to attend to the banking matters for which I came here, first." Hamid glanced out the window. Low clouds scurried darkly across the sky, and the slate roofs of the city were gleaming. Rain beat steadily against the glass. "In any case," he said, "I prefer to wait for more clement weather conditions before I entrust my life to an infidel who probably takes liquor."

Alexander Mackenzie was exhausted. He had slept little since he left for Europe, and now, back in Washington for one day, he was suffering from jet lag as well. He looked with disfavor at his four companions, at the rolling green fairways of the golf course which General Hardanger had insisted was the safest place to talk, and at the sky, which threatened at any moment to loose upon them a heavy shower. They were approaching the ninth green, the farthest possible distance from the clubhouse.

Hardanger was a grizzled, thin-lipped man with shaggy eyebrows and a head thrust aggressively forward in a fashion that reminded Mackenzie of an ill-tempered eagle. Of his three fellow conspirators, General McClintock was smooth-shaven and bland as a successful surgeon; the missile expert, Weiss, was short, tubby, and red-faced; and Tom Argyle was something of a dandy, with a Prince-of-Wales checkered suit, yellow shoes, and iron-gray hair curling over the collar of his tattersall shirt.

"I'm disappointed, Mackenzie, that these fellows you praised so highly haven't come up with anything yet," Hardanger said gruffly. "I should have thought by now . . ." He left the sentence incomplete.

Mackenzie's reply was tart. "With respect, sir," he said, "neither the Agency nor the outside elements to which you refer would have been involved at all if you and your colleagues had abided by the NATO agreements and refrained from . . . ah . . . meddling in affairs that are never less than tricky. Positioning a strategic weapon, without permission, in a supposedly abandoned site can lead only to recriminations from the Pentagon at the best of times."

Hardanger coughed. "Yellow-bellies," he growled. "Fools, quaking behind a wall of defense when they should be attacking! Only thing the Reds understand: a show of force. Should have put them out of business immediately after Korea. Preemptive strike, they call it now, or some such balderdash. Cleaning up the blasted commies, I call it. Prophylactic operation. Disinfectant. If I had my way—"

"If you had your way, sir," the CIA chief cut in irritably, "there would have been no American site on Mount Ararat, and I'd have had no Middle Eastern sector to supervise."

"Exactly. No need for 'em. World would have been a cleaner place, right!"

"That's not what I meant, General. A nuclear war—"

"Oh, come, Mackenzie," McClintock interrupted. "Let's not get into arguments on strategic policy now. We have a problem situation here: let's concentrate on that, eh?" He sank a seven-yard putt and picked his ball out of the hole. With Weiss, he was affecting to play a friendly twosome, to give them an excuse to be on the course, out of earshot of anyone else. "That leaves me three up and nine to play," he said.

"In any case," Mackenzie pursued, "it's not the communists we have to deal with here."

"Out of the same goddamn drawer," said Hardanger.

"Terrorists, extremists, anarchists. People who break the rules. Get rid of them all, I say. Hit 'em where it hurts."

"Unfortunately, they're in a position to hit *us* where it hurts."

"Well, whose fault is that?" Hardanger grunted.

Mackenzie forbore to comment. McClintock teed up his ball and surveyed the 375-yard fairway that led to the tenth. "Ask me, I'd say let them fire the missile," he said. "Wind in the right direction, that Tabun's a good, clean weapon: no damage to buildings, vegetation, oil installations. And we could do with a few less of those gentry. Khomeini's bunch, the Mussulman rent-a-crowd, Arabs in general, I mean." He addressed the ball and swung—a good straight drive with a flat trajectory. The ball hit the center of the fairway, bounced and rolled to within a hundred yards of the green. "But I accept that right now it wouldn't be politic," he added. "Now, if only these merchants had left the damned thing targeted on Moscow . . ."

Colonel Weiss was preparing to drive. "This targeting nonsense," Hardanger said. "The man Healey—he really could make the necessary . . . alterations? Substitute Tehran for Moscow?"

"No doubt about it, sir," Weiss said. "The experience he has in all control systems, his knowledge of the Minuteman guidance techniques, the computer data available to him . . . Dammit, that's what he's trained for: to check out those systems." He drove off. The ball came to rest ten yards wide of McClintock's and some way nearer the green.

"Yes, yes," Hardanger said as the two golfers picked up their bags and began to walk. "Theoretical targeting's one thing; the actual technique of getting the thing out of the silo, into the air, and on that course—it's not just a question of thumbing a button, is it?" He turned to Tom Argyle. "You're confirming that one man, this man, could do it? If necessary, with the help of these sons of bitches, if they've coerced him into showing them how?"

"Absolutely," the Rand Corporation man agreed. "No question. It's the sequential knowledge that counts. Once you have that, your actual manipulation of the controls is a piece of cake."

"And your progress report?" Hardanger turned to Mackenzie.

"As I have told you, gentlemen"—Mackenzie was keeping his temper with difficulty—"the . . . er . . . outside help we have called in, with your consent and approval, I may say, has at the moment not been able to find a way of neutralizing the terrorists. They have, however, infiltrated a man—if only temporarily—onto the site. I am awaiting his report. Although I have to say that preliminary reconnaissance appears to rule out any direct assault."

"And the alternative?"

"You are aware," Mackenzie said, "that I have stipulated, as a condition of Dean's employment, that he recruit a man supplied by the Agency? And that with this man—a renegade Palestinian—he evolve a contingency plan for the elimination . . . let us say for what may have to be done if we cannot best the hijackers and the ransom demand has to be met?"

Hardanger nodded. McClintock stopped by his ball, glanced toward the green, and selected a number-four iron from his bag.

"And we are still agreed that the most important, the most vital consideration is that the President remain in ignorance of your . . . miscalculation? And, further, that if the ransom does have to be met, no breath of suspicion attaches to him—or to the United States?"

"Yes, yes, of course. Get on with it, man," Hardanger said testily.

"Then I can reveal," Mackenzie said, "that any plan of assassination that Dean and the Palestinian concoct will simply act as a blind. To put it crudely, they will be there as fall guys, to be blamed if anything goes wrong, or if the terrorists fail to keep their bargain and leak the story."

McClintock straightened up, his club poised over the ball. "What are you saying? If Mubarak has to go, it won't be Dean . . . ?"

Hardanger said, "You mean there is *another* contingency plan? That *somebody else* would be doing the job?"

"When I inherited this position," Mackenzie said, "I discovered that my predecessors had instigated a number of contingency plans, at various potential trouble spots, for the possible elimination of influential men. Sleepers were installed at each of these places, people with genuine cover jobs there, whose sole purpose was to perfect plans for the . . . removal . . . of these men. If and when the necessity ever arrived. The sleepers have no other reason for existence so far as we are concerned; they are unknown to other Agency operatives working in the same area. One of the areas was Egypt. The target at that time was Anwar Sadat; now it is Mubarak."

"Good God!" Weiss exclaimed. "Do you mean it was a CIA operation, the murder of Sadat?"

"No, no. Quite the reverse. He was a great man: we wanted very much to keep him alive. Unfortunately, others felt differently. I repeat: this is very much a *contingency* plan; we should like President Mubarak to remain alive too."

"But if he does have to be killed? How would it be done?"

"I have no idea," Mackenzie said.

Hardanger stared at him. "What the devil do you mean, man?"

"Just that, General. The sleepers are left entirely to their own devices. They make their own plans, without reference to us. It's better that way: there's no comeback; we are genuinely in ignorance of their M.O."

McClintock lofted his ball toward the flag. It hit the bank on the near side of the green and rolled down into a bunker. "Shit!" McClintock said. He turned back to Mackenzie. "If you don't know what means these sleepers of yours are to use, how do you manage to—?"

"We have a countdown system," Mackenzie forestalled him. "Nothing happens until the operative is warned—usually at a box number—that he *may* be required to act. After that, if he *is* alerted to go ahead, his plan, whatever it is, is set in motion. Once that happens, there is no way we can call him off except at prearranged contact times, once every twenty-four hours. He calls a 'safe' number, identifies himself with a voice print and a code word that changes each day, and is told either Go or Stop—the order controlling his movements for the next twenty-four hours, after which he calls again."

"And if it's stop?"

"That's definitive. He goes underground until the next time he's warned. If he ever is. Should the decision be to go ahead, he continues calling until the appointed day. If it's still the green light . . . well, after his call there's no way to stop him."

Weiss chipped his ball neatly onto the green, where it came to rest a few feet from the pin. "Specifically," Hardanger asked, "has your agent been given this preliminary alert in this case?"

"He has. Instructions have been given that the existing plan be set in motion on Day Ten, forty-eight hours from now. The phone calls will commence at noon on that day."

"Security-wise," Tom Argyle said, "that seems foolproof. A very sound idea. Both the Agency and the administration are kept out of it . . . yet you continue to control the whole thing." He frowned, looking at the sky. A few drops of rain had begun to fall.

Weiss sank his putt. McClintock wasted three strokes getting out of the bunker, and then two-putted from the far side of the green.

"So the Palestinian you've foisted on Dean will be there simply as a dummy, a decoy, to be found out and blamed if the killing has to take place?" Hardanger asked. "So that no dirt will brush off onto the CIA?"

Mackenzie nodded, sighing. "That's the kind of business we're in," he said.

"And this fellow Dean knows nothing about it? He thinks his plan's the real one? He doesn't know about your sleeper?"

"No," Mackenzie said. "Dean knows nothing about it."

Colonel Weiss was heading for the eleventh tee. "I guess we'd better call it off now," McClintock said. "I could do with a drink, and it looks like it's blowing up a storm."

The Greek noncommissioned officer at the frontier post remembered the last time the U.S. Army command car had passed through very well. "It was unusual," he told Wassermann. "Must have been something very special on; they had a full colonel with them. Normally it is just the crew with the civilian technician."

"And it was the usual crew this time?" Wassermann asked.

"No. Now that you mention it, he had different men with him. I thought maybe they were training new recruits, at first. Then I realized that they'd hardly send a senior officer along with them if that was the case. Just the same, the new team looked somehow . . . well, somehow less *experienced* than the others."

"Too bad I should trouble you more," Wassermann said, "but do you happen to remember the *way* they looked? I mean, what sort of men?" Mackenzie had furnished him with a cover and important-looking papers, placing him as a staff major checking up on roster arrangements in the European theater. "There have been suggestions that certain grades of soldier might be overworked," he explained. "Could these new men have been, well, say, Puerto Ricans? Or perhaps from the Philippines?"

The Greek shrugged. "I do not know so much about people from those places, sir. They were perhaps darker than the usual crew—more the Mediterranean than the type customarily considered as American."

"Or Arab?"

"Arab perhaps. I was not especially noticing."

"You didn't notice anything bizarre or unusual about the car or its occupants?"

"I do not think so. But I was about to go off duty. I had an appointment that evening in Edirne. Perhaps my colleague remarked something." He turned and called to a man who had been scrutinizing the papers of a driver whose articulated truck was on the way from Ankara to Athens: "Hey, Cristoforou! Here a minute, will you?"

The soldier came across, saluted Wassermann, and tilted his cap to scratch the back of his head when the same question was put to him. "Bizarre?" he repeated. "I don't think so. Except perhaps that . . . Let me see . . . Yes, I don't know if it was exactly *bizarre*, but it was unusual. The young American, the scientist, was in army uniform. I had always seen him in civilian clothes before."

"Was there anything else about him? Did he seem at all . . . tired? strained? off color in any way? Did he say or do anything odd?"

The guard frowned. "I don't think so. He looked as if he hadn't slept too well. I kidded him a little. Like about bringing in substitutes for a football team. Mind you, he did say . . . No, that can't have been of any importance." He shook his head.

"What did he say?"

"I don't suppose it meant anything. He said something about being obliged sometimes to make changes. I . . . It's silly, but I thought at the time that he lingered over it a little, like he was kind of underlining the point. And it was a strange word to use in there, 'obliged.' "

"Thank you very much," Wassermann said. "You have been a great help."

Sean Hammer called Mackenzie from Luxembourg. Mackenzie was staying at the Pera Palas in Istanbul, waiting to hear Dean's progress report when Mazzari and the two Turks returned from the Ararat site.

"I'll not be wastin' too much of your time, sir," Hammer said, "but it seems there's a quare ould collection of facts lyin' around here for the pickin' up. I doubt not we'd find some kind of a lead, if himself could be persuaded along here to sort out the clues."

"What kind of facts? What clues?" Mackenzie asked.

"Clues I'm thinkin' might give us a lead on who the bloody hell we're fightin' against," Hammer said.

"Such as?"

"Healey's wife's car—a BMW, it was—got bashed outside their house by a small Volkswagen sedan. The sedan was rented in Frankfurt the previous day by two Turks with an address in Berlin. It was left next to the BMW after the kidnap, so there must have been a third vehicle involved."

"The local police found out most of that already," Mackenzie said.

"I know, sir. They discovered since that a second vehicle was rented that day from the Hertz people in Luxembourg itself. It was a closed panel truck. The truck was found two days ago, abandoned in a parking lot in Baden-Baden, Germany."

"I still don't see . . ."

"Witnesses," Hammer said solemnly, "who live in the same street as the Healeys, speak of seeing a panel truck parked in the driveway of an empty house opposite theirs not long before the snatch. One woman swears she saw this truck actually parked at the Healeys'."

"Very well, that looks like a getaway car. But—"

"Finally," Hammer said, with the flourish of a conjurer who keeps his most mystifying trick until last, "there was a third entry that could interest us on that day, June 27. It came in from the southwest, driven by a French couple—one of those big motor homes on a Mercedes chassis. It hasn't left the country . . . and it hasn't bloody well been seen since. There's a deduction there to be made, but."

"Yes," Mackenzie said slowly. "I see what you mean. What are you suggesting, Mr. Hammer?"

"There's little enough time, sir. And we have not so far been successful in any plan regarding yon site where the . . . where the Ark is rested. Wassermann's in Greece, Kurt Schneider's following the trail back through Italy, Novotny from Baden-Baden to Berlin. There's only himself and Alf Daler waiting to bring Mazzari back from the mountain. Unless Mazzari has some whicker plan for us to do these buggers somehow from the inside, I'm sayin' that it'd be better for the all of us to come here to Luxembourg, put the whole bloody team on it, and trace the kidnappers—rather than the boyos on the site—step by step until we locate them. For it's sure I am that they're here someplace in that camper. An' if we could get at them, rescue the woman and the kid maybe, then they'd have no hold over Healey, would they?"

"No," Mackenzie said. "They wouldn't. If, that is, we could find some way to let the hijackers—and particularly Healey himself—if we could let them *know* the hostages were in our hands."

The little Ulsterman's sigh was clearly audible in the earpiece of Mackenzie's phone. "Aye," Hammer said. "I'd not thought of that. Thon's a fly in the bloody ointment, that is!"

"It's a big if," Mackenzie agreed. "But it's an idea."

"What d'you say we have a go, sir? Will I call Novotny and the others back to Luxembourg? For there's too much to investigate here for one man. In the time we have available, I mean."

"In the time available, yes. We're already at Day Nine." Mackenzie passed a hand wearily over his forehead. Was it only yesterday that he'd been talking with Hardanger on a golf course? "Dean is not due to contact me by radio until seventeen hundred hours. Unless he reports that Mazzari has a better plan, I'll put your suggestion to him. Alert the others but tell them to hold it for the moment. Call me back at seventeen-thirty and I'll be able to give you a definite answer."

"Thank you, sir. And good luck to you." Hammer hung up.

"Christ knows we may need it!" Mackenzie said to the dead instrument.

# 10

# Unhappy Returns

The Zastava flatbed truck appeared around the lowest of the hairpin curves just after dawn on Day Eight. Dean, who had been waiting with Daler in the jeep since the evening of the previous day, heaved a sigh of relief. He had been worried since midnight when the truck had failed to return from the site. But there was nothing he could do but wait. Any kind of raid on the premises with only two men was out of the question. If they climbed the shoulder of the mountain in the dark to survey the gorge from above, they might not see Mazzari and the two Turks if they were still there—and if they left while Dean and Daler were high up among the rocks, they might miss them altogether. A direct approach to the gates, pretending to be messengers from the restaurant, asking were the waiters still there, would arouse the terrorists' suspicions and almost certainly endanger the lives of the three men.

It was therefore with an enormous sense of release from tension that Dean sighted the Zastava. He hated inaction. The present mission, with its endless conferences and radio reports, its inferences and deductions and hypotheses, the insistence on part of the background remaining secret, and the gnawing realization all the time that they had gotten nowhere, were driving him crazy with impatience. His credo had always been: digest the brief, check out the risks, quickly in, do the job, and get out before the enemy knew what hit him. Although this was perhaps the most perilous assignment he had ever accepted, he was finding it more and more the most infuriating. Hell, he didn't even know who the enemy *was* yet!

At least now, he thought, lying prone on top of the boulder behind which they had concealed the jeep, he would know something about the extremists who had taken possession of the site and the missile based there.

He unslung the field glasses from around his neck and

focused them on the truck. From below, Daler, who had been resting with his back against the jeep's offside front wheel, called out, "Signs of the prodigal, cock? Or did you flush out a girl in a bikini?"

"Truck's on the way down," Dean said tersely. For a moment he thought he had seen men on foot behind the tailboard, but when he refocused the lenses there was no sign of anybody. Daler scrambled up beside him, first reaching into the jeep for his own binoculars and a long-peaked forage cap. Beyond the great conical bulk of Ararat, the sky was shading from red through orange and pink to a pellucid green; there was already a faint glare above the crest: in a few minutes the rim of the sun would appear and blind them.

The truck lurched around the bend, almost ran off the road, and then rolled down the long, straight blacktop grade that led to the intersection and the state road from Iğdir to Doğubayazit.

"Looks like there's only one guy in the cab," Daler said, making a slight alteration to the milled focus wheel on his field glasses.

"Yeah," Dean agreed. "Maybe the others are lying down in back. They'd be hidden by the cab anyway." The group of rocks they had chosen was only a few yards to one side of the intersection, and their view of the Zastava was virtually head-on.

The truck sped toward them, gathering speed. "What the hell's that bastard playing at?" Daler exclaimed, lowering the glasses and pushing himself to his knees. "Is he smashed or something? Do you suppose those fucking terrorists have been feeding them liquor? Throwing a thanks-for-the-lovely-food party?" The truck was veering from side to side of the road in an erratic manner, still accelerating.

"Christ knows," Dean said, suddenly alarmed. "There's something screwy going on here." He slid from the boulder to the ground, loosening the flap of the holster clipped to his belt. A thin crescent of fire, incandescently brilliant, appeared behind the dark silhouette of the ridge, flooding the plain with light, throwing a long shadow dancing across the stony ground in front of the truck.

Dean shaded his eyes. He began running toward the intersection. After a moment, Daler followed him.

As the sun hoisted itself slowly into the sky, the light

brightened further, the shadow shortened and became more precise, swinging from side to side before the careering Zastava. They could see now that there was indeed a single man at the wheel, and two more lying on the tail, bouncing slightly as the tires thumped over irregularities in the road.

"He *must* be drunk—or stoned out of his mind!" Daler shouted. The driver too was sawing from left to right in his seat, wrenching at the wheel as the grade leveled off and the speed diminished.

"He's coasting," Dean yelled. "The motor's off. Quick—take the other side!" He raced across the road. The truck had run right off the macadam; it was skidding wildly among the shaly stones, crashing into small rocks.

Dean was running beside it like a madman, just contriving to keep up. The truck hit the U.S. Army divisional sign and snapped it off at the base. It leaped a small bank and headed for the boulders beyond the state highway as Dean sprang onto the step on the driver's side of the cab and seized the wheel. He hauled on the bakelite rim, turning the runaway vehicle enough to avoid a head-on collision with the rocks. The driver fell against the door.

There was a rending screech of metal on stone, and the Zastava finally stopped, the hood and left fender crumpled, the windshield starred. Daler ran up, panting, and looked inside the cab. "Jesus!" he said. "Holy Mary, Mother of God!"

Mazzari's broken hands had been wired to the steering wheel with electrical flex. Thick cords around his hips retained his body in the seat. Blood had soaked through his pants at the crotch, and there was blood caked too down the front of his ripped bush shirt. Through the rents in the material, multiple bruises and lacerations were visible. His face was unrecognizable, only the whites of the eyes showing among the puffy discolorations of the gashed flesh.

"Jesus!" Daler said again.

"Help me get him out," Dean said tightly.

Daler ran back to the jeep for wire cutters. Gently they eased the big African from the cab and carried him to the shade behind the boulder. "Is he . . . ?" Daler began.

Dean was kneeling with his ear to the savaged chest. He shook his head. With one hand he reached up and snapped the jeep's outside mirror from its mounting. He held it to the gap in the swollen jaw where Mazzari's mouth had been. Very slowly, the lower half of the glass misted over.

"He's alive," Dean said. "Barely."

"Thank God."

"But he's got to be taken to an intensive-care unit pretty damned quick. Take the radio; call up that contact in the military attaché's office in Ankara, give him our coordinates, and tell him we have to have a helicopter here within the hour. He won't ask any questions: he knows we're working with Mackenzie, and embassy people detest the Agency."

"Right away," Daler said. "You want me to call Mackenzie too?"

Dean shook his head. "He won't be listening in until seventeen hundred." With a commando knife he began slicing away the tattered clothes from Mazzari's torso. "Take a look at the other two on your way: from the way they were jounced around on the tailboard, I figure they're past saving."

He was right. The two Turks had been dead for some time. Their hands were bound together behind their backs with wire, and in each case the chest had been smashed in with a burst of slugs from a machine pistol fired at very short range. Unlike many of the dead, the faces were not expressionless but wide-eyed and openmouthed with horror and disbelief.

When Daler returned to Dean's side, the combat leader had cut away most of the stiff, bloodied garments from the unconscious man's body. "Jesus God!" Daler swore for the third time.

"There seem to be no gunshot wounds," Dean said, "and I can find nothing in the way of knife thrusts. He's just been systematically and very badly beaten. Beaten—and kicked—almost to death."

"I don't understand," Daler said.

"Either they knew he was coming or something went very badly wrong," Dean said. "Maybe Ed will be able to tell us later. They must have driven the truck to that last hairpin. Then, once it was in view, pushed it around the corner, lashed him to the wheel, and let it roll down toward us. I thought I'd seen some guys in back there when I first got the glasses on it . . . then, when it came on down, I figured I'd been mistaken. I wasn't."

"They let it roll toward *us*? You mean they knew we were here, waiting for Ed?"

Dean nodded. "Evidently. I found this in Mazzari's breast pocket." He held out a sheet of paper. It was crumpled and smeared with blood, but the two lines of printed capitals in the center were clearly visible. Daler read:

DEAN—THIS IS JUST TO SHOW YOU WE MEAN BUSINESS. NEXT TIME WE'LL REALLY TRY.

The message was unsigned. "They even knew Ed was connected with you?" Daler marveled. "And they knew we were here? How the hell do you read that, cock?"

Dean's face was very white. "I wouldn't know," he said. "But there's one thing I do know, Alf. Somebody"—looking at the brutalized body at his feet—"is going to pay for this. They're going to pay very dearly. And if it takes all of my strength and everything I've got to straighten out this fucking mission and find out who it was, then I'll still do it . . . and someone's going to be very sorry indeed that I did."

There was oxygen apparatus in the cabin of the Bell Huey AH-1S Cobra helicopter sent by the embassy. Dean squashed himself in with the white-coated intern and held the rubber mask over Mazzari's face while the young man busied himself with drip-feeds and tubes. Daler had offered to take the jeep and drive the bodies of the two Turks back to the mortuary in Erzurum.

"He'll live," the surgeon at the American hospital in Ankara told Dean. "But he must have a constitution like . . ." He shook his head. "Well, most men wouldn't have, a beating like that."

"What exactly is the damage?"

"Specifically, he has severe concussion, a cracked collarbone, five broken ribs, a fractured femur, a dislocated shoulder, and damage to the bones and ligaments of both hands and one foot. Preliminary X rays show no permanent deformation of the skull, and the superficial cuts and contusions, you can see for yourself. He'll have to curtail his sexual activity for two or three weeks."

"Don't tell me!" Dean said, overcome with a kind of hysteria to find that his friend would survive after all. "It'll only hurt when he laughs."

He waited until Mazzari had been cleaned up, the broken bones set and put in plaster where necessary, and the wounds dressed. There was a saline drip feeding into the patient's left arm; his head was spined with wires connected to an EEG recorder, whose function was to check out whether or not there was brain damage; and there were suction-cup electrodes attached to different areas of the thorax. Red and blue pilot lights winked from the electrocardiogram to which these were linked. There was no sound in the room but the insistent, regular bleep accompanying the EKG patterns traced on the machine's unscrolling graph-paper reel.

Dean was about to rise from the bedside chair and leave the reanimation theater when the unconscious mercenary's lips moved. His eyes opened deep in the weals of bruised flesh and slid toward the combat leader.

Dean thought he detected recognition. "It's all right, old friend," he said huskily. "You're still with us. You're going to be okay. Just relax and take it easy, huh?"

Lacerated lips moved. The rise and fall of the chest quickened. A thread of sound, half-whisper, half-groan, rattled from the throat. Dean leaned over the bed.

A rustle of starched material. The ward nurse keeping watch on the telltales that monitored Mazzari's pulse, respiration, and blood pressure appeared from behind a screen. "You mustn't talk to him," she whispered. "You mustn't ask him any questions."

"I'm just listening," said Dean.

"Fu . . . Fu . . . Fu . . . Furn . . ." The man in the bed was trying to speak. Dean leaned closer.

"I'm here," he murmured. "What are you trying to say?"

"You really must not," the sister warned. "It tires him."

"Furneux." Mazzari's voice was suddenly distinct.

"Furneux!" Dean exclaimed in amazement. "What the hell does that rat have to do with this?"

"Furneux . . . Canadian." Mazzari was struggling to get the words out. "Site . . . on site . . . Recognized, but . . ."

"But what? What happened, Ed? Try to remember. Was Furneux masterminding the deal, or was he just a soldier?"

"Mr. Dean, *please* . . ."

"Naturally he would recognize you. He knows you. But you said 'but.' But what? What else?"

The voice lapsed into an incoherent mumble, and then, very faintly: "But . . . they knew anyway. Before he . . . recognized . . ."

"Knew what, Ed? *What did they know?*"

Mazzari breathed harshly. The breath rattled in his throat. "About you. About us . . . Knew . . . even with . . ."

"Even with what?"

". . . out. Without me, they knew."

"I really cannot allow this . . . this cross-examination of the patient," the nurse said sharply. "It has been expressly forbidden by the doctor in charge. I must ask you to leave at once. The man doesn't know what he's saying anyway." She took Dean's arm and steered him firmly toward the door.

"Oh, he knows, all right." Dean smiled, allowing himself to be led. "And now, thanks to you, I know too."

# 11

# Flight into Flashback

"What do you propose to do now?" Alexander Mackenzie asked Dean when the radio report was made the following evening. "We are already at the end of Day Nine, and it seems to me the options are diminishing. Will you take up Hammer's suggestion and follow up the leads in Luxembourg?"

"Yes and no," Dean replied. "Mazzari's out of it, certainly for the remainder of this operation. I think Hammer's right: the rest of the team should go to Luxembourg and track back. Once the kidnap victims are found, we might be on a winning streak. But me, I'm taking the next plane to Washington."

"*Washington?* But why?"

"I'd like for you to be there too, if you could, sir. Because Mazzari did find out something. One of the hijackers is a mercenary who knew him. But he says they knew my group had been hired—were almost expecting us—*before this man saw Mazzari*. Remember, too, that attacks were made on my life at Istanbul and at Erzurum, where I'd reported I would be—but not at other places along the way. In other words, I wasn't being followed, but waited for. To me that can only mean one thing."

"Namely?"

"The hijackers have been one jump ahead of you—and, once I was employed, of me too—all along the line. Evidently they have outside help also. *But the only occasions on which that help has been used have been those when I reported in advance to you what I was going to do and where I would be*."

"What are you saying, Dean?"

"I'm saying the hired assassin, or assassins, who must have been briefed by the hijackers themselves . . . well, they obviously had advance information. In other words, the hijackers are in touch with your Washington hawks."

"Of course they are in touch," Mackenzie said irritably. "They use the communications at the site to make their damned ultimatums, ask for food supplies and that kind of thing. You know that as well as I do."

"I meant," Dean said, exercising what patience he could, "that the communication is two-way. The terrorists have been warned in advance of every move we make."

"But that's not possible!" The CIA man was thunderstruck.

"It is if there's a traitor—a mole, if you like—among the people in the U.S. who are in the know." Dean paused, and then, seeing the disbelief on Mackenzie's face, he added, "It's the only explanation that fits the facts. One of those so-called hawks is passing on every scrap of information that you give them—is possibly even the brain behind the whole conspiracy."

"Impossible!" Mackenzie cried again. "What would be the point? What could they get out of it? These are all what the British call top people, holding down important positions. Why would they want to harm their country?"

"That's why I have to go to Washington," Dean said. "To see if I can find the answer to that question. And that's why I want you there—to get me into the places where I can make the necessary investigations. As you say, time's running out. If my guys in Luxembourg can locate and rescue the hostages, and if you and I can find the mole and choke the truth out of him, there's a chance we could get Healey off the hook and spike the terrorists' guns at the same time. It may be a slim chance, but I can't see any other approach right now. And if it came off, you and the other hawks would be off the hook too: neither of the alternatives would have to be considered."

"But all these people have been extensively screened, more than once; they have top security ratings. They wouldn't be holding down these jobs if they didn't. If your mole theory is correct, is it not more likely that one of them has been . . . indiscreet . . . and that the leak comes from some third party?"

Dean shook his head. "I don't think so. That's the whole basis of the blackmail, isn't it: that these guys have activated an illegal missile silo, and they're shit-scared to let *anyone* know about it, because it would cost them those jobs if it ever came out."

"I suppose so." Mackenzie still sounded dubious.

"As for the screening," Dean said, "just think. What would have been the main object of the investigation, of *any* investigation, into security in the U.S.? To make sure the subject had no communist affiliation or political leanings that could work against the country, right? But we're not dealing here with dedicated comrades or terrorists from the extreme left. The aim of the operation seems to be, first, to discredit at any cost the U.S., and second, to create a dangerous instability in the Middle East—which works against the Soviets almost as much as it does against us. Whether you met the ransom demand and eliminated Mubarak or dug in your heels and allowed them to fire the Ark at Tehran, the results would be much the same in the long run."

"If there was any long run," Mackenzie said somberly.

"Exactly. What we're looking for, I would guess, is someone whose background, loyalties, interests, whatever, would be served by that instability; someone nonaligned politically in the normal East-West sense, but with some kind of Arab or Muslim connection someplace. What I'm getting at," Dean explained, "is that such parameters might not show up in the records of the usual security screening, which would be angled toward the discovery of any leftist tendencies in general. The right questions might not have been put. So the information, the leads we require, may not be stored in the data banks. But we have to run a check to see."

"And you want me . . . ?"

"I want you to fix it so that I have sight of any and every report ever made by any security agency on Hardanger, McClintock, Argyle, and Henry Carpenter."

"*Carpenter?* But surely you don't think the President's National Security assistant . . . ?" Mackenzie left the unsayable unsaid.

"I don't think anything. Yet. But the exercise is pointless unless it's complete. I want you to give me access to all CIA—and especially to all FBI—files, dossiers, and data-bank material on these men. I'd like afterward to run checks on the Pentagon's associative-memory computer. Maybe, that way, if we program in questions that normal security investigators wouldn't have thought important— vacation trips in adolescence, non-American college friends not politically committed, library reading, that kind of thing—it's just possible we might come up with some lead."

"And during the investigation, my name, doubtless, would be run along with the others?" Mackenzie said dryly.

"Certainly." Dean was unabashed. "I said complete. But I wouldn't expect to dig up anything on you. You didn't have to drag me in, after all. And if there was anything to find, *you'd* find some way to deny me access to those files, wouldn't you?"

Mackenzie laughed. "Very neat. That way, you make doubly sure I *will* give you access to the files. Otherwise it smacks of guilt on my part!"

"There's one other thing." Dean's face remained grave. "I want you to let your hawks know I'm coming. And hint, just hint, at the reason."

"Good God! Whatever for? Surely that would risk—"

"If anything happens," Dean interrupted, "it'll prove to you that my hunch was right."

"But if you *are* right, you'll be in great danger, surely?"

"I'm booked on the TWA flight that's routed across the Atlantic. I want you to tell them that. Flight number, time of arrival, and so on. In fact, I shall be going via Pan-Asiatic, on the great circle route that's due at Kennedy two hours earlier. That way I can keep an eye on any . . . arrangements they make, unseen."

"Very well," Mackenzie said reluctantly. He was going to add (by way of involuntary pleasantry), "It's your funeral!"—but thought better of it. Instead he said, "I'd better follow you as soon as possible, so that *I* can keep an eye on *you*. In any case, I cannot guarantee to fix you up at all those places by phone and radio. In some—the FBI and the Pentagon, for instance—I'd have to come with you personally."

"I already booked you on the TWA flight leaving early tomorrow morning," Dean said.

The Pan-Asiatic Boeing 747, with its improbable route that overflew Moscow, central Norway, Iceland, and the tip of Greenland, was more than two-thirds full. For the first hour of the long flight, the stewards and stewardesses were occupied settling in the elderly, distributing food and drink, answering questions, and readying the movie program for showing. Dean had found a seat by one of the rear ports, just aft of an emergency escape hatch—one of two that permitted him to stretch his long legs. And to his satisfaction, nobody had claimed the one next to him. The frightening equation he had been asked to solve had far too many variables, too many horrific X-factors for him to consider wasting time in the exchange of trivialities with some well-meaning bore.

Chasing the sun, the Boeing was extending his day by several hours, and he had been idly watching steppes and cities, forests and bare mountain ranges, slide past below while he attempted to impose some kind of order on the chaos of theories evolving from the latest turn in events. Forty thousand feet below, the sea was showing through drifts of cloud as a gray sheet of wrinkled crepe paper when the stewardess's voice broke through his thoughts.

"Would you like the earphones, Colonel Dean? To watch the film?"

"No thanks," Dean said absently, still gazing through the double glass. "I'd rather watch the night fall." And then suddenly it hit him.

Dean? *Colonel* Dean? Only those who knew him as a combat leader used this title; he never made use of it himself. In any case, he was booked on the flight as Hiram C. Webster, an electronics software salesman, of Minneapolis. He turned to look at the girl.

Slate gray uniform. Good breasts thrusting out the cream silk shirt. Short, dark hair with bangs. A wide, generous mouth with equally wide, clear brown eyes. A short, straight nose . . . and something that was nevertheless vaguely familiar about the whole. He knew so many air hostesses; apart from the fact that Mazzari's girl was one, he seemed always to be getting involved with them. And yet this one . . .

She smiled. "I don't expect you remember me, Colonel?"

The smile—and the personal as opposed to the professional voice—gave him the clue.

"Chloe!" he exclaimed. "Chloe Constantine! Of *course* I remember you. How could I ever forget? You saved my son's life, dammit—and you risked your own."

She sat down in the vacant seat. "How is Patrick?"

"Just fine," Dean said. "We were on vacation together only a few days ago. He's growing into a fine kid." With an inner twinge he had a sudden vision of the sand castle

112

on that New England beach . . . and then the stormy expression on Samantha's face when the CIA messenger arrived to see him. Chloe, he remembered, was a girl who found his occupation exciting, even glamorous, and not by any means contemptible. She had been the hostess detailed to look after Patrick when he was traveling alone on a jetliner that was hijacked—and which Dean, to his horror, had been hired to recapture, at any cost. It was through her courage, and the intelligence of his son, that he had been able to pass on to the crew instructions that allowed him to assault the plane without any loss of life to the passengers.

He looked at her now. Fine kid; great girl. The wide eyes regarded him warmly. She smiled again; she had very even teeth. Hundreds of years below, the sea, darkening from hammered pewter to gunmetal, withdrew beneath a cloud bank.

Dean, whose softer side knew about such things, recognized a fragrance, a faint breath blowing his way, of Givenchy III. All at once he felt desperately alone. The responsibilities of his brief, so heavy and alarming that he had pushed them out of his mind for days, had nevertheless weighed upon him, insidiously eroding that subconscious tonus that alone can bolster the conscious stamina which keeps a man going long after his body has cried a halt. Without knowing it, he was at a point of nervous exhaustion that required, that demanded, a stimulation as far removed from its cause as possible. What was the title of that movie? *The Loneliness of the Long Distance Runner*? He knew exactly what the man meant. And the fact that, in his case, the distance was short, and diminishing every hour, only made the problem more acute.

"What is it this time, Colonel?" Chloe Constantine was asking. "Another hijack? A well-earned vacation? Or shouldn't I ask?"

"The name is Matt." Involuntarily, without thinking, the gentler side of Dean's Gemini nature brought out the name by which until now Samantha, and only Samantha, had known him. As automatically, although it was against every instinct and tenet of his rigid professionalism, he added, "Yes. A kind of hijack. But I can't talk about it now."

The field agents of Britain's Secret Intelligence Service, which used to be known as MI-6, receive an arduous and rigorous practical training which includes—apart from the usual unarmed combat, cipher, and assassination courses —a series of practical exercises that have to be carried out without the knowledge of police or military authorities. These may include mock holdups, the secret penetration of high-security military installations, and actual burglarious entries. If the operative is caught by the forces of law and order, his bosses will not intervene to save him: he serves his sentence like any common criminal. Such a brutal apprenticeship breeds men with a very high regard for planning, security, and the other imperatives of their dangerous profession. But it is recognized that even such men cannot keep entirely to themselves the dark secrets of their calling, especially when they are working quite alone. Each agent on active service is therefore permitted one confidant (or confidante) with whom he is allowed, indeed encouraged, to discuss the problems of his current assignment.

The confidant (who will have been screened even more minutely than the operative himself) is customarily someone close to him—his wife, a college professor, his mother, on rare occasions a son or daughter—but never a fellow member of the organization. In the case of a marital split-up, the death of a confidant, or some other rupture in the relationship, the agent is withdrawn from active service and transferred to administrative duties. If a celibate operative wishes to get married, the new husband or wife automatically replaces the previous confidant—always provided the screening results are acceptable and the new spouse is prepared to sign the Official Secrets Act. If the newcomer is considered unsuitable or a poor security risk, the agent is again transferred to office duties. In default of such a system, psychologists have reasoned, the agent burdened with life-or-death decisions, the terrible secret responsibilities of espionage, perhaps the strain of maintaining more than one cover or false identity, must ultimately crack or destroy himself.

It was precisely because Dean, in his present isolation, lacked such a "safety valve" that the softer, more vulnerable side of his persona triumphed momentarily over the hard professional shell.

"Matt! You look tired," Chloe Constantine was saying. "You look dead beat, in fact. Let me get you a drink."

The concern in her voice touched some hidden spring

114

deep within Dean's psyche. He didn't reply directly. Holding the gaze of those brown eyes, he asked huskily, "Tell me, Chloe, do you have a stopover in New York?"

"No," she said. "The flight-deck crew are relieved there, but I ride on to Washington. I have a stopover there until thirteen hundred hours the day after tomorrow."

"Better still."

"Why do you ask?"

"Why does any guy ask a girl if she has an evening free?" For a moment the old rakish, devil-may-care look softened Dean's haggard features. "I shouldn't say this, but I damned well will," he added. "Because I want to go to bed with you more than anything else on earth."

# III

There are only two kinds of strategy: the good and the bad. The good fail almost always through unforeseen circumstances, which often make the bad succeed.

—Napoleon Bonaparte

# 12

# Alarms, Excursions, and a Dead End

Day Ten. At 0900 hours on Wednesday, July 13, 1983, the concierge of a Victorian apartment building halfway up the Rue St. Georges, in Paris's ninth arrondissement, walked to the sub post-office in the Rue Taitbouf, one short block away. She took from her worn purse a key, as she did every working day of the year, and opened the small scrolled ironwork door of P.O. Box 157. From the interior of the pigeonhole she removed a single letter. There was a letter there every day. Sometimes it bore a typed address, sometimes it was handwritten in green ink or blue, sometimes in black. The envelopes were in different sizes and shapes, some buff, some white. The postmarks could be from Belgium, Germany, Holland, or France. But the contents of the letters were always the same: a single sheet of 64-gram, $8\frac{1}{4}''$ by $11\frac{3}{4}''$ A4 office paper, watermarked "Extra Strong" and folded in four. For more than two years now, the sheets of paper had been blank. But today—the concierge saw with no particular interest when she slit the flap of the envelope and removed the contents—the paper bore a message.

Just above the lateral fold, there was a single penciled line (typewriters could be traced): the word "APPLE," followed by two groups of figures, one consisting of three digits, the other four.

In accordance with her instructions, the concierge had taken the letter around the corner and opened it on a wooden seat in the Square d'Orléans—a diminutive rectangle of withered grass with a single access lane from the Rue Taitbouf. The square was only used on the odd dates of the month. On the even dates, she alternated between a café in the Rue St. Lazare and another seat on the sidewalk outside the church of Notre Dame de Lorette. The invariable routine, she had been told, was so that anybody who wished to know where she was could give her further instructions. Nobody ever had.

There were, however, existing orders in the case of a letter that contained a message. The concierge memorized the word and the figures. She tore the paper and envelope into small pieces and retained the fragments of each in separate hands. She rose to her feet, left the square, and walked the three hundred yards to the Place St. Georges. On the way, she dropped the pieces of torn paper; the remains of the envelope went into a litter basket in the Rue d'Aumale.

In the southwestern corner of the Place St. Georges, there is a Métro entrance—one of the few still left with the original art-nouveau ironwork and lettering. The station, on Line 12, which runs from the Porte de la Chapelle in the north to the Mairie d'Issy in the southwest, lies between Pigalle and Notre Dame de Lorette. Outside it, a public telephone booth stands against the railings surrounding a small shrubbery. The concierge went into the booth and shouldered shut the door. She dropped a coin in the box and dialed a Montmartre number. There was no reply. An hour later, she returned to the same booth and tried again—a short, stout woman with wispy gray hair and down-at-heel shoes. Again the phone rang and rang until the connection was automatically cut, the coin returned, and the dialing tone resumed in the earpiece. At the third attempt, the concierge had to wait almost ten minutes while a teenage boy in a leather jacket talked interminably and mouthed kisses at the handset. But this time the Montmartre number replied at once.

A deep, crisp voice said simply, "Yes?"

The concierge uttered a code word. She repeated it, and then said, "You are to call New York. Here is the number." She passed on the seven figures she had memorized.

"Understood," the crisp voice acknowledged. There was a click and the line went dead.

The concierge left the booth and walked home. It had begun to rain and her feet hurt. It was a nuisance, this apparently meaningless daily chore she had been doing for so long, but the small retainer she was paid came in useful. It appeared without fail in her checking account on the fourth of every month. With a part of it she paid her social security and bought her weekly bottle of white port;

the rest she sent to her widowed daughter, who was struggling to bring up five children on a farm in the Auvergne.

The person who had taken the call in Montmartre phoned for a cab and went to the main post office in the Rue du Louvre. A lean hand fed six ten-franc coins into the yellow box in one of a long line of international booths. A forefinger dialed 19. When a second, deeper tone hummed in the receiver, the finger spun 1, the code for the United States; 212, for New York; and then the number quoted by the concierge.

The connection was immediate. The caller said slowly and distinctly, "Cain. On the subject of Abel. Shepheard's Hotel in Cairo was burned to the ground."

After a pause of some twenty seconds, a featureless electronic voice declaimed, "*Identi-fication and voice print ac-cepted. Speak.*"

"Message received. Awaiting instructions."

There was a whir. A faint clicking noise, and then what was obviously a continuous tape loop was cut in to the circuit:

"*. . . each day when instructions to proceed or abandon will be issued. Operation Tarboosh is to be activated, repeat activated, as of today, July 13, repeat 13. Subject in Paris, leaving Pan-Asiatic Flight PA717, repeat 717, for Tel Aviv on Day Fourteen, July 17, repeat 17. You are to call this number at 1430, repeat 1430 hours local time each day, when instructions to proceed or abandon will be issued. Operation Tarboosh is to be—*"

The caller replaced the instrument gently, left the post office, and walked to the gunsmith's in the Place André Malraux, on the corner of the Rue de Richelieu and the Avenue de l'Opéra.

One hundred and seventy-four miles to the east, Sean Hammer sat with Wassermann, Schneider, and Novotny at a table in one of the green-rexine-lined booths of the Hotel Cravat's brasserie-bar in Luxembourg. "Yon phony Interpol passes given us by your man Mackenzie have been useful, sure," he said. "The pollis here have helped all they bloody could—but what have we come up with so far, tell me that?"

"A gang of facts that show the kidnappers were pretty damned smart," Novotny said. "But fuck-all to show *who* they were."

"Well, we know there's a Turkish connection, man," Kurt Schneider pointed out. "These two characters hired the Volkswagen Rabbit in Germany, the one abandoned outside the Healey place, they did come from Berlin like they said; they did give their real names to the rental company. So we know this Turk thing is true because the police have checked and they are coming from Erzurum all right: Nesuhi Ertegal and Paul Tabor. Criminal records both. Maybe we better concentrate on that?"

"There's a slight hint of that connection—not much, perhaps, but an indication already—in the fact that the missile they hijacked, and its site, happen to be in fucking Turkey," Wassermann said sourly "Also they didn't go *back* to Berlin, did they?"

"All right, Abe: cut the sarcasm," Hammer said. "What else do we find? Aside from these two Turks who were careless enough to give their real names—or who just didn't give a damn—we have five guys not yet accounted for who booked into the country on June 27. Two Lebanese and a Belgian who arrive on the morning flight from Brussels; and a couple drove in from France in one of those motor homes. There's no check on the first three: just the names on the passenger list, one first-class and two tourist. The Belgian, name of Chapattier, took a cab and stayed one night right here in this hotel. The desk clerk says he was a fat guy. Two men answering to the description of the other two rent the Hertz panel truck abandoned in Germany, though the names they give the hire company are different. Interpol tell us the name and number on Chapattier's passport are genuine enough, but the clerk never saw any photo: the guy filled in the register out of his head. Lots of folks do—nobody ever checks the bloody things anyway, leastways not unless there's some query about the person. But it could be a pointer."

"And the couple in the motor home?" Novotny asked.

"Just heard from the local police," Hammer said. "So far as the immigration records go, the camper never left the Grand Duchy. It never showed at the vacation park where they said they were going, in Ober-Eisenbach, neither." He shrugged. "Of course that don't mean it may not have gone right on through and left the same day: they don't log every damned vehicle that passes. But the frontier guards did note the couple's passport details. The address they gave is fake, and nobody of that name ever had a passport with that number, according to the central computer of the Police Judiciare."

"A guy wouldn't be too much out of line he should suggest that camper's in a hideout someplace here, then?" Wassermann offered. "And that maybe the woman and the kid are in the same place?"

"I would think," Hammer agreed.

"They couldn't have been smuggled out in the panel truck?" This was Schneider.

"Sure they could." Hammer sighed. "There's no record of that truck leaving. They must have just waved her through, the way the Rabbit came in. But in that case, why is the camper still missing?"

"Okay, okay. You made the point," Novotny said. "So what exactly do we have, as of fucking now, on this goddamn snatch?"

"Healey's wife is a prison visitor. She brings knitting patterns and candy and glad tidings to the lady cons of Luxembourg city. One hour in the evening each Monday and Thursday. At the same time, the kid goes to dancing class. But she does it *three* times a week: Monday, Thursday, and Saturday."

"Any special reason the kidnappers chose Monday?"—Novotny asked.

"Sure. On Saturdays the kid gets a ride home with the mother of a friend, 'cause her own ma ain't at the big house. They wanted the wife and the daughter together. In any case, Healey would already have been in their hands by Thursday." Hammer pulled a sheet of paper from his pocket and spread it on the table. "We got witnesses who saw the panel truck by Healey's home, and later in the driveway," he said. "And another—a screw goin' off duty—who remembers seein' a VW Rabbit with a kraut registration stalled near the prison gates, just before Missis Healey left. No sweat workin' out that one! So here's the way it all stacks up." He spun the paper around so that all those in the booth could see. The timetable read:

*Luxembourg, 6/27/83—Sundown 2009 hours.*
*Clear.*
1910–1915 Chapattier leaves Hotel Cravat on foot.
1930 (approx.) Mrs. Healey seen leaving home in white BMW.

1945 BMW stops outside dancing academy to leave off daughter.
1951 BMW clocked in by guard at prison main gates.
1955–2005 (dusk) Chapattier arrives at Pavillon Royal.
2100 (dark) VW seen apparently stalled near prison gates.
2103 Mrs. Healey and BMW clocked out of prison by guard.
2110 (approx.) BMW collects Healey's daughter from school; panel truck seen opposite Healey home.
2120–2125 BMW struck by VW avoiding truck backing up out of driveway; VW passengers accompany Healeys into house; VW driver apparently hurt.
2130 Panel truck backs up Healey driveway. Not seen to leave but house left empty, open, with lights illuminated. VW (now driverless) abandoned.
2145 (approx.) Chapattier quits Pavillon Royal.
2327 Police, alerted by anxious neighbors, arrive at house.

"Shit, I don't know," Novotny said after they had all regarded it for some time. "All that seems to do is confirm and catalog what we knew already—and prove what a smart operation these bastards mounted here."

"By me it lets the fat guy out," Wassermann, who was always a little overweight, said with satisfaction.

"What do you say?" Schneider demanded. "He quits the hotel at a quarter after seven, but he does not arrive at the restaurant until eight—and it be no more than five minutes' walk away. What does he do with all this time between?"

"Jesus, how do I know? He goes for a walk. He stops by a saloon for a beer. He picks up a girl and has a quick *shtife*. You tell me. The important thing: he is inside that restaurant the whole time this kidnap routine takes place."

"Unless," Novotny said, "he happened to be Mr. Big, the brain behind the whole deal, who doesn't want to dirty his own fat hands and makes sure he is in the public fucking eye, eating, while all the villainy goes on."

"In that place? I should be so lucky to fix myself that kind of alibi if ever I needed one!" Wassermann said piously.

"Don't forget," Novotny urged, "that the girl on the cash desk told us he'd left in a hurry. Didn't even wait for a bill, but left a stack of folding money on the table and split. It seems he didn't even finish what was on his goddamn plate! Just a few minutes after the snatch."

"Yeah," Hammer said. "You could even be right, Emil. Where does it get us, but? Whoever these guys were, all we know is, we have to find a Mercedes camper in a heavily wooded country that may look small on a bloody map . . . but is nevertheless covering, it says in this brochure the barman gave me, 2,586 square kilometers. How the hell can four guys—six, if the Colonel and Daler come back—cover such an area when there's less than four days left, for Chrissake? Carve the place up into equal slices and buy half a dozen pairs of binoculars? Do me a favor!"

"Rent a chopper?" Schneider suggested.

"Aye, we'll do that. Not that we'll be the better for it. 'Tis the month of July, sure. Do you know how many caravans, and camping cars, and motor homes, how many vacationers there will be, a month of fine weather like this, even in a wee country like Luxembourg? And do you know how easy it'd be, locating one amongst all the others, when all we have is a rough description and the number on the license plates—which will surely have been changed?"

"The answer," Schneider said with a rare attempt at levity, "shall be in the negative."

"Right, lad. But we'll have to try just the same. So what do you say we prepare ourselves for the ordeal, stiffen the resistance like, with a drop of the creature first?" Hammer turned and called to the barman, "Hey, Mac! A quartet of *schnapps*, please, an' four steins of your fine local beer to chase away the flavor!"

Marc Dean stood beneath a peaked hat in a shapeless redcap uniform, with one foot raised onto a baggage trolley, in the shelter of one of the entrance bays beneath an arrival terminal at Kennedy field. There was a cigarette drooping from his lower lip; he looked exactly like any baggage handler at any airport in the world, remaining as inconspicuous as possible, hoping nobody was going to notice him and suggest he handled some baggage. Mackenzie could work wonders when it came to any kind of stakeout—even if his orders were given by radio.

Dean shaded his eyes against the glare of the sun and watched the Tri-Star take shape against a low cloud bank as it sank from the summer sky. The pilot of an executive Cessna, waiting on a perimeter track to receive the control tower's go-ahead for takeoff, throttled back his turbines and glanced up as the giant undercarts and nose wheel thumped down from the jetliner's belly. Construction workers manning a scaffolding on a site a mile away from the airport scarcely noticed the huge ship, air-braked now by seventy degrees of flap, as it roared overhead.

The Tri-Star's shadow undulated across rubble-strewn vacant lots, snaked over apartment towers and highways, and sped on past the huge maintenance complex of the airport. Soon it was hurtling toward the markers spaced out along the runway allocated for its approach.

As the dusty grasses on either side of the asphalt flattened beneath the ship's 300-mph advance, the shadow and the substance drew inexorably nearer: slowly the speeding jet sank toward the tarmac, and as slowly the skimming shadow moved out toward the center of the runway to join it. The only usual thing about the operation was the rapidity of the final junction: instead of leveling off, throttling back, and setting gently down with a scream of reverse thrust, the Tri-Star continued flying at exactly the same speed and inclination until the two, the aircraft and its shadow, met together. In ordinary terms, it flew straight into the ground.

At the shattering sound of the first impact, a mushroom of dust spurted from the ground. With its landing gear snapped, the jetliner bounced high into the air, slewed sideways when it crunched to the runway for the second time four hundred feet farther on, dug its port wingtip into the earth and cartwheeled in a slow arc for another 250 feet before it slammed upside down across the tarmac and burst instantly into flames.

Ambulances and tenders were racing toward the stricken plane while blue smoke from the scorched rubber still marked the place where the tires had first seared the runway, but the Tri-Star was outlined in fire long before they got near. On either side of the white-hot fuselage, the stressed metal of the wings buckled and curled like charred paper. Off to one side, the skeleton of the tall tail group, with its trefoil of jet engines, streamed flames and smoke into the air. "Holy Christ!" someone exclaimed just behind Dean. And then: "Lie down and roll, man! For Jesus' sake, get *down!*"

Dean turned around. A man wearing a fatigue cap and yellow coveralls was staring aghast at the holocaust. A single figure, thrown to the ground by some chance of mechanics when the tail and the blazing fuselage parted company, was zigzagging crazily among the trail of spilled baggage, window frames, and the crumpled fragments of auxiliary controls that littered the field. Flame licked the pants and sleeves of his lightweight suit, his tie was on fire, and thin plumes of smoke streamed from his hair. "Roll on the ground to smother the *flames!*" the man in the yellow coveralls shouted impotently.

But the injured man was still running, staggering now, falling to the sun-drenched runway, dragging himself to his feet and stumbling on. Beyond him, one of the giant landing wheels which had been rolling away from the inferno came slowly to a halt, wobbled, and fell over onto one side.

To the horrified watchers at the terminal, the survivor's pumping legs seemed hardly to move him across the immensity of the apron (one of the ambulances had changed course and was speeding to intercept him). But at last he was near enough for the airport workers sprinting toward the wreck to see his open mouth and staring eyes. He was screaming. And then something behind him exploded, and one of the lazily spinning fragments of debris brushed him with its incandescent tail as it flew past and dropped him once more to the ground. This time he did not get up.

Dean turned away, sickened. The Tri-Star was the plane he had originally been booked on in his own name. He had installed himself at the airport to spy on what he imagined might be an attempt on his own life, but this multiple horror was beyond anything he had envisaged.

"It proves your point," Mackenzie said heavily some hours later. "The ship was using Murchinson-Spears assisted-landing gear, which depends on the accuracy of the altimeter reading. The Tri-Star altimeter had been sabotaged: it recorded a height of fifty feet when the wheels were about to touch the ground." He shook his head. "As you said, one of our four hawks is in fact a mole, a traitor."

In Paris, the CIA sleeper who had been instructed to activate the contingency plan for the assassination of President Mubarak took the RER suburban subway to Orly, and then the connecting bus to the air terminal. Being in uniform, the sleeper occasioned no comment, moving through certain doors, along certain corridors, and out onto an apron where at times VIP's who were guests of the state could embark or disembark from their special planes not too far from the building and without the inconvenience of curious crowds rubbernecking.

In a washroom reserved for personnel connected with the airport, the sleeper—having made mental notes on the disposition of various installations on, around, and near the apron—changed into civilian clothes and took an elevator to that section of the airport authority which dealt with the issue of official press passes.

The pass applied for, duly stamped, franked, and signed, together with the accreditation documents presented in support of the application, was delivered to an address in Montmartre by registered mail the following day. It was valid for the twenty-four hours commencing at 0001 on July 17, 1983.

Edmond Mazzari ached all over his huge frame. Despite the painkilling drugs injected into him every six hours, each movement of any limb or muscle sent twinges of agony flaming through one part of his body or another. Mazzari was a stoic. He was prepared without complaining to suffer this, now that the doctors had assured him that the damage was not permanent, his skull was not cracked, he would not be left with a limp or an arm that he could no longer use. But he suffered too the impatience of the man of action forced to lie on his back half-immured in plaster. And in that position perhaps the worst of all was the complex of injuries to his mouth and jaw, which hurt when he spoke, and rendered the voice escaping through his swollen lips unrecognizable even to himself.

He was trying it out when Daler returned from the embassy, where he had been talking to Sean Hammer in Luxembourg on the ambassador's scrambler phone. " 'The devil damn thee black, thou cream-faced loon,' " Mazzari shouted as Daler came through the door. " 'Where gotst thou that goose look?' "

Daler halted with his mouth open. "*What* was that, cock?"

"Sorry, old lad," Mazzari croaked with a painful attempt at a smile. "What you might call a dry run. The jolly old bard, you know. Line from *Macbeth*."

"Of course," Daler said. "The messenger who brings him the unwelcome news that Birnham Wood does appear to be en route for Dunsinane. I should have known." Mazzari laughed—and was obliged to stop suddenly. Daler was always surprising everybody.

"What news from the Emerald Isle's gift to the New World?" he asked.

"Mainly routine and confirmatory," Daler said. "But all neat and tickety-boo, as you'd expect. There's even a timetable to go with the notes! Want me to read you the saga?"

"Might as well. They've got *Little Nell* and *Little Women* and *Eric, or Little by Little* in the hospital library, but I can't turn the bally pages until my hands are healed. Can't even move the little fingers!"

"All right, matey, you're on," said Daler. He began to read the summary of Hammer's researches that he had taken down, and when he was halfway through the kidnappers' timetable, he stopped abruptly and exclaimed: "Hey, hey, hey! What the hell d'you think you're doing?"

Mazzari was doing his best to sit up in the narrow bed, grimacing with pain as his cracked ribs came into play. "What was that?" he cried hoarsely. "Read that again, Alf!"

"What—the whole bloody lot?"

"No, no . . . the . . . timetable. The bit . . . where . . ."

Daler eased him back onto the pillows. "All right, all right," he said good-humoredly. "But only if you promise to lie still. If you make yourself cough, you'll do yourself an injury, never be able to screw again."

"That's it!" Mazzari gasped. "Screw! . . . What was that place—on the timetable? Read . . ."

"The Pavillon Royal?"

"Yes, yes . . . where the fat man was. What did you say the date of this snatch would have been?"

Daler consulted his notes. "Last month. June 27."

"Oh, God! Of course! Why the devil didn't I . . . think of it . . . before?"

"What are you talking about? You're delirious, Ed!"

"I was *there*!" Mazzari groaned. "In the Grand bloody Duchy. In that very restaurant, dash it all. On that night. My little . . . that is to say, my bird had a stopover in the city. She works for Lufthansa. I went to meet her there. We had dinner at that place—and I even remember this outsize johnnie at the next table."

"No kidding!" Daler was impressed.

"I was never really into the kidnap end of this mission, or I'd have realized before, as soon as I knew the date . . . I remember the fat chap leaving; he steamed out like billy-o the moment we sat down. Didn't even finish his grub; left a sheaf of bills on the table and legged it as fast as he could. And now of course I know why."

"Oh," said Daler blankly. "Yeah?"

"Must have recognized me. We'd met before, you see. Bugger almost tricked the Colonel into starting a war in the Middle East. He's probably the brains behind the kidnap, the hijack, the whole bit. Thought I was onto him when he saw me, of course."

"But *you* didn't recognize *him*?"

"Remember he looked vaguely familiar . . . thought nothing of it. I was . . . kind of occupied that night. 'Course, if I'd known about the mission then . . . or known about the fat man in Luxembourg when I did hear about the mission . . ." Mazzari, falling silent, looked stricken.

"Don't let it bug you, Ed," Daler soothed. "So you knew the guy. It doesn't really add anything, does it?"

"Oh, but it does, old lad. It does. It's not just that I met him before: I know who and what he is. If only I'd blasted well *realized*," Mazzari lamented again, "we'd have known who we were up against all the time, and the Colonel's job might have been easier."

"It may still not be too late. Who is this character anyway?"

"Cove by the name of Hamid. Something-or-other Arnaghi Hamid. One of the world's richest men . . . and one of the craziest. Got the bloody power complex, you see. Despot of the world, and all that. It's almost like the kids: tear everything down, destroy it; we'll dream up something to put in its place later."

"He's an anarchist?"

"Not to say in the Spanish sense. In a general way, yes: uses his money to finance a terrorist group, Marxism for Asia Organization, they call it. Anti-communist, anti-American, anti-Muslim, antieverything. You'll notice the acronym is MAO. Some affinity with the cultural revolution, then—but the hell with Moscow and Warsaw and even Brother Castro. My guess is, he doesn't give a shit which of the options are taken up on this Ark caper . . . either one means chaos for everybody. Except of course the MAO."

Mazzari subsided, exhausted by his speech. "I'll go right on back to the embassy and call up Dean in Washington," Daler said.

Andrew Healey was almost at the end of his tether. Since he had been forced by Furneux and the Palestinian Ahmed to watch the torture of the surviving guard, his life had become a nightmare with no letup. The boy, screaming and writhing against the straps that secured him to the trestle table in the gatehouse, had finally parted with the secret of the master control that overrode the security dispositives in the interior of the silo. But he had died from shock and cardiac arrest soon after the improvised electrodes carrying 240 volts of electric current to his genitals were transferred to his nipples. The duty officer and his noncommissioned companion had been shot down without mercy as soon as the armored doors to the lower levels of the silo were opened. But they had of course been warned—by the guardhouse and by the automatic sealing of the doors—that the site was under attack. Unable to obtain a comprehensible reply to their SOS on the direct line to Hardanger, they had done what they could to defend the top-secret installation entrusted to them. And this time the hijackers did not have it all their own way.

Before he fell under the hail of bullets, the officer managed to loose off two shots from his Browning, one of which took the sullen Palestinian, Kamal, between the eyes, killing him instantly. The NCO already had the pin drawn from a grenade, which he lobbed into the passageway before he fell. Nesuhi snatched it up and hurled it toward the entrance, but it exploded beneath the jammed steel shutter, wounding two of the terrorists who had arrived in the helicopter.

Since then, Healey had not been allowed to leave the silo. Retargeting the missile had taken time and application. At first he had considered trying to trick them, aiming the Ark either at a stretch of open sea or a city whose destruction would be against what principles they had. But since he had no idea who or what they were, what organi-

zation they represented, the latter idea was not feasible—
and anyway, the taciturn Japanese, Matsuzaki, was enough
of a mathematician to check up on his calculations.

There remained the firing of the missile. It had taken
him days to convince Furneux that this was a complex
routine. "I *can't* show you how to fire it," he repeated
again and again. "I can only show you to how to act as
assistants if I were to fire it myself."

"You better not be stringing me along, Bright Boy,"
Furneux said menacingly. "There's plenty of juice left in
that generator. They're fitted up with electricity too in that
—where your wife and kid are held. Maybe we should
give you a demonstration?"

"No!" Healey shouted desperately. "I'll do what you
want; I promised. Only you must believe me, you must:
it's not as simple as switching on an electric lamp."

The Canadian grinned. "Making folks do what you
want is *just* as easy as that," he said.

Healey knew nothing of the attempted penetration of
the site by Mazzari and the two Turks from the embassy:
he had been a prisoner in the sterile, air-filtered, window-
less depths of the shelter ever since the last guard had
died. But the doors had been open and he had heard the
shots when the Turks were killed; he suspected therefore
that there was still some kind of reaction in the outside
world. But the only things he knew for certain were that
Furneux and his terrorists were in UHF radio contact (a)
with someone to whom they deferred (in other words Furneux was not the ultimate boss); and (b) that they received regular reports from some contact in the United
States. These—Healey deduced from the fragments of
conversation he heard—seemed to be giving daily, sometimes almost hourly reports of what the Americans were
doing in their vain efforts to counteract the hijackers'
maneuvers. It was clear, therefore, that they had friends in
the supposedly "enemy" camp.

Psychologically, Healey was by now in too poor a state
to make even an attempt to rationalize this. Numbed with
horror, disoriented by continual isolation from what he
considered the world of reality, bludgeoned mentally into
submission by the terrorists' total rejection of any normally humane considerations, he thought only of his wife
and daughter and what he could do to save them. Curi-
ously, it had not occurred to him as a solution to make a

suicidal break-free attempt and get himself killed—which, after all, was the one thing that would have rendered his captors powerless.

"Leave them alone, leave them alone!" he sobbed when the daily radio contact was made with the terrorists' holding Margery and Carole. "What have they done to you?"

"Our guest is regrettably naive," the KGB-trained Turk, Nesuhi, said to Paul. "The concept that any kind of violence has to be *reciprocal*—that one only hurts *back* if one has been hurt oneself—is so outdated as to be ludicrous! Pain and distress are nothing but *weapons,* my friend," he said to Healey, "as you shall hear once again now, to make absolutely sure that you keep in line."

As outdated, Healey thought dully, as his colonel's ludicrous suggestion that one should get on *personal* terms with a hijacker. How was a man expected to obtain a personal reaction from a nonperson, an animal? He stiffened, the hairs on the nape of his neck prickling. Another of those intolerable radio contacts.

The high, crazed, hysterical shriek of his daughter, Carole: "*Leave my mommy alone! Don't do that to her! Don't, don't! Oh, please—*"

And then Margery's scream.

"Abdul Arnaghi Hamid!" Dean said softly. "Of course. I suppose I should have guessed. Who else is that ruthless?" He turned to Mackenzie. "The MAO," he said. "Conscienceless bastards. It would have been no good trying to reason with them anyway. But at least it's a lead."

"How come?" Mackenzie asked. They were sitting in one of the field agents' reading rooms next to a lecture theater at Langley, sorting through transcripts of all the printouts that had resulted from the query programs fed into the CIA data banks when the call from Daler had come.

"Because although Hamid himself is careful enough to keep his nose clean most of the time, there must be *something* on him in the files—and there will certainly be plenty on the MAO. They've caused more damage than the PLO and the Red Brigades and the Baader-Meinhof successors put together, mixing it in Indochina and the Middle East. We can cross-check that material now with all the stuff we've dug up so far, give the whole works to the associative-memory computer, and see what it comes up with in the way of psychosocial patterns, probably behavior, and even M.O. possibilities."

"Yes," Mackenzie said. "And now we know who we're dealing with, we can rerun programs on Hardanger, Weiss, Argyle, and General McClintock, searching for connections with this man Hamid, the MAO, or anything *they* have been connected with. That way, we could get a lead on which of those hawks is your mole!"

Dean nodded. "It's the best chance we have," he said.

They worked through the night. There were a helicopter and a Cessna executive jet waiting to take them to Washington when they had squeezed all they could from the CIA computer complex and the data banks to which it had access. Certain circuits under Pentagon authority were denied to them, and to gain the use of a console and be furnished with the correct access identifiers—especially without a military supervisor—it was necessary not only to fly to the capital but also to be accompanied by Henry Carpenter. And for this, the President's National Security assistant had to be called out of bed in the middle of the night and carted off to the building next to the Capitol, where many of the live-or-die plans affecting the rest of the world are hatched out.

"It doesn't seem to be getting us anywhere," Mackenzie said despondently as the darkness beyond the east window of the big room began to pale. "They all have Middle East connections—but so have a hundred million other guys. Two of them have been in major cities at the same time as Hamid when certain disturbances were reported: Paris, Vienna, Antwerp. But what the hell does that prove?"

"Try the family-background circuit," Dean urged, "the one that's housed in your old offices on the East Side in New York. Cross-check the education and vacation programs on that job-application file. Bank, that is to say. See if you can find any correspondence at all, geographic or chronological."

Mackenzie was white and haggard. He seemed to have aged ten years during the night. At first he seemed about to protest; then he shrugged, repunched his access identifiers, and—seeing that they now had overall system control—tapped out the necessary reference signals to connect them with the required circuit. "Try a couple of straight queries," Dean said, "feeding those parameters into the references we already have."

The screen above the console flickered. Then a line of green lettering appeared at top left: "PROCESSING QUERY. RESPONSE IN 18 SEC."

The screen went blank. Henry Carpenter, who had stayed silent through most of their night-long vigil over the machine, cleared his throat and said, "Let's hope this one will bring us—"

But the sentence remained unfinished. Responses to the questions fed into the circuit were beginning to unscroll across the screen. They read:

RECOVERY SYSTEM SUPPLIES FOLLOWING ANSWERS
    YOUR QUERIES.
QUERY 1 NEGATIVE ALL SUBJECTS A THROUGH F;
QUERY 2 NEGATIVE ALL SUBJECTS A THROUGH F;
QUERY 3 NEGATIVE SUBJECT A
        POSITIVE SUBJECT B DAMASCUS 1975 1977
          BEIRUT 1978;
        NEGATIVE SUBJECTS C THROUGH E
        POSITIVE SUBJECT F ATHENS 1974 1975;
QUERY 4 NEGATIVE SUBJECTS A B
        POSITIVE SUBJECT C ISTANBUL ANKARA
          ERZURUM 1981
        POSITIVE SUBJECT D ANKARA 1981 1982
        NEGATIVE SUBJECTS E F;
QUERY 5 POSITIVE ALL SUBJECTS A THROUGH F;
QUERY 6 NEGATIVE SUBJECTS A B C E F;
        POSITIVE SUBJECT D LONDON 1966 1967
                CAIRO 1970
                TRIPOLI 1970.
      CROSSREFER ADMIN/EDUC/40521/FBI
        CONTACTS/6AB7.
        GRADE TS CLASSIFICATION SIGMA 3 F/O/E/O.
END DIRECT RESPONSE. PLEASE ENTER NEXT QUERY.

"May I?" Dean's face was all at once eager. Suddenly, almost at the end of the chase, he had scented a trail. He took Mackenzie's place at the console, repunched the access signals they had been using for the FBI circuits earlier, connected the computer outpost with the data bank specified, and then tapped out at some considerable length the two highly specific questions that the printout had suggested to him.

The three men said nothing, their faces intent in the livid light diffused by the blank screen. Then the information from the top-secret F/O/E/O* data bank began to unroll. The format was different from the one disseminated by the old CIA machine in New York.

YOUR 7/14/83 SIGNAL 769813 RE CONTACTS/6AB7 OUR 40521:

SUBJECT GGG ASSOCIATE LECTURER LONDON UNIVERSITY SCHOOL ORIENTAL STUDIES 1965-6-7 ADVISER WAFDIST RADICALS CAIRO AFTER NATIONALIZATION FOREIGN ASSETS DISAPPEARANCE NASSER 1970 SUBSEQUENTLY ARMS CONSULTANT QADAFFI TRIPOLI 1970-1 ENDINFO SUBJECT GGG STUDENT ADVANCED ARABIC SUBJECT DDD LONDON UNIVERSITY SCHOOL ORIENTAL STUDIES 1966-7 FOREIGN CORRESPONDING CHICAGO GLOBE ALEXANDRIA CAIRO 1970 SPECIALIST ARAB AFFAIRS TRANSFERRED TRIPOLI OCTOBER 1970 PRE-RAND ADMITTANCE 1971 ENDINFO SUBJECT DDD TRANSMISSION ENDS.

Dean expelled a long breath. "Got him, by God," he said quietly.

"It's incredible," Henry Carpenter said. "No question of a mistake, I suppose?"

"Look at the evidence, sir," Dean said. "Examine the facts. We know someone has been feeding information to the terrorists: the latest attempt on my life—together with the cynical and ruthless murder of several hundred innocent people—proves that beyond doubt. It had to be one of the men in the know here; details of the flight were transmitted to them and only them. Now we know which one it is."

"He's right, Henry," Mackenzie said heavily. "No other interpretation fits the facts supplied by the computers."

Damn right it doesn't! Dean thought to himself. Subjects A to F on the first printout were the four hawks plus Carpenter and Mackenzie. The initial queries were routine: were there any physical contacts recorded between the subjects and the MAO? If not, were there any suspected communities of interest on file? Negative in all cases. The third question related to business or professional visits to the Middle East during the past ten years.

*Security classification: For Official Eyes Only.

The answers showed that Subject B (Mackenzie) had, as they all knew, been in the area between 1975 and 1978, when he was laying the foundations of the CIA network he now directed; Subject F (Weiss) had been sent to Athens in 1974 and 1975 as NATO's nuclear-missile liaison with Karamanlis when the Greek colonels' junta was finally ousted from power.

Query 4 was a repetition of the previous one, but restricted to visits that were specifically military. Subject C (Hardanger) had been in Turkey in 1981—doubtless laying his plans for the secret and unauthorized reinstallation of the Ark. His assistant had remained there until 1982, presumably tying up loose ends, arranging for transport of the missile, pulling wool over Turkish eyes. The fifth question showed that all the subjects had been to Europe on a nonprofessional or vacational basis at least once during the past ten years.

Subject G in the second printout was Abdul Arnaghi Hamid. Taken in conjunction with the sixth question on the first, the answers to this questionnaire underlined Hamid's extremist leanings and showed clearly that Subject D—who had probably been a student of Hamid's in London in the mid-sixties—had maintained contact as a journalist specializing in Arab affairs over a number of years. He had, moreover, visited Turkey with Hardanger and then stayed on in Ankara for another year after the general had gone.

Since no such liaisons with Hamid, actual or presumed, occurred in the case of any of the other five subjects, the conclusion was inescapable.

Subject D was Tom Argyle, the Rand Corporation nuclear expert.

"Oh, my God!" Carpenter said. "What do we do now? Congressional inquiry? Grand-jury indictment? Senatorial committee?"

"You do nothing at all," Dean said swiftly before Mackenzie could reply. "If you did, the results would be almost as bad as either of the hijackers' alternatives. Think of the publicity! How could you keep the President out of *that*? And shit, we're at Day Eleven already! I thought the whole idea of keeping it to ourselves—"

"Yes, yes," Mackenzie interrupted, "but what the devil—?"

"I said you do nothing at all," Dean cut in. "Either of

you. You weren't here tonight. You've seen nothing. You've heard nothing. No queries were programmed into any computer. Do you have the means, sir, to delete all signal identification, reference, and cross-reference to the work we have done here and at Langley tonight?"

"I guess so," Mackenzie said after a moment. "After all, we fed no fresh information *into* the data banks."

"Good. Do that at once, then. If this lead's to be any use, things have to be choked out of this bastard Argyle," Dean said. "Now! So go home, forget everything if you can . . . and leave this to me."

"So he wasn't on the plane," Hamid said silkily. "That was careless of someone, wasn't it? Very careless. I like working with people who behave like professionals. It was unprofessional of you to telephone me at this time . . . whatever the urgency. The usual channels—as we say— are there to be used."

"He was *booked* on the plane. It was a last-minute reservation, not like something planned in advance. I thought—"

"You are not paid to think, Tom, but to act. And to act rationally. The presumption, with a last-minute reservation, is that there is urgency involved, as you say; that the place booked will be taken. But presumptions are not facts. To translate one into the other, *observation* is required. To put it vulgarly, one checks. Who was posted at the airport to verify that the place booked was taken?"

Silence hummed over five thousand miles of telephone wires.

"Exactly," Hamid resumed finally. "When making presumptions, it is well sometimes to place oneself in the position of the adversary and imagine what one would do, were one in his place. There is a chance—faint, I agree, but within the bounds of possibility—that some lapse somewhere may have suggested a feedback between the site and your headquarters. If such an idea had occurred to you, Tom, and you were in the position of our friend, what would you do? You would wish to check, would you not? Ah, but no"—Hamid interrupted himself—"you do not check, do you? Anyone else, nevertheless, would check."

"Arnie, I've said I'm sorry."

"There are no apologies in the world of professionals.

The word does not exist because there is no need for it."

"Look, I don't see how—"

"How would they check in such a situation?" Hamid continued as though there had been no interruption. "Would they not perhaps feed a piece of false information—the supposition that a certain person might be on a certain aircraft, as it might be—to their adversaries? And if that information was acted upon, then they would know for sure, would they not, that among those to whom the information had been made available there must be someone playing a double game?"

"Oh, God!"

"We already," Hamid went on remorselessly, "have information that the purpose of our friend's visit is to plow through the contents of certain data banks—information which undoubtedly is *not* false."

"Arnie . . . ?"

"I should imagine that by now they will have discovered that you were once a student of mine. Even the Central Intelligence Agency would be unlikely to miss such an obvious link. The fact that we were at Cairo and Tripoli at the same time is a matter of public record. Add to that your two-year sojourn in eastern Turkey—"

"But both Hardanger and Weiss—"

"No names!" Hamid said sharply. "Have you forgotten *everything*? The fact that you are almost certainly . . . I believe the term is 'blown,' is it not? . . . this fact will scarcely affect the long-term results of our project, or alter in any way its eventual success and the hoped-for effects in the European and Asian theaters. The short-term results in the North American theater may, however, prove to be exceedingly unpleasant . . . for you."

"But what are we going to *do*? What do you intend to—?"

"I? There is nothing *I* can do. It is, I regret to say, far too late for me to do anything." Hamid's cold voice did not sound regretful at all.

"But, Arnie, you can't just leave . . . I mean, what sort of action should I . . . what am *I* going to do?"

"That is entirely a matter for yourself," Hamid said. "You must find your own way out of the mess resulting from your own foolishness." He put down the phone.

It was only a few blocks to the apartment building from

the information center where Dean and Mackenzie and Henry Carpenter had spent the latter part of the night. Dean took Mackenzie's black Cadillac and the chauffeur-bodyguard that came with it, and made the distance in less than ten minutes, door to door. But it was already almost full daylight by the time the big sedan slid into a space beside a fireplug halfway along the service road that ran behind the building.

"Apartment 37B, third floor," Dean told the man. "Flash your Agency identification, or any other law-and-order ID papers you have, if there's any trouble with doormen or janitors. You know what to do?"

"Yes, sir. Mr. Mackenzie told me." The bodyguard was a beefy young man with a crew cut and a heavy jaw. He grinned. "Station myself outside the door of that apartment, pay no mind to any noises I hear from inside, and make sure nobody gets in there."

"Right," Dean said. "Or out. See you later."

He nodded and hurried toward double gates leading to a yard in back of the apartment building, which had been left open for the garbage collectors who were due to pass within thirty minutes.

It had been raining for several hours, although now there was nothing but a faint blown moisture left below the scudding clouds, and the streets and sidewalks and slate roofs gleamed in the early light. Dean saw no one, crossing the yard, and ducked behind a stack of wooden crates as soon as he saw through the open gates that Mackenzie's man was heading for the awning over the main entrance. According to the words stenciled on the crates, the building had recently taken delivery of a new heating plant that had been imported from Germany. Dean was glad of the cover. He jumped upward to grab hold of the counterweighted ladder that led to the fire escape, well out of sight of anyone passing in the street. The ladder swung down—silently because the amalgam of rain and soot and grime was acting as a lubricant—and he climbed rapidly to the first of the perforated iron platforms that separated each flight of the metal stairway zigzagging up the rear of the building.

The building was shaped like an E without the center section. There were three fire escapes: one at the end of each wing, and the third, which Dean was on, serving the wall that rose from the yard enclosed by these wings. The advantages of this last were that anyone climbing it would be invisible from any passerby unless they were directly opposite the open gates to the yard, and that it led directly to a window that Dean knew lit the hallway of the apartment he wished to enter. The disadvantages were that anyone climbing it would be visible to anyone looking out of any of the windows on any floor of the two wings' inside walls. Dean hoped that this was not yet a real danger: light showed through an area window which presumably formed a part of the janitor's flat, but the building housed high-income-group apartments and it was unlikely that many of the tenants would be awake at this early hour. If they were—or, which was more likely, if they were just staggering home from some all-night carousel—Dean hoped they would find no reason to draw back the drapes and stare out at a rainy dawn. Certainly all the windows he could see were either lightless or masked on the inside. He trod silently up the stairs to the second floor.

Somewhere, only just audible, a bright radio voice was declaiming an early news bulletin. From time to time, Dean heard the greasy swish of automobile tires along the wide street passing the front of the building. The clatter of garbage cans was still two city blocks away.

Halfway between the second and third stories, Dean paused: a man and a woman were quarreling; suddenly the embittered voices were loud—perhaps a door had been opened inside one of the flats? He held his breath. The voices were to his left, slightly below. A light came on in the wing beyond; an electric kettle shrilled. He continued to climb, glanced upward . . . and froze.

The hallway window through which he had hoped to gain the inside of the apartment was brightly illuminated.

Dean swore. He looked at his watch. It was a quarter to six. Two more windows—in the opposite wing this time, and higher up—sprang into relief against the stormy sky. It was possible, of course, that the light in Tom Argyle's hallway had been left on all night by mistake; it was possible that he was not at home and it had been left on to discourage any kind of break-in. It certainly discouraged Dean: he couldn't risk the chance that the man might for some reason or other be getting up early. The records showed that he was a late riser, something of a sybarite, but there could always be exceptions—and the plan Dean had roughed out in his mind depended on surprise, on his being inside the apartment when Argyle first saw him.

Dean looked to his right. There had been no time to obtain and study a plan of the apartment, but Mackenzie, who had been there, knew that it ran to the right of the hallway, as far as the junction of the outer wall and the wing of the building. There were five windows in that space. The first two were also illuminated, but feebly, with a diffuse light, as if it might be percolating through an empty room from some corridor or source on the far side of the building. The next two windows—bedrooms, Dean thought, from Mackenzie's description—were dark. And the glass of the last one was frosted. Clearly this was the bathroom.

Between the fire escape and the corner of the wall, as there was on each floor, there was a narrow coping—sandstone contrasting with the red brick, like the outside doorcases, the window embrasures, and the parapet that topped the eighth and last story. Two or three feet above the bathroom window, a painter's scaffold hung from pulleys that were supported by gantries on the roof.

The workmen who used the scaffold had not yet arrived, and the scaffold itself was too high to be of practical use to Dean, but it could act as a blind, an apparent reason for him to be near that bathroom window—if he could get there without being seen first. The coping was some five inches wide; he was dressed in jeans and a black turtleneck sweater—not the ideal costume for a painter perhaps, but believable maybe if it was a painter surveying the work to be done before he donned his white coverall.

The traverse was not all that difficult: balanced on the balls of his feet, a man in good shape can easily move along a five-inch ledge, but he must keep himself pressed very firmly against the cliff face or wall in front of him, because if the muscular tension thrusting him that way slackens, or his center of gravity moves beyond the outer margin of the ledge, he will fall backward. The problem of course increases tenfold if there are no handholds whatever and he has to rely on the pressure of his calf muscles to keep him flattened to the wall. Any kind of paunch renders the exercise impossible; a cramp in the calf could be fatal.

Dean had no paunch and he did not suffer from cramp, being a physical-fitness freak always in tiptop shape. There were, however, disadvantages: the four windows were too far apart for him to stretch from one to another, so between each pair there would be an agonizing gap where he would have nothing but the thrust of those calves to stop him falling; there had been no rain for some time, so the light showers during the night had made the weathered sandstone slippery; he was wearing thin leather-soled loafers (for he had had no time to change those either), and these were slippery as well after the climb up the grimy fire escape. Finally, although the ledge was at a negligible height—perhaps no more than thirty-five or forty feet—the fact that a fall among the crates below would certainly break his back and probably kill him made the maneuver mentally as hazardous as a simpler exploit at a far greater height.

There was no question, nevertheless, that he would do it.

He stepped off the iron stairway, slid a foot experimentally along the ledge, and grasped the sandstone projection framing the first window. He moved his left foot up to his right, slid the right onward again, and then supported his weight on the sill as he transferred himself carefully from one side of the window to the other—after which, still gripping the window embrasure with his left hand, he inched his way to the right.

But the fingers of his outstretched right hand were still three or four feet short of the next window.

This was the nerve-racking part. For a second Dean hesitated, his spine tingling, brain agonizingly aware of the void behind, the mind willing the muscles to overcome that weariness that was threatening to sap his strength. Then he took a deep breath, let go of the embrasure, and continued his perilous advance.

A yard and one third, four feet, forty-eight inches, 1,220 millimeters—whichever way you looked at it, the distance seemed unending, the wet-brick space between fingers and sandstone a universe to be conquered. And yet mechanically it was so simple: a foot to move, feeling for the roughness, the lip that might crumble, the slippery patch; the transfer of weight from the ball of the other foot; the sliding of hands along the wall; the first foot to move again; the breath to be held, because inflated lungs might push the body away from the wall enough to topple—and all the time press, press, press with the toes and the muscles of the calves. The muscles that were suddenly aching. *God, let it not be a cramp!* Dean's fingertips brushed the next window embrasure. He gripped, held on, expelled his breath thankfully, and hauled himself to the next space.

The second traverse was easier: Dean was able to wrench his mind away from the drop and what would happen if he fell, concentrating on the smooth transitions of weight, the coordination of fingers and toes. But during the next, rain began to fall again; gusts of wind plucked suddenly at the legs of his jeans; water soaked his hair and ran down inside the neck of his sweater, chilling his back and making him aware once more of the space behind it.

Between the fourth window and the bathroom, as the blood trapped by his held breath hammered behind his eyes, he received a vivid mental picture of the sandstone breaking away under his weight. He saw himself plummet downward, grab despairingly at the ledge as the upper part of his body shot past, cling on for a moment, hanging by his fingertips over the drop, and then fell again when the numbed muscles of his hands gave way and the sandstone crumbled once more.

In fact this didn't happen until he was actually beneath the bathroom window, where part of the ledge had rotted through the effect of decades of rainwater falling from a section of decayed guttering five floors above. But there was a sill below the window. At the expense of barked knuckles and most of the skin from the palm of his right hand, Dean scrabbled for another part of the ledge and clung on. For a moment he rested, panting, and then dragged himself back level with the window.

To his surprise, it was not only unlatched but ajar. He eased it open. A moment later he had dragged himself over the sill and landed inside the apartment.

The bathroom was remarkable. The tub, which must have been nine feet long by four feet wide, was sunk into a surround of onyx and agate; like the handbasin and the bidet, it was of a deep, deep, submarine-blue-green porcelain. The walls and ceiling had been covered with squares of dark brown nonreflecting glass—though seven-eighths of the inner wall was occupied by a pink-tinted mirror below which there was a marble shelf loaded with colognes and bath oils and deodorants and hair conditioners in a variety of luxury containers. A gilt-framed cheval glass stood in one corner.

Clearly communicating with the adjacent bedroom, a door was set into the remaining eighth of the inner wall. Another, on the far side of the cheval glass, presumably led to the corridor. Dean tiptoed across to the former, leaving a trail of wet, sooty marks on the white fur rug that covered most of the floor.

He listened, head on one side. The apartment was silent. There was more traffic in the street now, and the banging of trashcans was close. Rain drummed stealthily on the open window.

Dean had had no time to prepare for his invasion. All that he carried was a pencil flashlight and a miniature Beretta long .22 automatic, which was tucked into the waistband of his jeans. He took out the gun and the flashlight now and tried the handle of the door.

It turned easily, noiselessly in his hand. Very gently he pushed the door open a crack. He knew at once—he could not say why: long experience? a more total silence? some sixth sense?—but he knew with a certainty that was absolute that the room was empty. He went inside and switched on the small flashlight.

Mirrored doors along one wall, pulled back to show dozens of suits, topcoats, cardigans, sports jackets. Rows of shoes. A bed with apricot-colored silk sheets that had not been slept in (which was odd, since these must, next to that bathroom, be Argyle's own sleeping quarters). Gold-backed hairbrushes on a dressing table.

Dean switched off the flashlight and opened the door to the passageway. The entrance hall at the far end was brightly lit by a crystal chandelier, but the diffuse lights he had seen came, as he had imagined, through an open door that led to a room on the far side of the apartment, overlooking the street.

He crept along the thickly carpeted corridor, gun in hand. As he approached the hallway, he became aware of a strong, bitter odor: if Argyle was making himself an early cup of coffee, either he had spilled some on the flame or the saucepan had boiled dry. It didn't matter: now was the time for Dean's dramatic surprise entrance.

"All right, Argyle!" he shouted. "The time has come to talk . . . and there are guns trained on you right now!"

There was no reply. No indrawn breath, no creak of a chair pushed back, no footstep.

"Come on, man: we know you're here. There's a guard posted outside the door!" Dean called.

Silence.

Dean ran through into the lighted room. White leather armchairs, a white grand piano, decanters winking on an inlaid table. Beneath a carved stone Citizen Kane-style chimneypiece, a mass of papers that had been burned still smoldered. The body, suspended by a length of telephone cable ripped from the wall, hung from an art-nouveau cluster attached to a hook in the center of the ceiling. There was an overturned chair beneath the dangling feet.

Tom Argyle had, as instructed, found his own way out of the mess he had created.

# 13

# Dean Decided

At 1017 on Day Eleven, Marc Dean was woken by the telephone on the night table. "Sorry to disturb you." Mackenzie's voice. "Think you ought to know, though. Now that we're wise to the fact that it's Hamid and the MAO that we're up against, we can set teams to work wherever, without them knowing why we need the information."

"You didn't waken me to tell me that."

"No. The researchers we have digging into Hamid's business affairs and commercial contacts have come up with what looks like pay dirt."

"Such as?" Dean yawned.

"They found it in the register of companies at Somerset House, London." Mackenzie was not going to be stampeded into giving away his punch line until he was good and ready. "You know that by law all the directors of a corporation must be listed."

Dean knew. But it was a statement rather than a question, and he didn't feel obliged to answer.

"Hamid," Mackenzie continued, "is executive director of a small holding company that has a controlling interest in certain iron-and-steel works in Longwy—rolling mills, blast furnaces, that kind of thing."

"Longwy in Lorraine? In northeastern France?"

"That's right. The company's called Lorraine Holdings. The other directors are figureheads. Lord This. Admiral That. Sir Somebody Something. Names that look good to investors when they're printed on the company letterheads."

"Okay, so Hamid's the real boss. So what?"

"Lorraine Holdings is a thousand-dollar company registered, as I say, in London. But the works at Longwy are only a few miles from the Luxembourg border. And the company headquarters, the offices and so on, are in Luxembourg city."

Mackenzie paused. Dean waited. Mackenzie said slowly, "Apart from the mills, the company owns a certain amount of real estate. The largest property—ostensibly for company personnel vacation use but actually at the disposition only of our friend Hamid—this property lies between Ettelbruck and Esch-sur-Sûre, in the center of the Grand Duchy."

"All right," Dean said, "I'll buy it. What kind of property?"

Mackenzie said, "A fortified castle, built in the seventeenth century and surrounded by sixty acres of dense woodland. It's in the Luxembourg Ardennes."

"Oho!" Dean said, sitting up in bed. "And you think maybe there might be a white trailer home, French-registered, on a Mercedes chassis, hidden somewhere among those trees? And maybe prisoners in the dungeons?"

"There's a helicopter taking off from the U.S. base near Saarbrücken, less than fifty miles away, within the next half-hour. I'll call you the moment I have his report."

"I'd better get back there right away," Dean said. "This could be the break we need. If that kid and her mother are being held on that estate . . . We could go in right away. And then—if that poor bastard Healey can be convinced that his family have been zapped—make it back to Ararat and deal with the motherfuckers there, knowing that Healey will no longer cooperate in launching the Ark." He looked at his watch. "Shit! In Europe, Day Eleven's almost over . . . and there isn't a plane leaving here until eleven-forty-five. I'd better call—"

"I already made your reservation," Mackenzie said.

Chloe Constantine's body was warm and scented. Dean slid back down beside her. She stirred sleepily and reached for him. He was still marveling that she was there.

There had been one hour and a half—ninety precious minutes—while Mackenzie and Carpenter had been organizing access to the computers, when he had been free the previous night. Over a candlelit dinner in an Italian restaurant, he had pitched the brashest, most outrageous woo of his life: he had exerted every last ounce of his charm, persuading her to share his bed . . . knowing full well that he himself was unlikely to be in it before dawn, if then!

And she had fallen for it . . . or perhaps for him. Amused at first, then intrigued, and finally—once she saw that he was not pulling the usual macho air-hostess-is-an-easy-lay routine—convinced that Dean really was interested in *her* and not just another scalp to add to his collection, finally she had succumbed. Chloe had spent the first twenty years of her life in Phoenix, Arizona; her father had been an outdoor man, and she had been brought up among healthy, hardworking folk successfully farming the land west of the city. For five years she herself had been doing a job where the surface glamour was far outweighed by the responsibilities of the position and the imperative need never to panic, whatever the circumstances. She admired men of action like Dean, men who made up their minds and held to their decisions. She admired courage; she admired daring—and Dean's pitch, she had to admit, was daring enough!

Apart from which she found him damnably attractive.

Staring into those steady blue eyes as the waiter slid the coffee cups in front of them and poured the Strega, she said quietly, "I'm at the Metropolitan. Room six-one-eight. I'll tell the night clerk my husband will be arriving late."

"Honey," Dean said, "it may be very late. The job I have to do . . . I've really no right to expect—"

"I understand about your job," she cut in. "Or at least the *kind* of job it is. You don't have to explain. I shall be waiting."

And she was. The computer revelation, the dash to Tom Argyle's apartment, and the discovery of his body had left Dean no chance to call her, and it was past six-thirty when at last he tried the door of Room 618 at the Metropolitan Hotel. The handle turned; the door opened; the room was softly lit by an amber glow from a lamp on the night table. Chloe was lying on the bed, propped up on a pile of pillows, reading.

She didn't say, "I thought you'd never come!" The wide mouth smiled, dark eyes sparkled. She said, "I'm glad to see you, Matt." She laid down the book and stretched out her arms.

Dean strode across the room and held her. "What are you reading?" he whispered in her ear.

*"To Have and Have Not,"* she replied. "There's something of Harry Morgan in you, anyway!"

His fingers clenched on the smooth, cool flesh of her upper arms. She was wearing a simple nightgown of dark, dark red cotton, with wide shoulder straps and a scalloped top. The sheets on the bed were cotton too, in yellow and white stripes. "I've kept you waiting the whole damned night. I couldn't call you; I can't explain why. I need a shave and I need a shower. I don't know how I have the nerve to come near you," Dean whispered, feeling his stubbled chin rasp against her cheek.

"You don't have to explain. Forget the shave. Have your shower. Then come to me."

She was pulling the red nightgown over her head when Dean came back from the bathroom wrapped in a white terry robe. "Shall I be your scarlet woman?" she asked. "But you must be dead beat—you must want to sleep for at least twelve hours!"

"Out of all the things in the world," Dean said, "sleep is the very last that attracts me at this moment." He dropped the robe.

Chloe eyed the lean, tanned, muscular hardness of his body with approval. There were pouches below the eyes now, and fatigue had etched furrows across the brow, but there was no trace of sag to the jawline, and the contours of Dean's rugged face were taut and alert. "Out of all the things in the world," Chloe asked, "what does attract you at this moment?"

"I'll show you," Dean said, and he climbed into bed beside her.

Slender, trim, almost boyish in the gray Pan-Asiatic uniform, Chloe's body was surprisingly voluptuous naked. The breasts were soft but well-shaped, the hips broad and firm, the wonderful, subtle curve of the belly a joy to caress. On either side of a wide, crisp triangle of pubic hair, her thighs were resilient. Dean felt the tiredness lift from him and dissipate as effortlessly as the bubbles from a glass of champagne.

Making love, Chloe was warm and pliant and demanding, though her adventurousness and her demands never exceeded the limits of his desire. Finally, on a tide of shared rapture, they drifted into sleep.

After Mackenzie's call, Dean took her again, forcefully, needfully this time, the knight paying a last compliment to his lady before setting out on his personal crusade. She was still smiling when he came out of the bathroom, dressed, and called a cab to take him to the airport. "I used your little razor," he said. "I'll buy you another in Paris. A gold one. With a private message engraved on it."

She stretched luxuriously. The smile broadened. Her flight was not until 1300 hours; Dean's was at 1145. "I'll leave messages giving you my room number at every airfield in Europe," she said. "You better show at one of them pretty soon, whatever your job is, or I'll become a soldier of fortune myself and come looking for you."

"I'll do my best to be at all of them," Dean promised.

He fell asleep as soon as the plane took off, but awoke several hours later with the conviction that something was wrong, that he had forgotten something. They were flying over the ocean. Immeasurably far below, silvered by a three-quarter moon, islands of sea appeared between the clouds. In the twilit zone between sleeping and waking, Dean wrestled with his memory, striving to recover the thought, the idea, the fear, that had half-surfaced and then submerged again as conscious reasoning flooded his mind. And then suddenly he had it. Not a thought, but an image. It wasn't something he had forgotten but something he had remembered—something that his subconscious told him was important.

The image of a house painters' scaffold hanging just above a third-floor bathroom window.

But painters do not lower an empty scaffold from the eighth to the third floor of an apartment building and leave it there. When they have finished work, the scaffold is drawn up to the roof so that they can climb off and go home. Or, more rarely, lowered to the ground. What explanation could there be for an untenanted scaffold by a window that was open? Dean could think of only one.

The telephone cord had been ripped from the wall to make the noose for Tom Argyle. Hurrying from the apartment to find a phone and call for help, it had not occurred to Dean that the Rand expert's death might not have been self-inflicted. Or that there might have been a third person somewhere in the apartment, concealed in one of the rooms he had not searched.

# 14

# Knight Takes Castle

The assault on Grindeldange Castle was a model of its kind—if indeed any yardstick exists for the measurement of an illegal commando raid by foreign mercenaries on the territory of a peaceful country where no state of emergency exists.

Gaston Jammot, the watchmaker-turned-gunsmith who supplied Dean—and most of the "private armies" of Europe—with their hardware, lived in the university town of Mons in Belgium. He found the place, half an hour by train from Brussels, discreet enough for the necessary meetings with those entrepreneurs in the half-world between the law and the underworld who customarily required his services . . . and at the same time convenient for the forensic police of Amsterdam, Rotterdam, Antwerp, Lille, and the Belgian capital for whom he carried out ballistic tests and other esoteric offshoots of weaponry used in the detection of crime. For Marc Dean, on July 14, 1983, Jammot's choice of residence was doubly fortunate: it was less than one hundred miles from Luxembourg . . . and it was not, as in the case of neighboring France, paralyzed by a national holiday commemorating the fall of another, larger fortress exactly 194 years previously.

Considering the amount of time available—only seventy-two hours before the MAO ultimatum expired—this last was vital. Because all services were running normally in Belgium, the stores open and airline facilities unrestricted by holiday staffing, the multiplicity of arrangements Dean had been obliged to make at very short notice—and organize moreover by transatlantic telephone—dovetailed smoothly. The problems of the assault were in any case logistic rather than purely military. According to photographs supplied by the air-force helicopter, the geographical factors that made Grindeldange such an admirable hiding place worked equally well in favor of those who might want to mount a surprise attack on the castle.

The dense woods that covered most of the estate came to within fifty yards of the grassy open space circumscribed by the graveled curve that led to the main entrance; a stream that ran through the grounds curled between the building itself and a stable building—and this, without in any sense being a protective moat, nevertheless allowed would-be attackers to float unseen beneath a rocky shelf at the rear of the castle and position themselves at the center of the complex; finally, the driveway that led from the gatehouse was in the form of an S, and little of it was visible from any part of the castle.

According to Interpol, details supplied by the local police confirmed that the property had only recently been acquired by Lorraine Holdings. Restoration of the château, which was partially in ruins, had yet to be completed. A chain fence had been erected around the perimeter, but local villagers questioned had seen no sign of patrols or guard dogs—and the couple who acted as gatekeepers came from the town of Diekirch, less than ten miles away: there was no question of them being in any way connected with Abdul Arnaghi Hamid's terrorist organization. So far as the Luxembourg police knew, no permanent staff had so far been installed at Grindeldange, which had for many years been empty and neglected.

It looked, therefore, as though the place could have been chosen as a site for the detention of the hostages precisely *because* of its isolation and the fact that the restoration had not been effected. The supposition was strengthened by the rear view, on two of the aerial photographs, of a pale-colored truck or van that was clearly too big to be entirely concealed within the stable.

That and the evidence of an extremely sophisticated system of radio aerials mounted on the bell tower above the stable.

Dean's problem, therefore, was less the manner of a raid than the problems of getting a small but well-armed band within striking distance of the estate.

Even at night, the transport of half a dozen men, complete with modern military hardware, through the center of the European Economic Community in some kind of personnel carrier or armored combat vehicle was unthinkable. Equally out of the question was the technique—frequently used by mercenaries in Africa—of introducing a supposed hunting party: open season for hunters was not for another two months.

There was no time for Mackenzie to organize what might appear to be a genuine U.S. Army movement order: in the first place, the itinerary would not correspond with any known U.S. transport pattern; second, this would involve a formal notification to the NATO authorities, who must be kept out of the affair at all costs.

Dean was therefore left with two alternatives: a clandestine entry, smuggling in both the men and their arms; or an open passage of the frontier, posing as businessmen or tourists, with the attendant weaponry problems.

He decided on a compromise. Three of his men would drive in openly, using a rented Range Rover, on the main road from Liège and Bastogne, in Belgium. They would head for the tourist center of Wiltz in the Luxembourg Ardennes, where there were campsites, vacation hotels, sports grounds, and boating facilities. Two more would cross the border secretly, under cover of darkness, near a country lane where the frontier post was open and manned only in daylight hours. They would not attempt to crash past the post, but would navigate the headwaters of the River Sûre, which rose near Bastogne and followed the course of the frontier at that point, paddling a rubber dinghy which would contain the weapons for the whole group.

The Range Rover party, having hired a boat from Wiltz themselves, would then depart on an ostensible fishing trip, taking the craft on the roof of the Range Rover and embarking late in the afternoon at Esch-sur-Sûre, a medieval fortress village clustered beneath steep, wooded slopes in a loop of the river. Some way beyond the town they would wait until the rubber dinghy showed, unload their weapons, take them back to the Range Rover, and head for Grindeldange. The two men in the dinghy would then beat their way up the tributary stream that ran through the castle grounds. Dean himself planned to be lowered to the roof of the building from a helicopter. There was a small civil airfield at Wiltz, and planes passed continually over the property. A green Very light fired from the chopper once he was safely landed would be the signal for the assault to commence.

For the first time since the mission started, everything went right from the start.

Dean walked off the Sabena jetliner at Brussels not knowing whether the hasty directives, telephoned to Mackenzie from the departure lounge at Kennedy, had been carried out or not. He didn't even know if his own equally hurried instructions to Sean Hammer in Luxembourg and Gaston Jammot in Mons had produced results. But Hammer was waiting on the far side of the barrier, his nutcracker face split with a welcoming grin. There was a Range Rover in the parking lot. Daler was due on the Pan-Asiatic flight from Istanbul in one hour's time. And Wassermann was with Kurt Schneider, arranging the purchase of the dinghy at a scuba-diving and sports store in the city center.

"Swell," Dean enthused. "That's good to hear. Looks like we may be getting someplace at last. Where's Emil, though?"

"Novotny?" Hammer said. "Ah, he's away with your man Jammot in Mons. He was up casin' the joint at dawn this mornin'. Yon castle in Luxembourg, I mean. And, him bein' an ex-quarryman and explosives expert an' all, he figured maybe a wee shot of the ould plastic might come in handy, from what he seed of the place through his field glasses."

"Okay. Do we pick him up in Mons?"

Hammer shook his head. "Your man says, for the kind of caper we have in mind, it's better to keep to the less-specialized hardware. No need for the latest electronic aids an' suchlike. More like the riot-control material the pollis themselves use in hostage situations, he said."

"Yeah," Dean agreed. "He's right at that. In any case, the old guy never keeps any stock at his own place."

"So he has a buddy in Liège," Hammer continued, "who owes him a favor. Guy runs some kind of a sporting armory and safari-equipment place. We pick them up there, the both of them, an' Jammot will fix it so we get everything we want." The little Ulsterman looked up at the digital clock turning slowly on its axis above the information desk. "Abe and Kurt should have the dinghy deal ironed out by now. Daler won't be in for another fifty minutes. Will we drive into town and pick up the bloody boat while we wait?"

"We will," Dean said.

With the dinghy and its electric motor packed on the roof rack, and the five mercs comfortably installed in the fast, luxurious "utility," the fifty miles from Brussels to Liège were quickly covered. The armorer's establishment was on the southeastern outskirts of the city, just off the highway leading to Theux and the Spa-Francorchamps road-racing circuit. It was a single-story, double-fronted building set back from the road, its display windows filled with the usual selection of shotguns, alarm pistols, fishermen's waders, decoy ducks, hunting knives, and antimugger aerosols. But inside—especially in back of a glassed-in office and accounting section—the merchandise was considerably more esoteric than the stock to be found in normal sporting-goods stores. Dean saw racks of such exotica as "over-and-under" rifles, multibarreled shotguns, Gyrojet automatic pistols that fired tiny rocket grenades, and Dardicks that tipped revolutionary triangular cartridges into their breech.

Gaston Jammot's friend was a tall, pink-faced man with neat white hair and oversize shell-rim glasses. He was a character in marked contrast to his fellow gunsmith, for Jammot was short and wizened—a smiling gnome with eyes magnified by thick lenses rimmed in gold. A Congo expatriate like Edmond Mazzari, he had left the country when the Belgians withdrew in 1960. Dean had first met him while working with the Peace Corps in Biafra.

"My colleague Paul Claes," Jammot said when they were all gathered in the back room, "is professor of ballistics at the military college in Antwerp. Inasmuch, dear boy"—turning to Dean—"as I have been told of your . . . ah . . . mission, I fancy his expertise may be of considerable use to you."

"Naturally I shall be grateful for any advice," Dean said politely. Jammot had taught him almost all he knew about firearms, and if the little man was recommending this silver-haired authority, he wasn't going to turn a deaf ear.

"In close-quarters fighting, with a great deal of cover of the kind I understand you may be required to undertake," Claes began, "accuracy is as vital as speed. In such conditions, the long rifle and even the modern overhung-bolt automatics are too cumbersome to be of use: it takes too much time to get them into the aiming position. I do not need to remind you of the deficiencies of handguns. Except, of course"—he favored them with a wintry smile—"in the case of television serials and westerns. Your normal choice, therefore, will clearly be the machine pistol."

Dean said nothing. He knew this as well as Claes, but he was obviously hearing an extract from a prepared lecture; on Jammot's say-so he would listen and see what came out at the end.

"The machine pistol," Claes declaimed, "is unique in that its main asset is also its chief liability. I refer to the weapon's astonishing rate of fire. The Skorpion, the Stoner, the M3-A1, the Bergmann, the old Schmeisser used by the Nazis, the modern Stechkin—they all hose out slugs at anything from 150 to 750 rounds per minute. One copy of the Mauser military pistol made by the Spanish—it was called the Royal—actually exceeded one thousand rounds per minute, which meant that the entire magazine was loosed off in less than a second!"

Claes paused to survey his audience. Most of them were waiting for what was coming. He hadn't told them anything yet that they didn't know already. Wassermann was staring at a stun gun and an M-79 grenade launcher in a display case.

"At such speeds," the Belgian continued, "an extended pressure on the trigger makes the weapon virtually uncontrollable: violent recoil action and muzzle blast cause the barrel to jerk up so fast that only the first shot is anywhere near the mark. The 'climb' of the gun in this way wastes a great deal of ammunition. It was because of this that the idea of 'burst-fire facility' emerged among designers in the mid-sixties."

Wassermann turned around to stare at the speaker, who sensed a quickening of interest now in his audience. Dean repressed a smile and avoided Jammot's eye. "The theory behind this concept," said Claes oracularly, "is that if a weapon is on single-shot action and the initial round misses, the soldier naturally takes longer to aim the second . . . during which time the target may have moved to an escape situation. But on automatic, as I have shown, if the first shot misses, the 'climb' of the gun is likely to spray the slugs harmlessly into the air. 'Burst-fire facility' reduces the number of shots released by any single pressure to three or five. The reasoning here is that if the first misses, the second and third, since they are fired without pause, will still be dispersed—but only slightly—and may thus hit the target. A gun with a thirty- or sixty-round magazine will naturally remain effective—*constantly* effective, that is—if each burst is confined in this way to those three or five shots."

The speaker moved to a locked cabinet with polished oak doors that was placed between two racks of sporting rifles. "There are of course arguments against this theory," he said. "Doubtless you are all familiar with them. Nevertheless, the West German firm of Heckler and Koch have produced a machine pistol with this capability." He removed from his pants pocket a bunch of keys on a chain, and inserted one in the lock. When the doors were open, they could see inside four squat and businesslike weapons supported horizontally on felt-sheathed pegs. The guns, still coated with the maker's grease, carried folding stocks and deep magazines incorporated into the pistol grip.

"The Heckler and Koch VP-70," Claes announced. "A blowback machine pistol, chambered for the 9mm Parabellum round. The burst-fire facility takes the form of an additional position for the safety catch. In this position, an internal mechanism is engaged which limits the number of shots fired by a single pressure of the trigger when the gun is on automatic. Once this plastic holster stock is attached, a connection is made with the trigger complex to bring the refinement into play.". .

"*Very* interesting," Dean murmured, moving up to the cabinet and reaching out a hand. "*Vous me permettez, Monsieur Claes?*"

"Of course, of course." The Belgian waved his hand. "Help yourself."

Dean removed one of the machine pistols and hefted it from hand to hand. "Nice balance," he said. "You have a range in back?"

"Naturally."

"Then subject to our being allowed to try them, I should like to buy half a dozen of these guns."

"*Hélas*," said Monsieur Claes, "the design is still being evaluated by the NATO military commands, and until they have decided whether or not to place orders for the general issue of these weapons, very few have come onto the market. The four you see there are all I have."

"Okay, so I'll take the four," Dean said, "if they prove satisfactory." He turned to Wassermann. "Abe, you're the marksman; is there anything you see here in the precision line that might suit your talents?"

"Oh, sure," Wassermann replied. "There's a .458 double-barrel competition rifle with a Winchester lever action. Made by Abbiatico Salvinelli in Italy. You would need no more than half the reserves in Fort Knox to buy it. I should be so lucky even to handle such a gun."

"You can have it," Dean said. "Uncle Sam's paying the bill."

Both Jammot and Claes looked puzzled, but Dean made no attempt to explain the remark. The weapons all proved satisfactory. Together with two loaded magazines for each of the machine pistols, a full cartridge belt for Wassermann, half a dozen concussion grenades, and a fuse pistol that Novotny required for his explosive charges, they were transferred to the Range Rover. Dean had chosen for himself simply a Beretta Modello 92, since any fighting he did was likely to be within the castle. This twenty-two-ounce blowback automatic, with its fifteen-shot magazine and double-action lockwork, was fast becoming his favorite personal weapon. A length of no more than six inches and the fact that it fired the same 9mm Parabellum rounds as the VP-70 machine pistols made it doubly suitable for the present mission.

Once the formalities had been settled—Jammot paid the bill and undertook to supply the necessary permits, for which he would add a fifteen percent service charge when Dean settled up later—they piled into the Range Rover and took the road once more.

They took the E9 turnpike south to Bastogne, and then the Belgian Highway 15 to Martelange, on the Luxembourg border. Here, near a waterside campsite and canoeing stage—but not so near that they would attract the attention of the owners—they unloaded and launched the dinghy. Schneider, the professional helmsman, and Novotny, as explosives expert, stowed the weaponry and allowed the rubber craft to drift slowly downstream. As soon as it was dark, they would start the electric motor and head for the Grand Duchy.

Dean about-faced the Range Rover. With Wassermann, Daler, and Sean Hammer, he took the first turnoff east of the highway and drove through the twisting, hilly woods of the Ardennes along the network of minor roads that led eventually to Route 34, the customs post, and the town of

Wiltz. Behind them, the sun had already sunk below the trees, and a cool breeze blowing in the open windows brought them the piny scent distilled from the forest during the heat of the day. "Whicker settin' for an ambush, this'd be!" Hammer observed, staring at the darkening corridors between the massed trunks.

"That's what the Germans thought in World War II!" Dean said.

Twelve miles to the south, Novotny and Schneider pulled the dinghy in to the riverbank beneath the overhanging branches of a willow. The road was on the far side of the stream, half-hidden by a line of alders: with luck, nobody passing would notice them there, half-concealed in the thickening dusk. "You have cased this castle, man?" Schneider murmured. "Walking all around the place this morning, isn't it?"

"Sure." Novotny nodded. "Not much to see. Too many fuckin' trees. But I didn't see no sign of life anyplace. I mean, like I was there, one viewpoint an' another, long enough to tell there ain't no goddamn patrols or anything like that. I'd of figured the shithouse for abandoned if it wasn't for them aerials." He spit into the river. "Grindeldange! Hell of a name for a castle! Sounds like one of those war books on Germany where the writer fucks up on all the names, gets 'em wrong the way the French always get English names wrong." Novotny laughed. "You know: Dorothy Pronk, Lord Multiple, Elmer Middle, that kind of crap."

"The name she is okay," Schneider said in his solemn way. "*Ange* is a Luxembourgeois suffix, like *-burg* in America, or *-ton* in Britain or *-ville* in French. It probably *means* 'town' or something. And there is not just Grindeldange and Martelange, where we embark. There is Useldange, Erfeldange, Harlange, Birtrange, Dudelange; Wormelange on the Moselle, Frisange in the southeast; Wolferdange, Hesperange—"

"All right, all right! You sold me the fuckin' policy!" Novotny protested. "Jesus!"

"The final vowel is pronounced." Schneider grinned. "You say the end like '*anger*.' Anger as in 'sore,' or 'mad as hell.' You know?"

"You go fuck yourself," Novotny said genially.

A little later, Schneider started the electric motor and steered the dinghy out into midstream. The reach was around two hundred yards long, screened at the far end by trees. After that, the river curved north and east, forming the frontier with Belgium for three miles before it flowed into the Grand Duchy.

By 2100 hours Daler had taken over the wheel of the Range Rover, burdened now with the fiberglass outboard they had rented from the boating marina near Wiltz; Dean had hired a cab from the town center and been driven out past the brewery to the private airfield, where he was waiting for the helicopter ordered by Mackenzie from the U.S. base near Saarbrücken; Schneider and Novotny, navigating slowly and carefully in the dark, had brought the rubber dinghy to the confluence of the Sûre and the tributary that ran through the Grindeldange estate. Here they waited for the outboard that would be coming from Esch to collect weapons for Hammer, Wassermann, and Daler.

At Esch-sur-Sûre, the nocturnal sport of fishing for eels was still something of a novelty, but it was not so unusual that three men unloading an outboard dinghy from the roof of a Range Rover would stimulate a flood of telephone calls to the police and the local newspaper. Wassermann and Daler lit the stern lantern that was perched above the motor and chugged upriver, leaving Sean Hammer—who was wearing a peaked chauffeur's cap for the occasion—to guard the vehicle. In the airfield clubhouse at Wiltz, Dean received a phone call from Mackenzie, now back at the Ankara embassy. Mazzari was improving, he was told; he would be allowed to leave the hospital within the week. Everything else had been arranged according to Dean's plan.

"There's one thing," Dean said dubiously. "The . . . contingency plan. I'll mention no names, but the person concerned is still leaving Paris on the seventeenth. Your contact, the man I met in Istanbul, as far as I know is in Paris too, studying in three dimensions what he and I worked out just on a plan, a map. I have to get in touch with him tomorrow with further instructions. What do I say?"

"Tell him to keep going," Mackenzie said. "Proceed exactly as if the plan had to be carried through. It may have to be at that. It could be that you've located the place where the wife and child are held. I've every confidence, in that case, that you'll get them out and neutralize Healey. But that plan's not going to be called off until there's not a single damned . . . interloper . . . left, and the site is back in our hands. Is that clear?"

"Yes, sir," Dean said. "I'll tell him to carry on."

He was of course unaware that the CIA sleeper, having called for the daily red- or green-light instruction shortly before, had been given precisely the same orders.

At 2205, ten minutes later than planned, the boats rendezvoused. Daler took charge of the two machine pistols, the extra magazines, the grenades, and a coil of rope; Wassermann sat in the stern, the cartridge belt slung, one hand on the tiller, the other supporting his beautiful rifle. As they wheeled around and headed back toward Esch, Schneider turned the rubber dinghy into the tributary that passed the castle.

They had gone less than a hundred yards when he uttered a sharp *Tut!* of displeasure. "What's with you?" Novotny asked. "Them guys forget something, leave something behind?"

"No," said the German. "It is me. The towns. I forget Rodange, Schifflange, and Rumelange!"

The attack developed with textbook precision—which, considering that the planning had been purely verbal and based on incomplete knowledge of the defenses, was a testament to Dean's qualities as an improviser and tactician.

At 2300 hours, a single-engine Beechcraft airplane flew low over the castle, circled the civil field at Wiltz, and landed there. At 2312, a twin-jet executive Cessna took off and headed south, still climbing half a mile east of Grindeldange. Neither of these ships had anything to do with the assault: they had been organized by Mackenzie to accustom the defenders to the idea that there was a certain amount of activity, involving different types of aircraft, in the sky that night. Dean's Cobra helicopter would therefore—the reasoning ran—excite no special interest when it was heard in the airspace above the estate.

To avoid relying too much on this stratagem, the combat leader planned to climb to the bottom of a thirty-foot rope ladder hanging below the belly of the chopper sometime before they passed over the perimeter. A portion of the château roof had fallen in, leaving only a rafter skeleton over part of the building's east wing, and Dean hoped to be able to step off the ladder here, leaving the helicopter only a few seconds in which to hover before it flew away south and out of earshot.

The green Very light that was to signal the attack would be fired before the ship was over the estate, in the hope that the MAO kidnappers would then in any case be otherwise occupied when they heard the clatter of the Cobra's rotors.

Dean was gambling everything on his hunch that this *was* the terrorists' hideout; the way he saw it, there was no possible alternative. The thought that he might conceivably be mistaken never entered his mind. (Even if he was, he had assured an anxious Hammer when they met at the Brussels airport, the worst that could happen would be that they wasted time and ammunition on a deserted stronghold; the best, that puzzled caretakers inquired why the hell military maneuvers were being carried out on private property. In any case, they would know the moment the first shot was fired: if it was answered, Dean was right; if it wasn't, and querulous voices demanded what the hell was going on, he was wrong. In which case they would simply have that much less time to solve the problem of the Ark. "Bejasus, Marc," Hammer had said feelingly, "a person would give half his life's bloody span to be blessed with the fuckin' confidence you have, an' all!" And, "Sean," Dean had replied, "that's what I'm being paid for, isn't it?")

The moon, not yet full, was rising late, but there was a milky brilliance diffused already over the quilt of woods that covered the high ground undulating between Wiltz and Esch-sur-Sûre. Waiting by the hatch, Dean saw the silvered curve of river cradling the town beyond the tunnel that led the road beneath the cliff on which the silhouetted ruins of the fortress still stood. Farther south, the four squat towers of Grindeldange, with their pyramid spires, rose above the dark trees. Dean signaled the pilot that he was going down.

Clinging to the foot of the ladder, he tugged at the cord that was acting as his communication with the cabin. Two tugs. Please fire, Very light.

The star shell shot away from the helicopter, trailing a wake of green fire. It burst—as intended—over a village a mile and a half to the east of the estate, its livid radiance illuminating the tents and cages and kiosks of a traveling circus that was performing a one-night stand in the central

**163**

square. Dean had no intention of using the green light as a guide; he was having it fired purely as a signal to his men on the ground. By positioning it over the village rather than the château, he hoped that the terrorists would take it for part of the festivities. As the dazzling flare sank slowly from the sky, he lowered himself like a performer from that fair, until he was dangling, trapeze-fashion, from the lowest rung of the ladder at the full stretch of his arms.

He reached once more for the cord. Three tugs. I am ready to be flown in. The pitch of the rotors altered, the whine of the turbojet deepened. The somber outline of Grindeldange spiraled slowly up toward the chopper.

Where the chain fence was broken by the stream, Novotny scrambled up the muddy bank from the dinghy carrying his fuse gun. Twenty yards away, a small charge of plastic was laid at the foot of the wire. Some way beyond that, the Range Rover was parked in a forest ride. Once the fence was blown, Hammer, Wassermann, and Daler would have only a short stretch of undergrowth to break through before they were inside the grounds. Straining his eyes in the dim light, Novotny sighted the gun.

The pistol—it was not really a weapon—had a wooden butt that was curved almost into a semicircle, and a stubby 3½-inch barrel. It fired special .38-caliber blanks that were designed to ignite a black-powder fuse. An instant after the trigger was pressed, there was a streak of flame and a vivid orange flash by the chain fence. The crack of the pistol was drowned by the thumping roar of the charge exploding.

Schneider was holding the dinghy against the bank with the motor in neutral. As Novotny leaped aboard, he slammed it into gear and the craft surged toward the castle, which was around a bend in the stream. The stuttering whine of Dean's helicopter, audible now for several minutes, was growing louder. But as the gaunt outline of Grindeldange's turrets emerged against the green glow to the east, it was eclipsed by a burst of automatic fire among the trees—short, sharp volleys, only a few shots at a time, that signified Hammer and his men were through the blown fence and approaching the castle. There were angry shouts from the far side of the wood, and then a rattle of answering shots, longer bursts from heavier guns—Stechkin pistols and perhaps a Kalashnikov, Novotny thought.

Dean heard them from above and heaved a sigh of relief. He could see the muzzle flashes, pinpoints of light stabbing the gloom below. At his side, no more than three or four yards away, bare rafters printed the shape of the roof against the fading glare of the Very light. The chopper pilot was hovering skillfully just above the ruined spire. Dean waited for the ladder to drift nearer, stretched out with a foot, touched wood, lost it, touched again more firmly—and then, as he was able to transfer his weight, tugged the cord for the last time: two tugs—pause—two more. I am stepping off. *Ciao!*

He let go the last rung on the ladder . . . and then lost his balance as the rotted wood frame of the roof snapped under his weight. He plunged through in a shower of slate fragments, pulverized mortar, and splintered laths. It was a fifteen-foot drop to the floor of the attic below, but Dean had enough experience in parachute jumping to hunch up, protect his face, and roll over as he hit the ancient boards.

The noise of his fall seemed to him as loud as a bomb burst, but there was no pause in the cannonade below. He heard the diminishing flutter of the Cobra fade toward the south, a sudden final crash as a fragment of slate detached itself from the gap in the roof to shatter by his feet, and then just the stealthy trickle of plaster falling.

Half-choked by the dust, he stumbled toward an open door. The thin beam of the pencil flashlight that he still carried revealed a stairway twisting down to a broad corridor running the whole length of the wing below. Treading carefully, he crept toward it.

The corridor—it was more of a gallery really—was empty. Shafts of moonlight slanting through grimed Gothic windows illuminated darker patches on the peeling walls where paintings had once hung. Dust rose to hang in the beams of light as Dean hurried to the far end of the passageway. So far as the investigators could tell, this whole wing was deserted, but plans lodged in the local townhall archives showed that there was a connection between the corridor and a central gallery that ran around three sides of an entrance hall in the central block of the castle. And it was off this hallway that the few inhabitable rooms were thought to remain.

Dean turned the corner. Here the moonlight filtered down through the architectural feature known as a lantern—in this case a low octagonal structure with a domed top and each of the eight sides paned in colored glass. From the center of the dome, long chains supported an iron hoop ten feet in diameter, from which hung the remnants of a huge crystal chandelier.

Three floors below, the hallway too was octagonal, an immense lobby floored with checkerboard squares of black and white marble. Six of the walls were pierced by pointed-arch doorcases, the remaining two being built out at second-floor level to form a porch framing massive oak entrance doors. The gallery on which Dean found himself, like its twins beneath, ran around six out of the eight walls (rather than three out of four, as noted at the town hall).

It was an eerie sight, looking down into that vast space, half-lit by multicolored reflections percolating through the lantern, the shadows beneath the lowest gallery hiding antlered deer and boars' heads and other trophies fixed to the walls. It could have been, Dean thought, the set for a Gothic movie romance . . . if it wasn't for the shooting outside, and occasionally an angry shout in Arabic. At least, he reflected, he hadn't come to the wrong place!

Hammer and his two companions had no idea how many kidnappers they were fighting. There had been at least six involved in the actual snatch, not counting Hamid. Of these, only two—the men who had abandoned the panel truck in Germany—were known to have left the country. Others might have come in to replace them or swell the numbers of those left. There were half a dozen more, plus a helicopter load of reinforcements, believed to be at the Ararat site—so the MAO clearly had plenty of soldiers available. Dean had been of the opinion that they would use as few as possible at Grindeldange, especially as the place seemed to have been chosen for its isolation: the more strangers there were around, the more they were likely to be noticed. "Four to six," he had told Hammer. "I wouldn't expect to find more. Apparently the couple on the gate aren't allowed to go up to the house; they've been told there are one or two high-powered executives, from foreign branches of Lorraine Holdings taking a rest—camping out, as they put it—who must not on any account be disturbed."

"What about the wimmin, but?" Hammer had asked. "The bloody hostages, man?"

"We have to be brutal here," Dean said soberly. "In a

**166**

regular hostage situation, the rescuers' most vital consideration is to save the victims' lives. We don't have that priority."

"What the hell do you mean, Marc? You're not sayin'—?"

"I'm saying that we can attack without any fear of reprisals against Mrs. Healey or her daughter. They *have* to keep them alive, or the guys on the site don't have a lever on Healey anymore. Dammit, we're going to *pretend* they're dead when we've zapped the people holding them. It'd be to *our* advantage if they were killed, and they know it!"

"Good grief! You're not after tellin' me that—?"

Dean laughed. "I'm telling you that you can attack the way you would if the hostages weren't there, that's all."

"But they *are* there. If they should get caught in the crossfire . . . ?"

"That's where we have to be brutal," Dean said.

By the time Hammer, Daler, and Wassermann, moving from tree trunk to tree trunk, and then from bush to bush, had reached the edge of the gravel sweep in front of the château, the Irishman had begun to think his leader was right about the number of defenders involved. A lot of shots were being fired at them, from various different places—and, by the sound of it, from several kinds of weapons—but the frequency of the volleys, and the absence of any concerted counterattack, led him to think that he was faced with a few men moving rapidly from one gun to another in order to give a false impression of strength, rather than a lot of men each with a single gun.

Most of the firing came from three windows on the west side of the entrance, two on the ground floor and one above. The windows were glassless but heavily shuttered. The most dangerous defender, however, was a sniper, using a single-shot rifle, who was ensconced behind an ornamental balustrade above the porch: heavy-caliber slugs from his weapon—an AKM, Hammer thought—came uncomfortably close each time the attackers moved. Daler's face was stung by chips of stone when a slug plowed into the gravel driveway only an inch from his head when he flung himself down at the outer edge of the wood.

"You think maybe we should separate and make a rush

for the doors, cock?" he whispered. "Once we're under that portico . . . and if we zigzagged, in this light . . ."

"Later," Hammer answered. "We're to wait on the Colonel's grenade, remember? An' we'd be the better of it if Abe could down thon bugger with the Kalashnikov first!" Wassermann had been posted behind a bay tree on the far side of the open space. There was a Trilux infrared night sight on his competition rifle, and Hammer had ordered him to do nothing, to make no move, until a shift in the moon or an incautious maneuver by the man behind the balustrade provided him with the opportunity for the single decisive shot that was all he needed.

Inside the castle, Dean had come to the same conclusion about the number of defenders: he could hear three—maybe four?—male voices speaking in Arabic or heavily accented French, one man who clearly was French, and an angry Frenchwoman. They were calling to each other from different rooms, and the Frenchman, who seemed to be the leader, was shouting from different levels too (presumably there was another staircase in the far wing). Once the combat leader thought he heard a muffled cry, but it was not repeated.

He was wondering whether he should move around the gallery and try to find a way through to the second stairway, when one of the doors to the octagonal hall was flung open and the Frenchman cried: "*Ça n'va pas. Faut qu'on file. Hassan—va sortir la bagnole, vite!* It's no good. We have to split. Go fetch the heap, but fast!"

Light streamed across the checkerboard floor as another door opened. "*Marcel! Attend! Qu'on se planque derrière les garces, hein?*" the woman called. "Wait! Let's use these bitches as a shield, eh?"

"*D'accord. Alicia: tu les décarres de la piaule,*" the man replied. "Bring them out of the room."

Dean tensed. Already he could hear footsteps running toward the back of the building. He knew the Range Rover would be some way off in the woods; if the kidnappers once got into the Mercedes camper with their victims, the whole operation could turn sour on him. He knew also that Novotny and Schneider should by now have hidden their rubber dinghy beneath the bridge that crossed the stream and concealed themselves in the stable to foil just such an attempt. But dare he rely on it? And would it work anyway if the Healeys were marched out first at gunpoint?

Long shadows appeared in the fan of light spreading out from the open door. A young woman who looked in her late twenties strode into the hallway. She was wearing tight jeans and a sweater. Her hair was untidy, there was too much makeup on her face, and she carried an Uzi submachine gun. In front of her, she pushed a freckled woman of about thirty-five and a teenage girl. They were gagged with strips of plaster. Their wrists were bound and their arms roped together behind their backs. The woman's dress had been ripped open to the waist and the straps of her brassiere cut.

Dean hesitated. If the kidnappers managed to smuggle them out to that camper . . .

It was up to him to stop them. But how? He had the Beretta, but the man Marcel was somewhere beneath the galleries. He would undoubtedly be carrying a gun, and he was out of sight. There could be other members of the band within a few yards.

Dean bit his lip. The girl was pushing the captives toward a door opposite the entrance. It was now or never. The great iron hoop of the chandelier was suspended level with the handrail of the gallery; it was hanging only a few feet away. He climbed silently onto the rail, launched himself forward, and grabbed the curved iron with his outstretched hands as he fell.

For an instant he swung there. Then the remaining lozenges of crystal shivered and tinkled as the hoop swayed under the impetus of his dive. Several pieces fell to the floor below and splintered on the marble.

"*Merdel Qu'est qu'y-a . . . ?*" A man with a heavy black mustache ran out from beneath the gallery. There was a Stechkin automatic in his hand. Another man ran in through the open door. He too was armed. The girl backed off, raising the muzzle of the Uzi toward the captives.

The two men lifted their guns to aim at Dean. There was no time for the perilous surprise drop that he had planned: he would be a dead man before he hit the floor. The Douglas Fairbanks routine would have to wait for another time. He did the only thing he could.

Letting go of the hoop with one hand, he whipped out is concussion grenade, thumbed the switch, and dropped the device in a single swift movement.

Novotny heard the loud, flat thud of the detonation from his position on the riverbank. For the second time, he fired his fuse pistol. The orange flash as the charge under the bridge exploded was much brighter than the momentary glare that had outlined the windows of the château against the night. The *plastique* made a lot more noise too. Startled up from his knees by the first explosion, the sharpshooter above the porch rose half-upright as the second cracked out. It was the chance Wassermann had been waiting for.

His eye was already close to the rubber lens shield of the Trilux sight; the balustrade was clear in the illumination from the red triphium light source; the suspended vertical aiming point hung just above the stone coping; Wassermann had already taken up first pressure. The instant his target lurched into view, he squeezed.

The two barrels spat fire almost as one. The sniper's rifle hit the gravel before the echoes of the double report were muffled among the trees. It seemed a long time before the man's body toppled over the parapet, performed a slow cartwheel, and crashed to the driveway.

Hammer was already on his feet running for the steps and the entrance doors. Daler fired short bursts from his VP-70 to cover him. Wassermann remained on guard, reloading and keeping his eyes fixed on the facade until they were both beneath the porch. The Very light had long since faded and died, but the moon was bright enough to catch the swing of a shutter, the gleam of a metal barrel.

In back, Novotny and Schneider, half-concealed in the open doorway to the stable, stood one on either side of the trailer. The wooden bridge had collapsed into the stream, ruptured in the center. It was quite possible for an agile man to scramble across among the shattered spars, but there was no longer any question of driving the big Mercedes around to the front of the house: it would have to be steered around a grassy track to the estate's rear entrance, along the highway, and then in again by the gatehouse—a detour of at least a mile and a half. Two men ran out of the château and stood staring in consternation at the ruin of the bridge. Schneider pressed the trigger of his machine pistol.

The three-shot burst went wide. Before he could fire again, the two kidnappers themselves loosed off half a magazine each from their Uzi SMG's, spraying the slugs left and right across the stable opening. Bullets thwacked into the rear of the camper and splintered the wooden doors. Schneider was hurled backward into the darkness. His gun clattered to the brick floor. He lay against an empty oil drum, cursing and clutching at his left shoulder.

But Novotny had in the meantime used the burst-fire facility of his weapon to good effect. Aiming for the muzzle flash rather than the indistinct moonlit figure of the man behind it, he pressed the trigger four times in quick succession while the kidnappers were still shooting. One of the men fell to his knees, pitched forward over the bank of the stream, and slid down to lie with his face beneath the water. The other spun around, dropped his gun, and subsided slowly onto the steps by the open door. After a moment, he leaned sideways, sprawled on the ground, and lay still.

There was a sudden silence. Very faintly, Novotny could hear music from the village fair. There was no more movement inside the château.

Then a shout and a burst of fire from the far side of the building. Hammer, shooting out the door lock, had stormed into the front entrance, followed by Daler and Wassermann.

But there was nobody left for them to fight.

Margery and Carole Healey lay unconscious in the octagonal hallway, together with the two men and the girl who had been their original jailers. Of the four terrorists sent some days before to support them, Wassermann had accounted for one, Novotny for two more, and the last lay groaning in a second-floor room, nursing a shattered wrist.

Marc Dean, himself knocked out by the concussion grenade he had exploded, was stretched out among droplets of crystal, his crumpled form showered by hundreds of points of colored light reflected from the lantern above.

"Roll up, roll up!" Hammer said. "Welcome to the bloody fair!"

Under his supervision, Healey's wife and daughter were carried into one of the few furnished rooms in the castle. Among moth-eaten Louis Quinze armchairs and tables from which the polish had long since worn away, there were mattresses, and packing cases, and cartons of tinned food and Coca-Cola and instant coffee. Beyond it, a huge stone-flagged kitchen and scullery were choked with opened cans and dirty dishes. At one side of these offices, a small pantry housed a wooden table with sweat-stained straps at each corner, a truck magneto with a crank handle and two cables ending in bulldog clips, and a sophisticated transmitter-receiver in a large open case, with wires that clearly connected with the aerials on the roof. An open tape recorder stood on a chair nearby.

Margery Healey's body showed traces of electrical and cigarette burns on the nipples. The inner labia were lacerated where the clips had bitten into the flesh. The child's body was simply bruised.

Schneider's wound was a clean one: the bullet had passed through the hollow of the shoulder without touching bone or damaging the muscles. The kidnapper with the shattered wrist and the man by the steps in back of the château would survive. "Fetch them out the back with the two wimmin, you," Hammer instructed Novotny. "Take yon bloody camper and whistle out the back way. Daler can go with you. All of them need hospitalizing right away."

"That's all very well, cock," Daler said, "but which hospital?"

"Don't be an eejit all your life," Hammer snapped. "You go to the airfield at Wiltz, for God's sake! Himself already organized a plane to take us all away, sure. They'll be cared for someplace safe."

"Yeah," Wassermann said, "a guy he should be excused he was wondering how the hell we explain this to the Luxembourg law."

"They may not even connect it with the snatch," Hammer said. "It was never a big story: Healey wasn't important enough. But the press run a piece every few days, asking why the hell no bloody ransom demand has been made. Let them go on asking. The old couple on the gates have been squared already: they saw nothing and heard nothing. But the shooting will have been heard someplace. The pollis won't be too long coming. They will find two stiffs and an empty bloody castle. Some kind of gang war, maybe. Missis Healey and the kid will reappear quietly stateside sometime in the future. It was all a big mistake. This guy Mackenzie will fix it. Don't ask me how!"

Dean recovered consciousness before the others. He had still been in midair when the grenade exploded. But although he had missed the full force of the concussion, he had been out when he hit the floor, and Hammer feared that his left ankle was broken: the swelling was already extensive.

"We'll attend to it later," Dean told Hammer. "Right now, it's back to the Range Rover and get the hell out. We have to make that plane before the whole damned duchy is crawling with cops."

The three stunned kidnappers were handcuffed and bundled into the back of the Range Rover. Dean, unable even to hobble, was given a chair lift by Hammer and Wassermann. They left the château with the doors open and lights burning. Two dead men, a rubber dinghy crushed beneath the ruins of a blasted bridge, bullet holes everywhere, and a gap blown in the perimeter fence—let the locals work it out for themselves!

As Hammer piloted the big utility along the grassy forest ride, heading for a dirt road that would take them nearer to Wiltz, the seesaw wail of sirens was already audible over the tops of the trees.

"All we need now," Dean said as they swung onto a highway and saw the lights of the airfield on a plateau beyond the next valley, "is a surefire way of making these sons of bitches say the right thing on the radio to their buddies on the site."

# IV

It is of little importance what we hate, so long as we hate something.

—Samuel Butler, *Notebooks*

Hate is no more than a defeat of the imagination.

—Graham Greene, *The Power and the Glory*

# 15

# Ark in Orbit?

Day Thirteen. And a surefire way to make the prisoners say the right thing to Furneux and the others on the site was hard to find.

Computer analysis of all radio traffic to and from NATO countries over the past thirty-six hours—which involved only frequency, direction, and duration of messages, not their content or decoding—tended to show that two-way transmissions beamed from the Wiltz area toward Turkey had ceased soon after the discovery of Tom Argyle's body. And that since then all messages—transmitted roughly every eight hours—had originated from the Luxembourg end. It looked, then, as if no call-up could be expected from Ararat: it was up to Dean to persuade Alicia, Marcel, or Hassan to make the contact. Don't call us, Dean thought wryly; we'll call you.

Analysis just of the transmissions arriving one way in Turkey showed also a fairly regular pattern of broadcasts emanating from the Paris area. But there were so many radio hams and CB transmissions operating from the French capital that this was of little use.

"We've *got* to make one of them contact Furneux," Dean said fiercely. "And after that we have to get across the idea that the wife and kid were accidentally killed in the attack. Healey's got to believe that. Otherwise those crazy bastards will fire that missile."

"Unless, of course, we knock off Mubarak," Daler said.

"Even if we get them to call," Hammer objected; "even if we did get across the idea that the both of them was deaded—how the hell do we make sure your man hears us? How do we know Healey will even be in the same bloody room? I mean, if he ain't, they're not goin' to tell him, are they?"

"We'll worry about that when we get through," Dean said. They were in a CIA safe house near Paris. The combat leader's ankle was indeed broken: his left leg was encased in plaster from the toes to the middle of the calf. Schneider was being cared for in Paris; the wounded terrorists were under twenty-four-hour guard in a U.S. military hospital; Alicia, Marcel, and Hassan were locked up in separate lightless, soundproof cells in the basement of the safe house. "In any case," Dean added, "we can be pretty sure that Healey *will* hear whatever is said. There are several different rooms on separate levels in a silo, but there's only one control room—and you can see from the plans of the Ararat-style silo that the radio installation, as well as the hot-line phone, is in that room. Those guys aren't going to have shifted all that, just so Healey can't eavesdrop on their talks. My guess is that the poor bastard will have been kept in there, where he can be of most use to them, the whole damned time."

"Okay," Hammer said. "So we go on with the persuasion."

It wasn't a job bringing immediate results. The afternoon was already far advanced. The prisoners, separately and together, had been brought up from the cells, threatened, coaxed, promised immunity from prosecution . . . all to no avail. None of them would even reply to questions, let alone discuss radio messages.

Reluctantly, to lend credence to their ploy—and in case the radio transmissions from Paris *were* connected with the conspiracy—Dean had allowed Mackenzie to release a story to the press, to the effect that the raid on Grindeldange had in fact been in connection with the kidnapped women . . . and that both Margery and Carole Healey had been killed during an exchange of shots. Since neither Belgian, nor French, nor local police knew anything of the affair, the newspapers made much of the mystery, the Parisian dailies of July 16 devoting a great deal of space to theories attempting to explain what could have happened, who could have been involved. The most popular solution was that a second gang had tried unsuccessfully to wrest the hostages from the original kidnappers. But as no ransom demand had been made public, and nobody knew why such an insignificant family should have been martyred in the first place, the enigma of the abduction was made more obscure rather than clarified.

The MAO ultimatum had threatened that the missile would be fired if there was the slightest press leak. Dean hoped fervently that, as there was no connection in the stories with Turkey, this would not count as a leak in the sense they intended. The risk was in any case partly balanced by the fact that any radio contact in Paris would certainly pick up the story and relay the news to the silo.

But he couldn't be sure that this would happen; there would be no way of knowing whether Healey knew. And the contingency plan to assassinate the Egyptian President —they dare not call it off until they knew for sure that any danger of the Ark being launched was over.

The papers, with headlines prominently displayed, had been left lying around in the room Dean used for questioning the prisoners when the Palestinian, Hassan, was brought up for the fourth or fifth time. "We know about Furneux," Dean told him. "Argyle's dead, so Furneux himself must know we're onto Hamid. He'll know we have you, simply because you haven't called him. Healey won't play ball anymore, because you've no hold over him now. Why not make it easier on yourself? Talk to Furneux."

"Who's Furneux?"

"Don't give me that!" Dean shouted. "We *took* you there, where the kidnapped women were killed, for Chrissake!"

"Which women?"

"They'll know at the silo that we raided the castle—and that they've lost out now the hostages are dead. Let's get it over with, huh?"

"I don't know anything about any castle. What silo?"

"You'll be gettin' nothin' outta him, faith," Sean Hammer said when Daler and Wassermann had taken the Palestinian back to his cell. "He's KGB-trained, or I'll eat me bloody hat. They never break."

Dean's strength lay in the fact that none of the captives knew for sure that Margery and Carole were *not* dead. All three of them had been knocked out by the grenade; for all they knew, the woman and her daughter had been caught in the crossfire when the absent members of the kidnap commando were killed or wounded. The point clearly was of no importance to the girl, Alicia. There were no ID papers on her; she refused to give any other name; she refused to say anything or do anything (even from the cell to the room where Dean was sitting with his injured leg resting on a stool, she had to be carried by Daler and Wassermann between them); and such replies as she made to their questions became after a time invested with a certain monotony.

"You're the little slut who allowed that child to watch her mother tortured; you're the bitch who helped burn an innocent woman with electrical current," Dean said tightly.

"No fuckpig of a mother means more than any other cunt," Alicia said.

"You're not the only ones to have a truck magneto handy," Hammer said. "Wire comes easy and we got clips, we got time."

"Piss off."

"It's easier and quicker from the electric current in the house," Daler said. "We got 220 volts alternating here. Let me strip the little sow and have a go, eh?"

"Piss off."

"I know a trick or two with tailor's scissors," Wassermann said. "She ain't interested in motherhood, she won't need the tits anyway."

"Piss off."

"We've nothing to do with the law," Dean said. "Nobody knows you're here. When we've finished with you, the body could be thrown in the Seine and there's not a person in the world would know. Even if we handed you over to the *flics,* you'd get twenty-five years—most likely with no remission. You'd be fifty when they let you out."

Alicia sighed. "You make me tired," she said. "Why don't you piss off?"

Marcel, the man with the heavy mustache, was the most promising material. He was the only one whose fingerprints were on record. Despite the French passport he carried, his name was in fact Marcel Tufik and he was Libyan. He was wanted in several countries for complicity in bank holdups, burglary, and extortion, and there was a suspicion that he had been involved in two lethal outrages in Paris in the summer of 1982, one in the Rue Marbeuf, near the Champs Elysées, where a Lebanese newspaper office had been destroyed by a bomb, the other at a Jewish restaurant in the Rue des Rosiers. Although at first he was no more communicative than the other two, Dean had a hunch that his silence was due more to fear than to conviction or contempt for society and its authorities.

"We have half the software in Europe analyzing anonymous radio transmissions over the past week," Dean told him. "It's only a matter of time before the central computer eliminates the rest and comes up with the frequency you were using. All you have to do then is talk."

"Why the hell should I do that?" the man called Marcel asked.

"To save your life maybe?" Dean suggested.

"What are you talking about? There are no capital crimes logged against me. Anyway, in this country—"

"We're not talking about this country," Dean said softly. "Or even Luxembourg. We're talking nevertheless about a murder rap."

"You can't pin that on me," Marcel blustered. "Those two skirts were okay when your damned grenade knocked me out, and you know it. They must have been KO'ed too. If they were killed, it was afterward. Anyway, there's no death penalty in France—"

"We're not talking about France; we're talking about Greece. Where they have a very good death penalty."

"What do you mean?" For the first time the man looked scared.

"I'm talking about a command-car crew machine-gunned to death in northern Greece a couple of weeks ago. American citizens. The United States government would like an example made of the people responsible. To discourage such outrages in future. The Greek government will be only too happy to oblige. NATO and all that, you know."

"But you can't pin that on me!" Marcel cried again. "I wasn't anywhere near Greece. *Merde!* I was hired just to organize a snatch and watch over the clients afterward. I was never out of Luxembourg."

"There are witnesses who saw you near the scene of the killing in Greece. At the material time. With an SMG."

"But it's not *true!* Jesus! I wasn't even—"

"There are nevertheless witnesses who will swear that it *is* true," Dean said. "Think about it." He turned to Hammer. "Take him away, Sean."

On the way back to the cell, a carefully planned charade was played out. An outburst of shouting from the cellars was followed by a cry of pain from Alicia, and then another from the Palestinian. There was a volley of shots. And then a total silence.

At the point of a gun, Hammer made Marcel wait for ten minutes in a hallway. Through an open window, they could see a courtyard surrounded by a high wall. By tall closed gates, a panel truck waited with its motor running.

"What is this?" Marcel demanded. "What the hell——?"

"Shuddup and keep quiet," Hammer snarled. "Or I'll plug you."

Finally Daler and Wassermann appeared, carrying between them something limp and heavy wrapped in tarpaulin. The bundle was tossed into the back of the truck. Less than a minute later, they reappeared with a second, which was similarly treated. Wassermann opened the gates. Daler climbed into the cab of the truck and drove it through the gates and out of sight.

"What's going on?" Marcel demanded uneasily. "Who——?"

"Shuddup and get goin'," Hammer snapped.

The Libyan was taken back to his cell and locked in . . . but not before he had been allowed to see that the cells previously occupied by Hassan and Alicia were now empty, their doors wide open.

"Okay, it's mental torture, according to the Convention of Human Rights, or whatever they call it," Dean said later. "But you can't treat these bastards according to any damned convention. They don't play by any rules; if you want to best them, you have to throw the rulebook out the window too. There's no other way. You can't reason with or reeducate guys who place no value on human life, who'll kill or maim anyone to make a political point, even if they've no connection whatever with the politics involved. The only thing you can do is beat the shit out of them until they cry quits. And that's what we're going to do here, even if the beating is mental and not physical." Dean paused. "Though I'd be perfectly tuned in to anyone who wanted to make it physical as well," he added.

"You want we should soften him up some?" Wassermann asked.

"I mean like this time for real?" Daler said.

He was referring to the scenario organized for Marcel on his way back to the cell. Alicia and Hassan had in fact been slapped around a little—but only enough to make them cry out (which was entirely justifiable, Hammer had considered, in view of the condition of Healey's wife and child, and the anguish they had suffered). As soon as their voices had been audible, they had quickly and efficiently been chloroformed—the unconscious bodies, once a few volleys of blanks had been fired, being transferred to locked rooms on the attic floor. The bundles with tarp coverings loaded into the truck had been dummies: the vehicle had simply been driven around the corner, and then returned as soon as Marcel was back in his cell.

"I'm thinkin' maybe we should scare the bejasus outta thon bugger," Hammer said. "An' if he happens to fall down once or twice first . . ." He shrugged.

"I don't like the way those dames were treated," Daler said. "Believe me, cock, it would be a pleasure."

"I'm not paying too much attention to what you guys are saying," Dean remarked. "I have other things to think of. I'd like this man Marcel brought to the radio room— say, in about a half-hour, okay?"

The radio room housed one of the most powerful and sophisticated noncommercial transmitters in Europe. Apart from the computer console, a telex machine, and a row of filing cabinets, it now held a scrubbed table fitted with straps at each corner—a replica of the one the mercs had found at Grindeldange. Two electrodes at the end of a long lead that was plugged into a wall socket lay on the table next to a roll of adhesive tape and a pair of surgical scissors.

Marcel was naked when he was brought into the room. There were a large number of reddened marks on the upper part of his torso, some of which were already bruising yellow and brown. His lower lip was split, one of his eyes was blackened, and blood from his nose had dried on his chin and matted the hair on his chest. Hammer, Daler, and Wassermann slammed him face-upward onto the table and fastened his wrists and ankles so that he was effectively spread-eagled by the straps. He shivered slightly as the electrodes were taped in place.

Daler moved to the switch by the wall socket. "Which is stronger," he asked, "a household-cable jolt or the current from a generator when the handle's turned as fast as possible?"

"You'll have to ask your man there," Hammer said. "He'll be in a unique position to know, will he not?"

"This," Wassermann said, "I think I am going to enjoy."

Dean had not turned around. He was sitting, with his injured foot stretched in front of him, watching a printout unrolling across the computer screen. "They have it down to three frequencies," he said. "But there'll be a call sign—won't there, Marcel?"

The terrorist was sweating. His whole body glistened. "Look," he said thickly. "For Chri' sa'e . . ."

Daler's hand moved toward the switch. "The call sign?" he asked. Before Marcel could reply, the phone rang. Dean picked it up.

He listened for a few moments, said, "Yes, he's here," paused again, said, "Very well, sir. Right away," and replaced the receiver on its cradle.

"The Greek embassy," he said. "Sending for him at once."

Daler's hand dropped to his side. "Too bad," he said regretfully. "I was hoping . . ." He shrugged. "Oh, well. Guess the treatment there will be much the same."

The naked man on the table was straining against the straps. His eyes were staring. "You can't!" he croaked.

Wassermann, Daler, and Hammer moved toward the door. "Might as well leave him here," Hammer said. "They can pick him up easier."

"*No!*" Marcel shouted. "You can't let them. *Je n'ai rien à foutre avec ce turbin. Faut pas me faire porter le bada. Merde!* I'd fuck-all to do with that affair. Shit, you can't pin it on me!"

Beyond the shuttered windows, brakes squealed somewhere below. Heavy feet clattered across a sidewalk. A moment later, there was a heavy pounding on the entrance door. "Quick," Daler observed. "Must already have been on the way when the embassy called."

"Aye," Hammer agreed. "They must want this one badly."

"You got to get me out of this!" Marcel yelled desperately. "All right, all right, all right. Get me Furneux. He knows."

Dean still had his back turned. "The frequency and the call sign," he said.

Marcel babbled the necessary information. Hammer and Wassermann left the room and went downstairs. In the distance, voices could be heard. Daler picked up a hand mike and stood by the head of the table while Dean twirled tuning knobs and moved the controls of the directional aerial.

"You got to get me out of this! You got to get me off

the hook!" Marcel said frantically once the connection had been made.

"*What the hell are you talking about? What happened? Why didn't you call us?*" Furneux's rasping voice was immediately recognizable to Dean.

"You know what happened! Sandra reads the papers, doesn't she? She must have told you. You must know that—"

"*Shut your mouth!*" Furneux interrupted.

"You know those two bitches were knocked off; you know they were carried out feetfirst; you must know it wasn't me; it was strictly written out of the scenario. I wasn't even with it when it happened. But that's not all—"

"*Shuddup!*"

"—not they're pinning the Greek bit on me. I won't fall for it: I wasn't even there. You know that. You must tell them." Daler held the microphone near the frenzied man's foam-flecked lips. "I could even plead accessory to the killing of the Healey dames," Marcel shouted, "though I didn't do a thing. But you got to tell—"

"Be quiet!" Furneux roared. "*You stupid, senseless prick: don't you cotton on to anything?*" There was a click and the speakers died, leaving a radio silence humming in the ether.

But the Canadian failed to cut the transmission before Dean and Daler heard a voice—an unmistakably American-accented voice—gasp in the background: "Oh, no! *It can't be true! Oh, Jesus! Oh, God! The murderous, filthy bastards!*"

For the first time since Marcel had been brought into the room, Dean turned around. For the first time in several days, he smiled. "You can tell the CIA boys downstairs that they're off parade now," he said to Daler. "Take this character back upstairs and lock him up with the other two. Mackenzie can decide what to do with them later."

"Right you are, cock," Daler said. He grinned. "You got what you wanted, eh?"

"Oh, I guess so," Dean said. "It's still no more than a hunch based on character reading, but I'd put my shirt on the fact that Mr. Furneux will get no more help from Healey now. The Ark won't be going into orbit just yet!"

On the table, the man called Marcel had started to cry.

# 16

# Race Against Time

"I've been trying to contact you all afternoon," Alexander Mackenzie said crossly. "I don't know what the hell's the matter with radio communications today. Sun spots or something, I guess."

"Yeah," Dean said. "There's been a certain amount of activity here, too: we've been using the embassy channels fit to bust. But nobody's going to light the blue paper now."

"Thank God." Mackenzie's phrase was almost perfunctory. Dean realized at once that he must have known already. Radio contact might be poor, but the monitors wouldn't stop feeding information into the data banks. "You just have time to go on in and retake the site," Mackenzie said, "now we know there's no risk to Tehran."

"Look," Dean said, "Mazzari doesn't come out of the hospital until tomorrow. Schneider's in Paris with a bullet hole in his shoulder. I'm left with Hammer, Daler, Novotny, and Abe Wassermann—and in case you didn't know, I happen to have a broken ankle myself."

"Yes. I'm sorry about that—"

"There's anything up to eighteen men on that site. According to your original satellite information, they have automatic arms, grenades, bazookas, maybe even a mortar or two. Plus the weapons the murdered guards would have been carrying. For all I know, Furneux may have been able to raise Hamid and have reinforcements flown in: after Marcel's giveaway, he must know we'll raid the site."

"Yes, yes, Dean. All that will be taken care of. All we want you to do is *plan* the operation, since you have been there more recently than . . . than any of the few people who know about this. And your colleague Mazarov—"

"Mazzari."

"Yes. Your colleague has actually been inside the perimeter since it was taken over. It's more practical therefore for you to work out the best method—"

"What do I use for men?" Dean interrupted.

"If you'd just listen: a company of paratroopers from the Third Army at Erzincan will be at your disposal as of midnight. They can be flown in by Hercules transports from Elazig, supported by F-4 Phantoms; dropped by helicopter; or, if you prefer a straight ground attack, taken there in M-113 troop carriers with an escort of Leopard tanks."

"Turkish troops?" Dean was astonished. "What about this nobody-must-know-but-the-inner-seven routine? You've always said—"

"That stipulation related to a crisis situation where there was a risk of a nuclear launch," Mackenzie said. "It was predicated on the absolute necessity of keeping the President and the administration in the clear if . . . if the crisis developed. Now that the situation no longer exists, no ultimatum can be enforced, and the problem at Ararat can be presented simply as the theft of American property by a band of extremists. The fact that there is a missile there—and in particular the nature of its warhead—need not enter into it."

"Why not fly in American troops?"

"Too many questions would be asked. Illegal acts committed on the territory of an ally—even if directed against U.S. interests or involving U.S. property—are best dealt with by the forces of that ally. It remains in such a case simply a matter for local commanders. And it gives the ally a sense of importance. They don't feel," Mackenzie said, suddenly dropping his oracular tone, "that we're trying to pull any Big Brother shit."

"At least why not have the operation planned by an American officer?"

"As an American yourself, you already provided the answer: again, too many questions!"

Dean laughed. "Okay, okay. Where do I liaise?"

"An embassy car will call for you in a few minutes. The company commander will be in the military attaché's office. I need hardly say, the ambassador knows nothing of this."

"Hardly. Where are you? I thought you'd be here too."

"In Paris."

"Swell. If I give you the contact, will you call off

Yusuf? Now it's no longer either-or, I'd hate for a mistake to be made."

"Er . . . yes." There was a silence, and then the CIA regional director's voice, slightly tentative in the speaker, as though he had turned momentarily away from the microphone. "We . . . ah . . . we do have a problem there."

"What do you mean?"

"I wished Yusuf on you, to be sure. But there is also . . ." Mackenzie cleared his throat. "The fact is, a second contingency plan exists. Purely as a backup precaution, you understand. We—"

"Are you telling me that there are *two* assassins briefed to knock off Mubarak? In case we hadn't neutralized the missile, I mean? One organized by me . . . and another I didn't know about?"

"Well . . . not to put too fine a point on it . . . yes."

"You double-crossing bastard," Dean said. "I know just what you mean by backup: if we'd been forced to activate that plan, whoever succeeded, whether or not the MAO people reneged on their undertaking to keep quiet, we'd carry the blame, and you'd be in the clear. Oh, well—I guess you can't expect anything else from your kind of setup. Good thing we *didn't* have to activate it, eh?"

"I did say there was a problem," Mackenzie replied.

"Come again?"

"The second operative is a sleeper, a long-time retainer in Paris. He's been calling a number every day to check whether he's to go ahead with his plan or kill it."

"Well, call him off the next time he checks in—the way you'll call off Yusuf."

"That's the problem," Mackenzie said. "Marcel came across too late. The sleeper had already made his final call—twenty-four hours before zero—and he was still getting the green light."

"Shit! Then you'll have to catch him before he leaves home, or intercept him on his way to the airport—unless you know exactly what his movements will be when he gets there."

"You don't understand," Mackenzie said wretchedly. "*We don't know who he is.* He's just a code name and a voice print to us: we have no address for him, the M.O. he was to use was left to him. He has been in place for years, recruited for just such a contingency—but the guy who originally put him on the Agency payroll, the only person to know his real identity, was killed in a car accident last year."

"Oh, Jesus God!" said Dean.

Abdul Arnaghi Hamid was back in his suite at the Hotel Georges V in Paris. His pale, fat, hairless face was creased into folds of anger and discontent. He looked (the masseuse in her white clinic jacket thought) like an ice-cream sculpture that had begun to melt. She dripped more cologne onto the palm of her hand and began to knead the huge belly.

"Ghislaine," the fat man ordered, "bring me the phone."

He punched the button to connect the instrument with an outside line, and dialed a Paris number. "The fools have wrecked everything," he said when the call was answered. "I thought I was dealing with professionals." He listened for a moment, scowling, and then said, "Contact Furneux at once. He is to make every effort to . . . ah . . . to put the Ark into orbit at once. He is not, repeat not, to wait until the original time lapse has expired. He is to use every means within his power to obtain cooperation. . . . *Every* means, including the ultimate one. I do not intend my warnings to be taken lightly. If, however, the launch even then proves impractical or impossible, Furneux is to inform you, and together you and I will put the alternative option into motion ourselves, here in Paris."

He glanced at the red-headed masseuse—she was working alone today—busy with her lotions and vibro equipment on the far side of the room, and then added in a low voice: "The Americans? I have dismissed them from my mind. They can do nothing. The man Dean has succeeded in ruining my original plan . . . but one or the other of the alternatives in my ultimatum will be unleashed tomorrow, come what may."

Hamid hung up and handed the phone back to the girl. "Now we will go into the bathroom, Ghislaine," he said.

The woman who had taken the call in her Montmartre apartment replaced the receiver and climbed to the clandestine transmitter in her attic, as she had done so often during the past two weeks. She had been admiring a pair of emerald earrings in a morocco case when Hamid phoned. After she had transmitted his instructions, she came back down into her living room, closed the case, and put it away with a number of similar jewel boxes in the top drawer of an inlaid seventeenth-century escritoire. She changed into her uniform and left the flat.

Thirty minutes later she was at her desk in the Rue de Rivoli.

Alexander Mackenzie hurried down the steps of the American embassy, turned left outside the tall iron gates, and strode toward the Place de la Concorde, where he hoped to pick up a cab. But it was seven-thirty on a Saturday evening, a wind was blowing, the sky had clouded over, and an unseasonal drizzle gusted across the huge square. Theater-goers, executives working late to avoid rush hour at the stations, and early diners appeared to have commandeered every taxi in the capital. Each rank he went to was empty; at some the taxiphones attached to lamp standards were ringing impatiently, with nobody to answer. Mackenzie hastened along the arcades bordering the Rue de Rivoli in a fury of impatience himself. He had been forced to wait until midafternoon before the embassy switchboard could raise any personnel at his own filing headquarters: early on a Saturday morning (as it was then in Langley, Virginia) is not the best time to obtain coherent or efficient service, even from the most expert of organizations. And when at last he had been able to make them understand what he wanted, all they could come up with was an address and a post-office-box number in the Rue Taitbouf. The agent controlling the CIA sleeper received her instructions at the box number, he was told, but only the agent herself would know how she passed them on. The department responsible for organizing the letters that were sent to the box number was at Langley, but unfortunately the operative dealing with the routine was on vacation.

Mackenzie arrived at the intersection where the Rue de Rohan carried traffic streaming down from the Opéra across the Rue de Rivoli and through the Palais Royal to the riverbank. The cab ranks there and in the Place Colette were deserted. So was the one outside the Comédie Française. Finally he had to return to the Place Vendôme and bribe the doorman of the Ritz to find him a vehicle. Even then the cabbie grumbled. "Rue St. Georges?" he said. "What number?"

"I don't know," Mackenzie confessed. "All I know is, it's an old apartment building, the Residence Carnot."

"That's no good. St. Georges is one way, north to south," the cabbie said. "The wrong way for us. If you don't know the number, I won't know where to turn into it. We'll have to take Lafayette and Notre Dame de Lorette right up to the top, and turn into St. Georges at the far end." He shook his head disapprovingly.

"All right, all right," Mackenzie almost shouted. "Just so we make a start, okay?"

The concierge at the Residence Carnot wasn't able to tell him much. She went to collect the letter every day at the post office (long since closed, of course). Her orders were to go to different places on different days, where she was to open it to see if there was a message. There hardly ever was. But there had been one . . . oh, no more than three or four days ago. "What was the message?" Mackenzie asked.

"Not much," the old woman said. "Something about a fruit, and then some figures. I just telephoned them through."

"Would the fruit have been an apple? . . . Yes, I thought so. The Big Apple. That's New York. And the figures a telephone number."

"I daresay. I just pass them on."

"Do you remember the number?"

"Of course not. My instructions are to tear up the letter and throw it away once I've passed on the message."

"No, no. Not the American number—the number you call here to pass on the message: do you remember that?"

"Well, naturally." The concierge was indignant. "That's what I'm paid for, isn't it?"

But she had no idea what the person taking the calls looked like.

Mackenzie had to return to the embassy and have the first secretary pull strings before he could get authorization for the telephone service to divulge the name and address of the subscriber whose number he had been given. It was the Montmartre number, and the address was in a narrow street behind Sacré Coeur.

By the time Mackenzie had found another cab, and the cabbie had found the street, it was a quarter to ten. The concierge here was most helpful. The tenant of the top-floor apartment worked for an airline (she didn't know

191

which; it wasn't Air France), had called a taxi and left only an hour before the gentleman called, was not expected back until late tomorrow night.

The CIA chief was desperate. One of his own operatives, anonymous and unsuspected, was abroad in the city with uncanceled orders to assassinate the Egyptian President before he boarded the plane for Tel Aviv the following day. There was no way of getting in touch with him, no way of calling him off, no way of finding out how he proposed to carry out his deadly task. Mubarak could of course be warned—had already been warned—that there were *rumors* of an assassination attempt. But because of the source of the danger, it was impossible for the informants to be more precise, and Mubarak had refused to change his plans. All Mackenzie could do was warn embassy security men—numerous in most capital cities ever since the Tehran hostage crisis—to keep an extra-special lookout. And hope that maybe Marc Dean could come up with some last-ditch solution.

Yet had he only known it, the sleeper that it was so vital he contact was within fifty yards of Mackenzie when he was vainly searching for a cab near the Comédie Française earlier in the evening.

# 17

# Jokers Wild

Furneux had been drinking. Away from the disapproving gaze of his Muslim companions, in one of the hermetic fastnesses of the silo, he had been knocking back liquor from one of two flasks that he carried in the pockets of his U.S. colonel's uniform. Now the network of tiny veins on either side of his nose had flushed an angry red.

Enforced idleness, the isolation of the site, the claustrophobic confines of the underground redoubt itself, had all combined at the same time to enervate and exasperate a man accustomed to boast and brag and show off in front of admiring cronies. Like Marc Dean, Furneux was a mercenary; unlike him, he gave no thought whatever to the moral implications of what he was paid to do. The Muslims had their fanatic ideals, crazy though they might be, to sustain them; he had nothing but the thought of the end-money he would be getting once he had done the job and quit this shithole wilderness.

If the fucking job was ever going to get done. He was beginning to have his doubts. He turned to look at the son-of-a-bitch American whose pigheadedness was beginning to be such a pain in the ass. He grinned to himself, pleased with the mixed metaphor.

Healey lay sprawled on the floor, half-stunned, his head and shoulders against the filing cabinets where Furneux's last blow had sent him stumbling. There was a lump on his jaw, and his lower lip was split.

"You're gonna come across with that fucking combination," Furneux shouted, "and explain about them keys, and wise me up on the technics, boy. Or else."

Numbly, Healey shook his head.

"Just because someone fucked up and croaked your brat and her ma, that don't mean we ain't still got the means to make you talk," the Canadian yelled. "You think you can hold out just because you're marked up some and you ain't said nothin'? Brother, that ain't even a beginning! You saw what happened to that soldier kid? We can keep you alive a lot longer than that, believe me. Uncomfortably."

"It's no use," Healey was mumbling through thick lips. Margery and Carole murdered; his whole world shattered—and the senseless destruction, the nightmare into which he was plunged, apparently the fault of those he trusted, those upon whose help and final rescue he had relied. Nothing made sense anymore. "No use," he repeated. "You can't do anything. I've nothing to lose now."

"You got your balls to lose. Or maybe one eye, spread out over your cheek. Or your guts, with an electrode rammed up your asshole. It burns away quick, inside, with 240 volts." Furneux was losing his temper.

Matsuzaki, the Japanese terrorist, was sitting on the edge of a steel desk on the far side of the underground room. It was obvious to him that the increasing violence of Furneux's threats was only pushing Healey deeper into his apathy. "You don't need anything electrical or mechanical," he said, flexing his spatulate fingers. "There are points on the body where quite a small pressure suffices. Let me have him for half an hour, Furneux."

"Maybe later. First, the little bastard is goin' to agree at least to talk, okay?" A vein in Furneux's temple was throbbing angrily. He didn't like being thwarted. He took a Browning automatic from the waistband of his pants and pointed it at Healey's chest. "A slug in the belly or through one of the lungs," he rasped. "Just to show you I ain't kiddin'. Unless you get up and start to talk. Now."

Behind the ache splitting his head, through the darkness that threatened to engulf him, Healey saw suddenly the freckles in the hollow of his wife's shoulder, felt the soft warmth of his daughter's arms around his neck, her cheek against his own. Grief overwhelmed him. He was drowning in a sea of desolation and despair. Before he went under, he raised his head and spat out the words at his tormentor.

"Piss off!"

Furneux's lips tightened. He pressed the trigger.

In Paris, the sleeper hired a cab at the Gare de Lyon. It was late at night; the last suburban trains were all in; there was only one express from Bordeaux to come. From the automatic baggage check, the sleeper removed a japanned tin box of the kind used sometimes by professional photographers to transport their more complex equipment. There was, in fact, cushioned inside the padded interior, a television camera and a tripod with collapsible wooden legs. Behind the box was a burlap satchel with a shoulder strap. This contained two transistorized electronic gadgets, each about the size of a cigarette pack, a bleeper-type transceiver, and a remote-control television-channel selector in the form of a small panel with button switches. The four items were wrapped in a wool sweater.

The last object to be taken from the locker was a long leather purse with a zippered top fastened by a tiny padlock. Two fourteen-inch pistol barrels, rifled and bored out to take 13mm Gyrojet rounds, lay in the bottom of the purse. Above, wrapped in oiled silk, was a double breech and trigger mechanism from a Mainhardt and Biehl miniature rocket launcher together with certain clamps and radio components. The tiny rockets, little bigger than a standard .45 revolver cartridge, were fitted with explosive heads. Offset venturis surrounding the percussion cap that fired the fuel imparted a spin to the projectile that stabilized its flight. Two of these deadly little missiles were packed into a special pocket at one end of the purse.

The tin box was so heavy that the cabbie had to hoist it on his shoulder in order to get it to his vehicle. The sleeper carried the satchel and the purse. When the box had been stowed in the trunk, the driver climbed behind the wheel. "Orly, is it?" he asked. "Which terminal do you want?"

"Orly West," the sleeper replied, settling back on the cushions.

The driver nodded, swung out of the railroad-station yard, and drove through the wet streets in the direction of the city ring road and the tunnel that led, beneath the Porte d'Italie, to the turnpike linking Paris with the airport and the South.

The battle to regain possession of the Mount Ararat site was short and fairly sharp. In collaboration with the Turkish company commander, Dean decided that there would be no preliminary reconnaissance: detailed maps of the site were available at the embassy, and he himself had been there recently enough to recall the intangibles that could not be shown on any plan—the steepness of slopes, the amount of erosion in weathered rocks, the possible sight lines and areas of ground cover. In addition to that, the lack of obvious scouting activity should increase their chances of surprising the occupiers.

The most important thing, Dean reckoned, was to take the guardhouse the moment the attack went in. He knew from Mazzari that the steel-shutter mechanism designed to seal off the entrance to the redoubt was damaged and out of order, but the fail-safe controls that could block the inner core of the silo as soon as an alarm was sounded might still be operable by the men on the gate. Once that hazard had been taken care of, it should simply be a matter of getting enough men inside the perimeter to overcome the hijackers.

The gorge was too steep and too deep to risk a landing from helicopters: they would be too easy a target for the RPG-7 grenade launchers in the terrorists' possession. It was too narrow, with unpredictable cross currents and thermals, to allow a one-hundred-percent-successful drop by parachutists—who would in any case be sitting ducks for the gunmen beneath, once they sank below the cliff edge. Troops landed *behind* each lip of the defile would, however, once they advanced to the edges, be in a position to enfilade the defenders and give most effective covering fire to any force making a frontal attack on the gates.

This was the tactic Dean decided to adopt. A platoon of infantrymen would be landed from Super Frelon helicopters a hundred yards back from each lip; Dean and the Turkish commander would lead the remaining two platoons and attempt to storm the gates immediately before the choppers flew in; Hammer and the other three mercs, landed lower down the gorge at the same time, would advance to the cascade and block any retreat that way.

Had there been any observers, it would have looked like a textbook operation. The two M-113 APC's and the command car carrying Dean and the Turkish officer had driven as far as the entrance to the defile under cover of darkness. As the sky lightened to the east and the conical form of Mount Ararat slowly emerged from the night, they rolled forward to the place where the defile widened. Minutes later, when the first pale brush strokes of orange and then pink separated the earth from the sky, Dean barked a command into his radio and the three vehicles surged forward.

The order, a single coded phrase, was picked up by the helicopter pilots, who had been cruising some way north and south of the gorge (for the sound of distant engines would not alarm the hijackers: Soviet airplanes frequently flew near the frontier, ten miles away). The choppers turned and began their run in.

From the darkness that still filled the mouth of the canyon, the APC's burst out and roared down on the perimeter fence and the gates. Each of the tracked carriers had been fitted with a heavy steel bumper bar separated from the armor plate by plastic and rubber insulators. In tandem, they struck the junction between the two gates, and a length of chain fence a few yards nearer the guardhouse. The gigantic flash when the electrified wire short-circuited momentarily threw the towering faces of volcanic rock into lurid relief, an instantaneous multicolored glitter that far outshone the pastel light in the sky.

The gates burst open; the flattened fence buckled beneath the caterpillar tracks of the second carrier. Before the two vehicles were level with the guardhouse, bazookas were spitting flame over their armored sides. A well-aimed rocket grenade exploded with shattering force beneath the tail of the hijackers' helicopter, which was still parked on the pad, blowing off the rear rotor and stripping the stressed skin from the fuselage. A second made a direct hit on the nose of the machine, reducing the blister and its controls to a tangle of crumpled metal laced with fragments of Plexiglas.

From the second APC, a grenade flamed through the window of the guardhouse. Before the echoes of the cracking detonation had died away along the gorge, soldiers from both carriers had leaped to the ground, firing M3 submachine guns at the terrorists who were scattering— still wearing U.S. Army uniform—from the rear of the building. There was answering fire now from men around the huts farther down the site near the silo entrance. For several minutes the dawn air was stabbed with flashes of orange and the valley was loud with the stutter of automatic weapons and the thump of grenades. Then the two platoons of airborne infantry, who had advanced over scrub and shale to the edges of the gorge, began hosing lead down on the defenders from their M16 rifles.

An RPG-7 grenade struck the front of an APC and blew off the starboard track. The soldier manning the .50 machine gun mounted on the other carrier was killed by a long burst of fire from a Kalashnikov. The Turkish commander, leading his men at the double toward the silo, fell with a bullet in his thigh. Two more infantrymen who had been wounded dragged themselves back behind the guardhouse, and a third, struck by a lucky shot from below, toppled over the edge of the cliff and fell, arms flung wide like a drowning man, over and over to the rocky floor behind the cascade. But it was not long before superior force began to tell. There were bodies in the smashed guardhouse, beyond the helicopter, and around the huts. The concentration of the terrorists' fire began to diminish.

Dean, marooned in the command car because of his leg in plaster, kept in touch with the platoon commanders by radio. From here he directed encircling movements, forcing the defenders back as they sought shelter from the withering fire poured down on them from the clifftops. Before the sun's rim hoisted itself over the ridge and flooded the gorge with golden light, the only survivors were trapped in the depths of the silo.

The end came suddenly. There had been no more than a score of Furneux's men in the first place: the half-dozen left surrendered at once when a Turkish sergeant wormed his way facedownward into the redoubt and tossed a CS gas grenade in through the open doorway. The sullen prisoners included the two MAO men wounded by the grenade thrown by the original American duty officers in the silo, the two Turks, Paul and Nesuhi, and a couple of Palestinians who had crewed the helicopter.

Three more wounded were recuperated from among the huts. Ahmed, who had led the attack in which Healey's command-car crew were gunned down, had been blown to pieces by the first bazooka grenade in the assault on the guardhouse. The remainder of the terrorists were dead.

To the great relief of Sean Hammer, who had one artificial leg, nobody had attempted to escape by way of the precipitous rock shelves over which the cascade plunged. Furneux, however—together with the taciturn Japanese, Matsuzaki—had escaped somehow. He was not among the wounded, he had not been killed, nobody of his description had even been seen. In some way or other, perhaps the moment the attack started, along some hidden path or previously worked-out route, he had slipped through the net.

Right then, Hammer and his three companions were not worrying: they had a very special mission—to help the Turkish soldiers mop up by every means in their power . . . and at the same time tactfully ensure that nobody penetrated to the actual silo and examined the sinister finned silver shape pointed upward through the rock opening toward the brightening sky.

They found Andrew Healey in the main control room. He had been shot once through the chest. The slug had entered between two ribs at one side of the sternum, but the exit wound was clean, and neither lung had been touched. It would take him some weeks to recover, but he would live.

The thing that was to make all his suffering worthwhile, the moment he regained consciousness, was to see, on either side of his hospital bed, the faces of the wife and daughter he had believed dead.


At 0730 hours, in an airline office at Orly that would not be staffed or open to the public for another hour and a half, the CIA sleeper removed the television camera from the japanned box and set it on the tripod. The two pistol barrels fitted inside the lens hood, invisible from the outside. The breech mechanism was hidden by the body of the camera. But the normal action had been greatly modified. Ordinarily, the Gyrojet firing mechanism was a hammer mounted in front of the trigger which hit backward to strike the nose of the tiny rocket in the breech. This drove the projectile backward against a fixed striker, which in turn exploded the percussion cap that ignited the rocket fuel. The difference in the one-off device assembled by the sleeper was that the triggers for the two barrels had been removed and electromagnets substituted—and these in turn were actuated via transistorized controls subject to radio impulsions, so that the springs retaining the hammers could be released from a distance.

The sleeper left the office carrying the camera and its tripod over one shoulder. The leather purse, empty now, and the wool sweater were hidden in the burlap satchel that was slung over the other.

With camera, tripod, and satchel safely stowed in the

terminal's press room—a special pass was needed to enter—the sleeper returned to the airline office, unlocked a steel clothes closet, and changed from one uniform to another that was completely different.

Abdul Arnaghi Hamid swore. It was unusual for him; customarily he remained impassive even under the most extreme provocation. But the Montmartre number he had been calling for more than two hours still obstinately refused to answer.

The bitch must have gone out immediately after she reported that she had received a negative reply from Furneux. It was insufferable, working with incompetents, Hamid thought furiously. And he had specifically told her he would require her help if they had to act themselves, in case of failure to launch the missile.

He looked at the flat gold watch on his hairless wrist. The digital figures on the black face flicked from 0947 to 0948. His fat lips pouted in a *moue* of exasperation: as always, if you wanted a thing done, you had to do it yourself. He went to the built-in wardrobe, took out a black hide golf bag that seemed to be exceptionally well filled, and rang the Georges V reception for a porter and a cab.

By helicopter to the Turkish air base at Elazig, and then an army jet to Ankara, Dean managed to make the four-hundred-mile journey and fall into his hotel bed by 1010 local time. Chloe Constantine was waiting for him. "This time, you sleep," she said.

Dean showered, limped to the bed, hauled his plaster cast up onto the mattress, and pulled her warm body over him. "There's an old song," he said. " 'Just a little bit of loving . . . will go a long way.' "

She twisted her head and kissed him hard. A shudder ran through them both, and suddenly the longing was hard and urgent. In the moment of her orgasm she gasped, and cried out, and tore at his shoulders—yet even at her most passionately abandoned, there remained about her a certain inward calm, a still, cerebral center and a respect for herself and for him that elevated their coupling to something far above a mere physical hunger.

He was dozing, his hand pressed between her thighs, which were still warm and wet from their lovemaking, when the phone beside the bed shrilled him awake.

"You have forty minutes to make the airport," Mackenzie's distant voice said in his ear. "There's a military jet waiting, and a car will be outside the hotel entrance in a quarter of an hour. You've got to be here in Paris well before two o'clock, whatever happens."

# 18

# The Moment of Truth

Eight minutes before 1400 hours, Paris time. The U.S. Army jet that had streaked over the sixteen hundred miles of Europe that lay between Ankara and the French capital landed on a little-used runway and taxied to a discreet dispersal pan near one of the perimeter tracks. Mackenzie was waiting for them in a black Cadillac sedan that flew a Diplomatic Corps pennant from the right-hand-front fender.

Dean, Hammer, Novotny, Daler, Wassermann, and Chloe Constantine climbed down the steps from the jet's cabin and hurried across the wet tarmac to the car. It was no longer raining, but the atmosphere was close and the damp air heavy with the odor of kerosene.

"It's a woman!" Mackenzie shouted as Dean approached. The copilot of a Tri-Star was warming up his motors on the far side of the perimeter and it was difficult to make yourself heard.

"A woman?"

"The sleeper, man. Our agent in Paris. I found out last night; tracked her down to her apartment, but she'd already left. It seems she works for an airline. Name of Sandra Suleiman."

Chloe Constantine, very trim in the slate-gray Pan-Asiatic uniform, smothered a gasp of surprise. "Sandra?" she echoed. "But she works for us! At the information desk in our Rue de Rivoli office . . . and sometimes in Transit, here at the airport."

"Then she'll have access to the apron, the loading bays, the departure lounges, everywhere," Mackenzie snapped. "If you know her by sight, that's great . . . but she's got to be found and called off in the next fifteen or twenty minutes. We'll get on over there right away, and . . ." He gestured toward the concrete-and-glass terminal building a quarter of a mile away, and broke off in mid-sentence.

The radio speaker on the Cadillac's fascia had crackled and come to life. Dean was unable to hear the words over the roaring whine of the Tri-Star's jets.

Mackenzie looked up from the driving seat. His face was white. "The stupid bastards," he said bleakly. "The airport security people: they've switched Mubarak's flight from the western terminal here to Orly North. As an extra precaution!"

Dean swore. The broken ankle was paining him, and the cast had begun to irritate the skin on his leg. He stared at the long, low line of buildings on the far side of the huge field and shook his head. By the time they had threaded their way through the vast complex of maintenance hangars, baggage and freight conveyers, underground bypasses, and parked aircraft, there would be no time left to search the other terminal, let alone identify a single person in it. Yet to drive straight across . . .

"And just to make things easier," Mackenzie added, "they advanced the time of the flight ten minutes. Instead of two-thirty-five, it's two-twenty-five—in just over twenty minutes."

He followed the direction of Dean's gaze. A Boeing 747 hurtled across the field and climbed steeply into the sky like an arrow shot from a bow. Beyond it, a DC-10 that had flown UTA passengers from Johannesburg and Nice braked at the end of its landing run, and a Trident from the French internal service lowered itself to the ground with flaps down and the jets screaming on reverse thrust. "It would be suicidal," Mackenzie said, "with all those main runways, and feeder tracks and taxi lanes to cross, and ships coming and going every few seconds. Even if we survived, a pilot could see us in his way and take avoiding action that could result in a crash and cost hundreds of lives."

"I guess so." Dean sighed. "But what the hell—?"

"Go the other way," Wassermann said suddenly.

They turned to look at him. "I mean, like you should drive the long way around," he explained, "on the outer-perimeter track. It is much farther—but much faster, because it's uncluttered."

Mackenzie stared once more around the enormous expanse of the field, plucking at his lower lip. "I don't know . . ." he said dubiously.

"And on the way, maybe you can see places where a

driver he can cut corners. You know? Besides, look." He pointed to an area about halfway between them and the far terminal. On the outer edge of the field, iron gantries carried two lines of red marker lights across a sunken roadway that skirted the airport. Forty feet above the ground, each girdered structure bore near the lights an inspection platform reached by a ladder.

"Abe, you're right!" Dean exclaimed. "We have to assume the attempt would be made outside, between the exit from the VIP lounge and the plane. If anyone was crazy enough to try it inside, we'd be lost anyway, and so would he . . . I mean, she. But if I remember the layout correctly, that sector of the apron should be visible at that height from one of those platforms. Right?"

Wassermann nodded. He patted the long canvas case he carried. The other mercs had concealed their stubby weapons in valises that they brought with them, but his prized competition rifle could only be strapped inside a recognizable hunter's cover. "If we should see anything," he said, "it's well within range."

Dean looked at Mackenzie, who nodded. "It's a long chance," the CIA man said, "but let's go!"

Airport security officers are not the only people to suffer from second thoughts. Mahmoud Yusuf, the triggerman wished on Dean by the CIA in case a fall guy was needed after a successful assassination, had indeed been contacted and called off his lethal mission by Mackenzie. But Yusuf was a political animal: he had quit the Palestine Liberation Organization because he believed it was not being tough enough in its actions against Israel; he had welcomed the contract offered by Dean; he thought it only right that the leader of an Arab country who was prepared—like Anwar Sadat before him—to treat with the enemy should be eliminated. He felt, therefore, when the whole deal was annulled, a disappointment that amounted almost to a sense of deprivation, a feeling that he and the cause for which he had stood were being cheated.

And then, early that morning, he had thought: Well, why not? Why not carry on as though nothing had happened? He had, after all, been paid for the job. It would be virtually dishonest (he reflected, his black humor taking over) *not* to go through with it—whatever the American said. Who was to know that he wasn't in the pay of Israel?

Like many of his North African coreligionists, Yusuf had found work as a baggage handler at Orly. He could go where he wanted, beyond the customs and immigration barriers. Soon after 1300 hours, he absented himself, collected from its hiding place the Husqvarna Express that was his favorite long-distance weapon, and made his way to the roof of the terminal. Here, screened by an air-conditioning vent in the corner that he and Dean had chosen, he waited for his target to appear.

Ten minutes later, still carrying his golf bag, Hamid appeared on the roof. Unlimited money could buy you anything: from an alleyway attack in Istanbul to an arranged "suicide" in Washington, D.C. For the man who financed the MAO from his own fanatic pocket, bypassing airport officials to gain access to a door that led to a stairway marked "Private" presented no problem at all.

Behind a stack, he commenced to assemble his own weapon. A mashie-niblick with an unusually thick steel shaft supplied the barrel. What seemed a jumbo-size rubber-swathed grip to a putter fitted over one end as a silencer. The wire stock was dismantled from a small collapsible trolley that fitted inside the bag. The breech mechanism and a Russian-made NKA telescopic sight were in the outside pocket normally reserved for golf balls, and the cartridges were neatly taped to the inside of his billfold.

When the gun was put together and loaded, he stepped toward the edge of the roof and peered over. It was 14 hours 10. Already the activity below was increasing; newspapermen and television camera crews were assembling in the space between the exit from the VIP lounge and the El Al Boeing 737 that was to fly Mubarak to Tel Aviv. Security men mingled with the minor diplomatic officials on the apron. The big shots would come out with the Egyptian President.

Hamid crouched down behind a parapet, grimacing with distaste as his pale suit was smeared with the sooty damp of the roof. He turned his head to make a final check . . . and it was then that he saw, fifteen yards away beyond the vent, the back of Yusuf's head.

Marc Dean too saw the newshawks assembling. Most of the cameras were hand-held, but there were a few film cameras on tripods. Some of the sob sisters were paying out yards of cable from the hand mikes they were going to thrust at Mubarak when he appeared. For the moment Dean paid no special attention to the single camera tripod with no operator nearby.

He was standing on a gantry inspection platform with Chloe, Mackenzie, and Wassermann, staring at the distant group through powerful field glasses. Hammer and the others were on the neighboring gantry, scrutinizing every yard of the terminal facade with their own binoculars. An Airbus zoomed over their heads and touched down on a nearby runway, leaving puffs of blue smoke hanging in the damp air where the wheels had first hit the tarmac.

Dean looked at his watch. A quarter after. The Boeing was due to take off in ten minutes. The crowd milling around on the apron was now being marshaled by gendarmerie, pushed back to leave a gangway between the exit doors and the steps leading up to the open hatch at the front of the plane's cabin. "Better start squinting through that sight, Abe," Dean said. "Any little movement, anything at all out of line, wise me up right away, eh?"

Wassermann nodded and raised his gun.

Lewis Perissol, one of the security men sent out to Orly from the U.S. embassy, paced a narrow promenade in front of the terminal's mezzanine. Crowds lined the rooftop viewing terrace above the main departure lounge nearby, but the public had been denied access to this part of the terminal and there were only a few uniformed crew members, stewardesses, and airport staff watching from the balcony.

Perissol was fifty years old. He had picked up a girl at a *boîte* near the Champs Elysées the previous night and gone home with her. He had not returned to his apartment until after four. Now he had a cold and he was suffering from lack of sleep. The early order to come out to Orly had been in the nature of a last straw. Nevertheless, they had said to keep an *especially* alert eye open for anything, anything at all unusual. Perhaps it was because he was feeling itchy and disgruntled that he noticed the woman.

He wouldn't have if he had not chanced to see her an hour previously . . . and she had been wearing a different uniform then.

She was about forty, a neat, dark woman in Pan-Asiatic

gray. Or she had been. Now she was wearing a dark blue monogrammed pantsuit with the initial letters of a German press agency on the pocket.

That was odd, Perissol thought. He moved toward her. She appeared to be holding something like a small walkietalkie. A short length of aerial projected between her fingers.

Perissol's languages were good. "Pardon me," he said in German, "but do you mind telling me just what you are doing—?"

She turned and pulled a gun on him before the sentence was finished. The plane was due to take off in six minutes.

A great number of things happened in those six minutes. To begin with, the clouds parted and for a moment the sun shone.

Hamid knew that Yusuf had been briefed as the number-one assassin. He also knew that the Palestinian would certainly have been called off that mission once the missile was in no danger of being launched and the blackmail threat was no longer valid. Seeing him there, armed and above the apron, he therefore assumed that he had been rebriefed to *protect* Mubarak against any likely killer. Such, for instance, as himself. Yusuf must therefore be eliminated as quickly as possible.

Coolly, Hamid sighted his silenced weapon and shot Yusuf in the back of the head.

He lowered the gun, broke it, and inserted another round in the Winchester breech. As the polished steel barrel canted downward, a shaft of sunlight touched the roof.

Dean saw the bright flash reflected from the metal. Not unnaturally, he was paying special attention to a point he had himself chosen as a suitable site for a sniper. He thumped Wassermann on the shoulder. "There!" he rapped. "On the roof. Two o'clock from the entrance. Big man in a white suit. Quick!"

Swinging doors at the exit to the VIP lounge opened and President Mubarak walked out onto the apron, accompanied by the personal assistant to the French Foreign Minister, several Middle Eastern colleagues who had been attending the same conference, and a posse of security men. The crowd of media reporters pressed forward. Hamid returned to the parapet. He leaned his elbows on the coping and raised his gun.

Lewis Perissol reacted instinctively to the threat. Before Sandra Suleiman could fire the pistol she had produced, he shot her through the stuff of his jacket (his hand was already in the pocket) with the 9mm Beretta automatic that he habitually carried.

The slug took her between the eyes. She pitched forward and fell. As she hit the tiled floor of the terrace, her right hand, twisted beneath her, was forced against the remote-control panel she held. The button switches were depressed.

On the apron, electronically operated magnets actuated by the radio impulse released the retaining springs in the Gyrojet trigger mechanism hidden within the body of the lone TV camera. The hammers sprang up, the tiny rocket projectiles were driven back against the firing pins.

The camera viewfinder showed in close-up the open hatchway of the El Al Boeing 737. When the missiles left the twin barrels concealed by the lens hood, they shot flaming across the intervening space and burst with scarcely audible explosions against the edges of the hatchway door—at exactly the height Mubarak's chest would have been if he had turned at the top of the steps to make the obligatory farewell wave favored by departing diplomats.

The exploding Gyrojet rounds might have been scarcely audible, but they were powerful enough to tear the stressed skin of the Boeing's fuselage and buckle the door frame; and the sharp crack of the percussion caps was heard by every person on the apron.

Consternation. Mubarak's entourage scattered; the camera crews swung this way and that, searching for a picture; security men, French, Egyptian, and American, surrounded the President and began to hustle him back toward the shelter of the terminal. On the roof above, Hamid swore again and realigned the sights of the murder weapon.

Abe Wassermann too made a fractional readjustment to angle and elevation. The fat man was now a sideways-on target. Fortunately (Wassermann thought, visualizing his own comfortable frame), he was fairly substantial from front to back as well as from side to side. To make absolutely certain, the slug must strike below the left arm, where it was raised to support the gun barrel as the man leaned on the parapet. But it was not an easy shot. Wassermann estimated the range as 770 yards—more than 150 yards more than the ideal distance over which he could be one hundred percent sure. Add to that the fact that it was vital and it had to be quick. It had to be now.

The sweat running into his eyes, misting the telescopic lens and coating the thick finger curled around the trigger, was not due to the warm, damp atmosphere. The cross hairs moved down from a pale shoulder, centered on the six-inch gap between the jacket sleeve and the parapet. Hamid's gun was aimed at the knot of men below. Wassermann held his breath. He squeezed the first trigger. And the second.

The double report of the .458 Salvinelli rifle was lost in the roar of a Tri-Star under full boost as it took off from a runway to their left. The white-clad figure vanished behind the parapet, his gun discharging harmlessly into the air as he fell. Dean clapped Wassermann on the shoulder. "Got him, by God!" he exclaimed triumphantly. (Was it his imagination, or had he seen a sudden flowering of scarlet on that pale cloth a hundredth of a second before the man disappeared?)

On the platform of the next gantry, Alexander Mackenzie lowered his field glasses and groped for his handkerchief with a trembling hand. He dabbed thankfully at his forehead. At last the long nightmare was over.

President Mubarak was driven hastily to Charles de Gaulle Airport, on the far side of Paris, in an armored limousine. The plane that was now to take him to Tel Aviv was already waiting, and took off at once without any formal farewells.

When Dean and his men arrived on the roof of the terminal at Orly there was no sign of Hamid beyond the bloodstains smearing the parapet. The MAO has supporters everywhere, and his body—dead or alive—had been deftly removed. The organization was, however, blamed for the attempted assassination of Mubarak: French crime-squad police, following up the address on the ID papers carried by Sandra Suleiman, discovered enough evidence in her Montmartre flat to link her with the MAO and prove (if they had known the connection) that she had been the contact between Hamid and his hijackers. But nobody knew that the radio in her attic had also served her in her capacity as the CIA's sleeper in Paris.

The investigators were astonished at the amount of jewelry and antiques in the apartment of a woman who had worked as a simple airline hostess. They were not to know that it was an inborn craving for luxury rather than political conviction that had made her—like Tom Argyle in Washington—adopt the perilous life of a double agent. Her CIA contact, the concierge from the apartment house in the Rue St. Georges, continued to collect blank sheets of paper from the P.O. box in the Rue Taitbouf for another year.

When it was all over, Dean and Chloe Constantine climbed the stairs to one of the terminal cafés overlooking the Orly runways, in search of a drink. Mackenzie was sitting at a table near the door, an untasted cup of coffee before him. Dean hurried across, hobbling on his plaster cast. But the CIA chief rose from the table and cut him dead; refusing to acknowledge the combat leader, he strode past, saying only a brief "Have the coffee on me" as he left the café.

Frowning, Dean sat down at the table. Beneath the cup and saucer was a numbered key to one of the lockers in the baggage check near the arrivals hall below. Dean went down to open the locker. Inside was a single brown manila envelope bulging with high-denomination bills: enough and more for Dean and the mercs' payoff.

"That's the life I lead, you see." Dean laughed. "That's the mercenary story all over: reward but no recognition!"

"You'll get reward *and* recognition tonight," Chloe Constantine said.

# LOOKING FORWARD

The following is the opening section from the next novel in the exciting MARC DEAN—MERCENARY series from Signet:

## PASSPORT TO PERIL

Laigueglia, Italy. A small Riviera town, a fishing village between Imperia and the holiday resort of Alassio, with a single jetty, a twelfth-century watchtower, and an extraordinary, two-towered, wedding-cake church presiding over the nets from the lower slopes of the hills that rise from the Mediterranean shore. Not the place, on a late September afternoon at the end of the tourist season, where a man expects to be struck between the shoulder blades by a 14.6 mm slug from an elephant gun.

The ocean that Tuesday was oyster-colored and smooth. Every few seconds it gathered enough strength to flop listlessly into a miniscule wave, which sank into the sand before it could recede. Half a mile offshore, water and sky merged, horizonless, in a uniform sheet of gray.

Moisture beaded the white wrought-iron tables and chairs on the deserted café terrace at one side of the Piazza Garibaldi; it brightened the paintwork of the fishing boats drawn up on the damp sand and glistened on the crisp, dark hair of the black man striding into the café. The blond girl with him was wearing the blue uniform of a Lufthansa air hostess. Her short hair was covered by a cap.

The black man sat down at a table by the window. He was very tall, and there was a ripple of muscles beneath the red tee shirt that he wore over his jeans. "I can't ask

**211**

you what'll it be," he said, smiling. "Orders are that we must both drink Campari-sodas."

"Why all the mystery, Edmond?" the girl asked, smoothing her skirt as she installed herself opposite him. "Why could your friend not call by the hotel like anyone else and meet us for a drink at the bar?" She was a pretty girl with adventurous eyes and a long, rakish jawline. Her English was correct and almost accentless.

Edmond Mazzari's, on the other hand, was exaggerated to the point of caricature. He spoke like the leading man in a pre-war drawing room comedy. "Not a friend," he said. "A contact. In my racket you meet the strangest people—go-betweens, very often, for the johnnies who really do the hiring, with everything under wraps by order. If you don't know, you can't jolly well tell, what!"

She smiled. "They do the hiring—but you do the firing?"

Mazzari nodded. He was a soldier of fortune, a mercenary, and he was used to the secretive ways of those who offered him contracts. The present rendezvous had been arranged by someone who had troubled to track him down during a free weekend when his girlfriend had a stopover in Milan. Now, two days later, he was sitting waiting for the man to show—in the right café, at the appointed time, over the prescribed drink and in the right company (the girl's next flight did not leave until the following morning).

Sipping the bitter, refreshing cordial, he looked the place over. Even indoors the moist air was filming the shiny walls and misting the panels of the Gaggia *espresso* machine behind the counter. Apart from a couple of students necking in back, the café was empty. The proprietor leaned over the bar, reading a spread-open copy of the *Corriere della Sera*. Mazzari took a paper napkin and wiped a clear space in the center of the steamy window. He saw fishermen in shorts and tee shirts crouched over a seine net that was stretched out along the quayside. A small power boat nosed in toward the jetty. On the sand, a gray and white cat jumped out of a dinghy with a stolen fish in its mouth. "I think this'll be the merchant we're waiting for now," Mazzari said.

A chunky man in a windbreaker and sunglasses coasted a Lambretta motor scooter to a halt and leaned the machine against one of the empty terrace tables. He glanced quickly around and then walked to the open door of the café. A tuft of beard grew on his chin. His face was even darker than Mazzari's.

Another swift glance, and he was pulling out a chair to sit at Mazzari's table with his back to the door. "Kiri Ononu," he said. "Thank you for following these some-what . . . melodramatic . . . instructions. You know how it is. My principals . . ." He shrugged.

"I know," Mazzari said. "What can we do for you?"

"A mission, man." Ononu had the thickened articulation and broad vowels of an East African. He looked at the girl. "Excuse me," he said, "but although it was useful as a cover to have two . . . well, what I have to say is strictly for one. You know?"

Mazzari smiled resignedly. "Hannelore, my treasure," he said, "there are some rather fetching postcards outside the *parfumeria* in the Via Dante Alighieri, just behind the square. I wonder would you mind . . . ?"

The German girl got up and left. If Mazzari had asked her to jump off the jetty fully clothed, she would have done so with a smile.

"All right," he said, when they were alone. "Let's have it."

Ononu cleared his throat. "You've heard of Aston Clare?"

"Who hasn't?" Mazzari said. Clare, forty years old, with a doctorate in law from the Sorbonne, was President of the Afro-Asian Congress. Possessor of one of the world's strongest—and angriest—voices to be raised against the Apartheid policies of the South African government, he had won the right to argue a case for an independent black republic before the United Nations General Assembly when he was arrested and jailed on a trumped-up trea-son charge. The trial had been set for mid-October.

"You know how much chance a black man has of get-ting a fair trial in Pretoria," Ononu said. "Or Durban or Jo'burg or Capetown, for that matter."

Mazzari nodded. The café owner turned a page. The two students entwined themselves behind their cold *cappu-cini.*

"We have it on good authority that BOSS, the South African security service, plans to stage a 'suicide'—or perhaps have Clare shot down 'while trying to escape.' It'll be the Steve Biko case all over again."

"We?" Mazzari's eyebrows were raised. "You mean the Congress? The AAC?"

"I myself, brother, am a member of the Congress," Ononu said carefully. "But my principals are . . . let us say people of some influence who share the organization's aims and ideals."

"Right-o! Let us say that. And so?"

"We can't afford to lose Clare. The whole black movement needs him. And that's why we need *you*, man."

"You want me to . . . ?"

"We want you to infiltrate a small group of guerrillas into South Africa, bust open the jail, rescue Clare, and smuggle him out of the country."

Mazzari's teeth flashed white. "Just like that!"

"Within reason, you can name your own price. In the townships, you can have all the help you want—or you can choose to work on your own, without any reference to us. Are you interested?"

"Yes," Mazzari said slowly. "I think I am interested. But I'd want to collaborate with an old mate, a combat leader who's more used to planning this kind of caper than I am. He's a white man, too, which might be a help out there."

"Whoever you like. I told you. So long as you'll agree—"

Hannelore came back into the café. "I'm sorry to interrupt, Edmond," she said. "I left my purse hanging over the back of my chair, and I'll need it if I'm to buy—"

"Not to worry, love." He picked up the purse and handed it to her. "Go and break the bank . . . and get a couple for me."

"For more specific information," Ononu said when she had reached the door, "and details of payment, you must meet one of my principals. If you could be in the bar of the Hotel Splendid at nine—"

The sentence was never finished. Ononu reared up abruptly from his chair, overturned the table, and hurtled head-first across it to crash into the wall on the far side. He slid to the floor, blood frothing like a grotesque wedding flower beneath the collar of his windbreaker. At the same time Mazzari's shocked senses registered the crack of a distant shot. Shards of glass tinkled to the floor from the shattered window.

Mazzari was out on the terrace by the time the girl had reached the East African's body. The sound of a tuned engine accelerating fiercely cut through the babble of horrified astonishment from the fishermen and tourists among the lobster pots and nets. Beyond the jetty, riding high on its creaming bow wave, the power boat raced out to sea.

A fat man with a beard had dropped a shallow basket full of gilt-heads and sea bass. He was staring at the café window. "I can't believe it," he stammered. "Standing at the end of the quay, cool as you please . . . he had a rifle with a telescopic sight . . ."

Back in the café, Mazzari shook his head. "He must have sighted through the clear bit where I wiped the glass," he said.

There was blood on the girl's hands. "He's quite dead," she said, looking up. "But, my God, what kind of a gun is that—to send a man crashing over a table . . . ?"

"Big game stuff," Mazzari said. "A safari gun, probably a Mannlicher. The kind they use in Africa."

While he and Hannelore were identifying themselves to the *carabinieri*, the two students slipped out through the kitchen and left the café. A quarter of a mile away, they went into another bar in the Via Roma and the girl walked through to a telephone booth. She dialed a number and waited. Then, "Your man was a little late," she said. "Ononu had already begun to talk . . . but I don't think he had time to say much."

Feeling in some way responsible for the callous murder of his contact, Mazzari decided that he must stay in Laigueglia and make the date at the Hotel Splendid, even though he had no idea who he was supposed to meet, or whether he himself should carry some kind of coded identification. "I wouldn't worry too much," Hannelore said, staring appreciatively at his husky six-foot-two-inch frame. "There can't be too many in town who could be mistaken for you. I mean, don't trouble to call them; they'll call you!"

He laughed. "You could be right, sweetheart. But first I must drive you to an airfield, where you can grab some kind of shuttle and make your flight from Milan tomorrow morning. Nice or Genoa?"

"Nice," she said. "I have a friend on the Air France desk who can always find me a seat."

On the autostrada that wound through the coastal mountains it was just over an hour to the French city, but it was already dark when Mazzari parked the rented BMW on his return and headed for the Hotel Splendid. A salt breeze blowing off the sea carried a hint of fine drizzle along with the odors of fish and seaweed and the tiled promenade was deserted. Green shutters blinded the severe, rectangular facades of the waterfront houses, terracotta and Tuscan red, maroon and ocher and magenta in the lamplight. There was no sound but the hiss of waves and a desultory rhythm picked out by a guitarist in the empty depths of a disco-bar garnished with the sign HELL'S KITCHEN in neon red. Mazzari turned down a lane so narrow that arched buttresses had been built high above to keep the tall houses apart.

It was here, from a flight of stone steps half hidden behind a solitary palm, that the gunman fired his second shot that day—a shot that was aimed this time at the black mercenary himself.

But before that Mazzari had met the luckless Ononu's "principals" at the Splendid . . . and he had put through a call to his longtime friend and leader, the American Marc Dean, in Paris, France.

Mazzari's British English was the result of a sojourn at Oxford University, but once he had been an officer cadet in the old Congolese army. Dean was a Vietnam veteran whose military skills had been for hire since the seventies. The two of them had shared many hazardous adventures since—and now it was Mazzari's turn to lay a proposition on the line so that Dean could check out the pros and cons before a decision was taken.

Briefly, Mazzari sketched the outlines of Ononu's original offer, and added the details he had learned from the men at the Hotel Splendid. "What do you think?" he asked finally. "It seems to me a good cause, and the money's good. D'you fancy collecting together a small team and having a bash? If you ask me, it's a job we could pull off without too much trouble."

Six hundred miles away, in his Montmartre apartment above the Rue Cavalotti, Marc Dean was laughing. "What's so funny, squire?" Mazzari asked.

"Just this," said Dean. "Two hours ago a South African guy, name of Piet van der Hoek, came to me with a proposition. Know what he wanted me to do?"

"I can't wait," said Mazzari.

"He wanted me," Dean said, "to collect together a small team whose briefing would be to block any attempt by foreign mercenaries to spring Aston Clare from jail!"

## JOIN THE MARC DEAN, MERCENARY READER'S PANEL
## AND PREVIEW NEW BOOKS

If you're a reader of MARC DEAN, MERCENARY, New American Library wants to bring you more of the type of books you enjoy. For this reason we're asking you to join MARC DEAN, MERCENARY Reader's Panel, to preview new books, so we can learn more about your reading tastes.

Please fill out and mail today. Your comments are appreciated.

**1.** The title of the last paperback book I bought was: _____
_____

**2.** How many paperback books have you bought for yourself in the last six months?
☐ 1 to 3   ☐ 4 to 6   ☐ 10 to 20   ☐ 21 or more

**3.** What other paperback fiction have you read in the past six months? Please list titles: _____
_____
_____
_____

**4.** I usually buy my books at: (Check One or more)
☐ Book Store   ☐ Newsstand   ☐ Discount Store
☐ Supermarket   ☐ Drug Store   ☐ Department Store
☐ Other (Please specify) _____

**5.** I listen to radio regularly: (Check One)   ☐ Yes   ☐ No
My favorite station is: _____
I usually listen to radio (Circle One or more)   On way to work /
During the day / Coming home from work / In the evening

**6.** I read magazines regularly: (Check One)   ☐ Yes   ☐ No
My favorite magazine is: _____

**7.** I read a newspaper regularly: (Check One)   ☐ Yes   ☐ No
My favorite newspaper is: _____
My favorite section of the newspaper is: _____

For our records, we need this information from all our Reader's Panel Members.
NAME: _____
ADDRESS: _____ ZIP _____
TELEPHONE: Area Code ( ) Number _____

**8.** (Check One)   ☐ Male   ☐ Female

**9.** Age (Check One)   ☐ 17 and under   ☐ 18 to 34
☐ 35 to 49   ☐ 50 to 64   ☐ 65 and over

**10.** Education (Check One)
☐ Now in high school           ☐ Graduated high school
☐ Now in college               ☐ Completed some college
☐ Graduated college

As our special thanks to all members of our Reader's Panel, we'll send a free gift of special interest to readers of MARC DEAN, MERCENARY.

Thank you. Please mail this in today.

NEW AMERICAN LIBRARY
PROMOTION DEPARTMENT
1633 BROADWAY
NEW YORK, NY 10019